Us

THEY ARE HERE.
SURVIVAL IS UP TO US.

BILLY DIXON

Jan-Carol
Publishing, Inc

"every story needs a book"

The Origin Society: Us
Written by Billy Dixon

Published March 2021
All rights reserved
Copyright © 2021 by Billy Dixon
Skippy Creek
Imprint of Jan-Carol Publishing, Inc

ISBN: 978-1-950895-97-7
Library of Congress Control Number: 2021933815

You may contact the publisher:
Jan-Carol Publishing, Inc.
PO Box 701
Johnson City, TN 37605
publisher@jancarolpublishing.com
jancarolpublishing.com

For Robin, who rolls her eyes
every time Allie and I get started.

AUTHOR'S NOTE

Writing a series is fun. Writing a series you've dreamed about since you were in middle school is a little bit stressful. Series are more challenging that stand alone books. There's so much to keep straight. I have more than 20 pages of notes on my phone. Many, many times have I awoken in the middle of the night with an idea I didn't want to forget, so I grab my phone and start typing, but I wouldn't have it any other way. I hope you enjoy book two of *The Origin Society*. I'm trying my best to do justice to the idea that's been floating around in my head for more than 30 years.

"What in the world?"

Cameron Corman was reclined in his chair, feet propped up on his desk. He tossed a small stress-reducing sponge ball into the air, catching it over and over, blowing strands of his longish black hair out of his eyes and off his designer glasses with each throw. He had laughed at the purpose of the ball. Stress relief? Boredom relief was more like it.

He had been over the moon (so to speak) with excitement when he'd gotten the job offer from NASA. He had dreamed since childhood of being an astronaut, but a congenital heart condition had destroyed that possibility. It had not, however, quashed his love of astronomy and his deep-rooted fascination for the realm of space. The sun and moon, the planets, the stars, and the galaxies. The enormous amount of distance between it all. He'd never been able to wrap his head around it as he lay in his backyard at night as a kid, the rear of his house blocking most of the light from the street, staring into literal infinity.

The numbers were incomprehensible. One of mankind's first deep space probes, Voyager 1, had been launched in 1977 and had sped toward the great beyond at a mind-boggling 39,000 miles per hour. It had taken nearly 40 years at that speed just to break through the boundary of our very own solar system and enter the cold void of deep space.

40 years!

But that was nothing. At its current rate, it would need another 40,000 years to reach Proxima Centauri, the nearest star to the sun.

It had literally kept young Cameron up at night thinking about it.

The vastness of space was one thing to consider. The unlimited possibilities of what could be out there filling that space were something else altogether. It was awe-inspiring. It was a source of unlimited potential.

It was mind-numbingly boring.

The job had been a dream come true. His chance to be a pioneer. His opportunity to make THE discovery—the one that would change mankind forever.

Instead, he was tasked with monitoring the dullest of all satellite feeds.

At first, the Deep Space Climate Observatory (DSCOVR) satellite had been intriguing. Revolving around Earth a cool 1,000,000 miles away—four times farther than the distance between Earth and the moon—the view beaming back to his monitor was amazing. Earth from that far away was gorgeous, the deep blues and greens under the pure white clouds a more beautiful sight than anything created by an artist.

The novelty, however, soon wore off. The purpose of the satellite was to monitor incoming solar storms. Important, sure, but not exactly the type of thing likely to bend views of life as we know it and reshape the world.

So Cameron tossed his ball, over and over and over, with one eye loosely keeping track of the feed on his computer screen. Anything to keep from falling asleep at the wheel.

It was the same thing day after day. Week after week. Month after month.

Until it wasn't. Until something changed.

One of the coolest things about the location of the satellite was that the moon crossed the path between its position and Earth. Very few people had ever seen the dark side of the moon. Since the moon's rotational period was exactly the same as its orbital period, the same side always faced the Earth. DSCOVR allowed for a clear view of the other side. That was really cool until Cameron discovered that the far side of the moon was just as cold, gray, and lifeless as the half man had been able to see since the beginning of time.

The moon was transitioning across Earth today, and that was, perhaps, the only reason Cameron was paying close enough attention to see something move. From that distance, nothing ever moved. No object was remotely large enough to show up individually.

But he'd definitely seen something.

"What in the world?" he said again, planting both feet on the floor and leaning across his desk, getting closer to the monitor.

He looked at the time stamp at the bottom of the monitor and jotted down the numbers, then continued to stare closely for the next hour. He wasn't crazy. Something had moved. Flickered, actually. For another hour, he sat glued to the screen, hardly daring to blink for fear of missing something, the sponge ball dropped and long forgotten.

All remained still and normal. The moon moved ever onward and was soon clear of Earth.

Convinced after a while that there was nothing else to see, Cameron rewound the video feed to five minutes prior to the time he had jotted down. He watched. His jaw dropped, and his heart stopped beating for a moment. He couldn't believe it.

He rewound and watched again. And again. And again.

He fumbled with the receiver of his desktop phone and misdialed three times before getting his supervisor.

"Fr-Frank," he stuttered, "you bet...bet...better come t-t-t-take a look at this."

Cameron rewound the feed and watched again. The view of the moon was exactly as it always was. Gray, cratered, unremarkable. Then several things happened. The entire face of the moon flickered, like a TV getting bad reception. There was a blinding flash of red light. This, Cameron figured, had to be what had initially caught his attention. Then, for only a brief second, the scene changed. No longer was the moon perfectly spherical and lifeless. That was merely a deception—a moon-sized projection used to hide an incomprehensible project. The entire back side of the natural satellite had been scooped out, turned into a concave receiver. Giant beams extended miles outward from around the edges, converging to a single point, like a satellite dish. A massive spaceship materialized out of thin air near the tip of the beams. The ship itself was nearly as large as the moon. Impossibly large. And it wasn't alone. Several other ships, varying in shape and size, hovered nearby.

It was over in a second. The projection of a perfectly normal moon returned, with no trace of the abnormality.

"What in the world?" Frank, Cameron's supervisor, said, suddenly appearing over his shoulder.

After having some trouble dialing, as Cameron had earlier, Frank Mansfield finally managed to hit the combination of numbers he needed.

"Get me the President," he said into the receiver, his hands shaking. A brief pause followed while the person on the other end spoke. "I don't care what country she's in or who she's meeting," Frank said sternly but evenly. "Get her on the phone. Now!" While he waited, he poked Cameron on the shoulder and whispered, "Transfer that feed to the big board."

The big board was the array of giant screens in the Mission Control Center, the place in the space center that the general public would recognize from news reports during mission launches and other non-top secret events involving NASA. Rows and rows of seating and desks, which were individual workstations, faced the big board, each place equipped with smaller monitors and keyboards.

Cameron entered the command to divert the feed, but nothing happened. His monitor went dark, two white words blinking on a black background, taking the place of the million-mile view.

SIGNAL LOST

PART 1
FOREST

INTERLUDE, PART 1

4,000,000 Years Ago

Deep space. Cold. Vast. Dark.

A lone chunk of a hard, blue, rocky material streaked through the emptiness. Not even a speck of dust in the vast expanse around it. No reason to suspect how this little cosmic bit of randomness would reshape the galaxy through which it traveled.

Its journey had started millennia ago, when another, larger meteor crashed into a planet, dislodging this little piece of what would later come to be known as blulex. At impact, there was less than a one in a trillion chance that its trajectory would send it on a course to be captured by the gravity of another planet.

Infinitesimal.

Destiny, both good and bad, however, often starts with better odds.

Time and distance meant nothing. In the void of space, speed was meaningless. The meteor would travel until its progress was stopped, likely with another collision.

It passed just out of the gravitational reach of several stars. Its path was slightly redirected by the pull of a planet teeming with life in the form of both primates and reptiles, similar to the early history of the world called Earth. On this particular planet, evolution would eventually favor those of a reptilian nature, creating a species far worse than anything in the known universe—at that point or at any time in the future. Theirs is another story, though. A tale for someone else to tell.

Our story, however, is focused on the blue chunk that was headed for another planet, one also in the developmental stages of intelligent life.

Thousands of years after its brush with the first planet, the second neared. Like Earth, in another corner of the galaxy, this planet was rich in resources. Even from millions of miles away, the dark blues of deep oceans contrasted with the healthy greens of lush land masses.

The meteor picked up speed as gravity caught hold and reeled it nearer the planet. The star in the center of the celestial system was creating a heat on the surface of the blulex chunk, slowly burning off the ice that had accumulated, leaving a trail of vapor and dust behind.

Nearing the end of its fateful journey, the meteor entered the atmosphere and streaked toward the horizon. Most of the still-evolving animals on the planet were more concerned with food and survival than the quick but brilliant flash of light in the sky. There was, however, a spark of intelligence in the eyes of one group of creatures huddled near the entrance of a small cave. They saw the streaking meteor and followed its path out of curiosity.

The meteor crashed thousands of miles away in a salty marsh.

Now a meteorite after reaching the ground, the small chunk of blulex set into motion another unintended consequence. The curious mammals scurried after, having no concept of the distances involved. Their journey took them into an undiscovered valley. There, the water was fresh and food grew on trees. They discovered that by standing on their hind legs, it was easier to reach the hanging fruit. Using their hind legs for walking also made it easier to climb up the sides of the valley walls, where the caves there offered protection from the other, more vicious life forms roaming the surface.

The meteor long forgotten, the animals settled into their new home. They grew both in size and numbers, mentally and physically.

The chunk of blulex wasn't finished shaping the history of the planet Mondea, though. Time has no meaning to that which is not alive. A day is no different than a month, or a year, or...

3,000,000 Years Later

The salty marsh had long since dried up. The cumulative effect of 3,000,000 years' worth of ever-changing surface conditions had covered the area with a rich vein of mineable salt.

The people had changed drastically, as well. The band of mammals that had scurried into the fertile valley while chasing after the meteor thrived and evolved into one of the most intelligent species in the known universe. Their planet, Mondea, had become one of the jewels of the galaxy.

The Mondeans had recently secured a spot at the table in the Planetary Council, the ruling body of all things affecting the overall well-being and continued sovereignty of the galaxy. The Council consisted of representatives from the community of known planets hosting intelligent life. Membership currently stood at eight following the suspension of the Erdean representatives for repeated violations.

Despite the advancement of their species, the Mondeans still relied heavily on the natural resources of their planet. The discovery of a rich vein of salt relatively close to the surface was welcome. Complex tunnels were constructed for the excavation.

It was in one of these tunnels where a tired miner made a startling discovery...and a near-fatal mistake.

The small chunk of blulex would soon complete its role in our saga.

CHAPTER 1
What Was

To say 11-year-old Jess Grisham was shell-shocked would have been an understatement of Titanic proportions. She found herself scraped, bloodied, and bruised in a battle-scarred clearing in the middle of a dense forest. She cowered under the shadow of an immense transporter constructed out of a crashed airplane, aluminum ladders, copper wiring stripped from power lines, thousands of batteries, and a strange, white, blanket-like fabric that crackled with energy. The group she was with found themselves facing a giant alien grasshopper intent on destroying Earth by stripping it of its resources and enslaving every human. It was all part of a galactic war she had known nothing about until a day ago.

Some way to spend spring break, huh?

If there were any positives in this dire scenario, one was that she wasn't alone. In the pregnant pause between the battle they had just won and the impending war they seemingly had no chance of winning, she looked briefly at the rag-tag bunch standing with her. Jess allowed her left hand to slide down from her twin brother's elbow until she was clasping his hand, holding him steady.

Jace was struggling, as Jess had earlier, to come to terms with what he had done, to understand the potentially permanent damage he had caused while under the influence of the alien talisman. To his eyes, the piece of cloth had looked like Ranger Ron, his favorite toy as a young boy, but it was, in reality, a piece of alien mind control technology created by the invading Erdean race. Jace, like Jess herself, had been an unwilling pawn in the Erdean race's grand scheme. Finally freed from the mental stronghold of the EncephaLink, Jace was now feeling the torment and shame of being used. When he needed to be at his strongest, he felt frail and vulnerable. It was a true indication of just how bad things were that he didn't try to pull free from his sister's grasp. He didn't react at all aside from a light squeeze of his fingers.

On the other side of Jace stood their father's best friend, Aaron Bellamy. His dark skin was pale, and the man looked as if he could collapse at any second under the weight of his actions. Initially, his role had been to watch over and protect the twins, but when he'd gone under the influence of the EncephaLink, his role in the Erdean plan was the most unforgiveable in his eyes. He'd been stationed at the foot of the transporter, sending an unknown number of elementary school-aged children into the machine. There, the students were disassembled on a molecular level and transported into space to be reconstructed, chained, and forced into Erdean servitude. Free from the controlling blanket, Aaron now faced the reality of his actions, and he sank to his knees on the forest floor, weeping uncontrollably.

Also deeply affected by his actions, Jess's father, Rick, could barely stand to Jess's right. He had one arm wrapped around her, partly a loving embrace and partly for support. His inability to stand unaided was partially caused by the burden of his role in this tragedy, but it was also due to the returned crippling effects of the ALS, a disease that was stripping his body of functional control. While possessing his own piece of the EncephaLink, the symptoms of the disease had been reversed.

Supporting Rick on the right was Max, a double agent of sorts. Besides Jess, Max was the only one of their group clearheaded enough to feel the proper amount of fear. Unlike Jess, Max at least had an idea of what he was getting into when all of this started.

It all began simply enough. Jess and Jace had awakened on Monday morning to a quiet house. That was a little odd because their father always had a TV on and was usually talking loudly into a phone about his latest theory on aliens visiting Earth. The silence had been strange, but it just meant Rick wasn't home. Before they could find out why, though, "Team Creepy"—a military special ops team—had crashed through the windows of their house with smoke bombs, battle gear, and assault rifles. Max had been a part of that team, but instead of capturing Jace and Jess, he had helped them escape through a secret tunnel in their basement.

There was something about that tunnel that kept tugging at the back of Jess's mind, but now wasn't the time to sort it out.

Once out of the tunnel, the twins met up with Aaron, who had been helping their dad track down the answer to a conspiracy about a downed military aircraft. The plane supposedly carried out-of-this-world artifacts recovered from the crash of an alien ship in their hometown of Ridgeport in the 1950s. Using satellite images, Aaron had found a possible location of the military plane, along with knowledge that the government had covered up the incident and left the plane and its contents scattered in the remote forest.

Obviously finding out what Rick and Aaron knew, Team Creepy had crashed the house in order to capture and detain Rick, and keep him quiet, but their father had started his journey in the middle of the night, ahead of the siege.

Determined to catch up with and join their father, Jace and Jess, with Aaron in tow, had escaped more encounters with Team Creepy and caught up with Rick deep in the woods of eastern North Carolina. But before they could approach him, Max and his team of soldiers arrived on the scene and captured Rick right after he opened a trunk containing the strange white blankets.

Left alone in the forest, Jace and Jess had emerged from their hiding spot under a vine-covered mound and examined the trunk for themselves. That's when they had discovered the blankets, in the form of Ranger Ron for Jace and a Baby Molly doll for Jess. The alien technology embedded in the EncephaLink quickly took control of the kids and downloaded a mission into their brains. This was what ultimately led to the showdown they had just experienced.

The kids' first task had been to share their blankets with adults on death's door. Compromised by illness, the adults were easily manipulated by their pieces of the EncephaLink. Healed by the alien technology, they'd converged at the crash site in the forest to begin constructing the transporter.

Jace and Jess were moved like pawns in a game of chess on to phase two of the nefarious plan. Visiting a series of large elementary schools and sharing pieces of their blankets with principals, the twins had easily persuaded the administrators to take the entire student bodies on a field trip into the forest. Jace and Jess had been used to herd a young slave force like cattle to the transporter where they would be blasted off the planet and prepared for their new lives of forced labor and military sacrifice.

At the last school, however, a second special ops team had arrived to capture the twins. The aliens controlling their actions had deemed Jess as expendable and allowed her to be captured, giving Jace and Aaron time to escape. Shortly after, Jess came face to face with Max again. This time, Max was representing the Origin Society, a secret group that had protected Earth since the early days of man, back when Erdeans had attacked the planet in search of massive quantities of blulex, a rare natural resource that powered the Erdean civilization and their war machines. A friendly species from another planet called Mondea had masked the blulex, fended off the Erdean offensive, and erased any signs of civilization on Earth in an effort to discourage the hostile aliens from returning. The Mondeans had left a small team behind to keep track of the progress made by Earth's indigenous intelligent species: humans. The knowledge they possessed had been passed down through the generations, and the group of them, known as the Origin Society, infiltrated every major government and military force with the purpose of keeping the advancing humans' secret for as long as possible. At the same time, they were preparing for the inevitable return of the Erdeans.

While Max was explaining this to Jess, he had severed her connection with Baby Molly. Eventually regaining control of her own mind, Jess had been able to reveal that construction of the transporter was taking place in the same forest clearing where the old crashed military plane had been discovered.

Assembling a small team of fighters, Max had led an ill-fated charge against the construction site. But facing a superior technology being wielded by hypnotized and otherwise innocent humans they were unwilling to kill or injure—including Jace, Rick, and Aaron—the battle had quickly ended. The OS soldiers had been captured, and some of the elementary school kids transported off the planet in violent blasts of red light.

The battle, however, had activated a Mondean defense system in the form of a drone attack plane. To protect their mission and the transporter, the Erdean mind control blankets had severed contact with their human hosts and had come together to form a shield.

In the end, both the Mondean drone and the Erdean shield had been destroyed. Free from the EncephaLinks, the humans in charge stopped transporting the kids.

While members of The OS team had been shepherding the children and stunned adults out of the forest, the machine in the middle of the clearing transitioned from a transporter to a receiver. The device accepted seven transmissions in the form of an armed Erdean scout team. The giant insect-like beings had spread out on a platform overlooking the clearing and the five remaining Earthlings standing below. Five humans, two merely 11 years old, facing down seven of the most biologically superior creatures in the known universe.

Jess's appraisal of her friends and family recovering beside her, seeing the desperate reality they currently faced, occurred in the briefest of moments, like her life passing before her eyes. That was all the time they had.

The dust had barely settled from the first attack, and the concussive force of the Erdeans' arrival in the receiver, when the second battle began.

CHAPTER 2
What Is

There was no one word that could sum up the swirl of emotions crashing like a tsunami through Jace's mind. Pain, anguish, shame, guilt, confusion. He felt them all.

"This is my fault," he muttered, hanging his head.

"I know how you feel," Jess said, taking his hand and trying to squeeze as much compassion and comfort as she could through the tips of her fingers. "I felt the same when they took Baby Mol— When they took that *thing* away from me." She was determined to never again associate her favorite childhood toy with that evil bit of alien tech. "There's no way we could've known beforehand, and there was nothing we could do to stop it once we touched it," she continued. "But you're free of it now, and we have a chance to make them pay for what they did."

Jace stole a sideways glance at his sister. It was only a second, and then he returned his glare back to the threat standing before them. Still, Jess could see the conflict in his eyes.

He wanted to believe her, but the emotions were so overwhelming.

"In time, this will pass," she said. "But we don't have time. We need you—*all* of you—here and now. The world depends on it. Remember the dream? We have to stop that from becoming a reality. I'm sure you've been in this situation before in a video game. We need you to use that experience and lead us to victory."

Mentioning Jace's video game skills was pressing all the right buttons. Jace's eyes perked up. His jaw set. The confidence, bordering on arrogance, that had helped him drive Aaron's Tahoe out of Team Creepy's trap crept back, and he gave her a smug smile.

On the platform surrounding the transporter, the lead Erdean stepped farther forward. Long antennae protruded from the top of its head, jutting in their direction, twitching. Because of his antennae, his keen sense of hearing was refined to make up for his shortcomings in vision, and he had picked up the conversation between the twins. As their leader prepared to speak, the other six fluttered their thin, membranous wings in anticipation. The leader shifted his weapon to a middle set of arms and began rapidly swiping his front set back and forth over his throat. The motion created a vibration that the strange creature turned into sound. His mouth, looking like nothing more than stiff lines on a hard, smooth exoskeleton shell of a face, moved to form words.

English words.

"Yes," the thing hissed. The effect was strange, sounding almost electric, like static feedback from a microphone, but it was perfectly understandable. The speech pattern was rhythmic, like a mating call of a cicada on a late summer evening. "Remember the dream, Jace. Or should I call you Lysander? It is, after all, your destiny to be a liberator. *Our* liberator. Your destiny is to free us from the tyranny of the council." He shifted his attention to Jess. "And you, Axelia," he said. "You shall be the protector of Mother Erdea. Both of you on the throne. It was not merely prophecy. It was the future. It's your destiny to fulfill. Take back your EncephaLinks and see *all* that's in store for you."

The creature held out two perfectly white pieces of cloth. Thankfully, Jess saw it now for what it really was. She no longer saw Baby Molly.

Jace was less certain and seemed torn. Had Jess not mentioned the video games, a comment that had sparked a bit of life—a bit of his old self—in him, he might've fallen for it. He slowly took a step forward, but instead of approaching the transporter, he surveyed the clearing.

His autopilot was kicking in. He could sense the game controller in his hand. Instinctively, he took in everything. He sensed the movement behind him. Max and Rick were ever so slowly spreading out to avoid being grouped so tightly together. They were easy targets with the way they currently stood, like fish in a barrel. Moving also positioned them closer to the discarded weapons still lying on the ground from the earlier fight.

Jace, tuning in to the internal voice that did indeed make him a tremendous gamer, noticed other things, as well. The forest had gone unnaturally silent. No living thing wanted to call upon itself the attention of the mighty predator standing in its midst. Despite that silence, the Erdean squad had been too intent on listening to their leader speak to hear the two men approaching from the opposite side of the clearing. Jace recognized them from the battle.

Jess wanted to scream out to Brown Eyes and Mustache, the good cop and bad cop from her interrogation in the OS mobile command center earlier. She bit her lip and forced herself to keep eyes on the Erdeans. The last thing she wanted was to give away the secrecy of the soldiers' approach. If those two were back, it could only mean one of two things. Either the kids had been safely moved out of the forest and were being reunited with their families, or the remainder of the rescue team knew of the looming threat and needed more time. Since there was no way a handful of adults—some of which were undoubtedly still feeling their own side effects from being withdrawn from the Encepha-Links—could have gotten a couple thousand kids to safety that quickly. Jess knew the whole group needed to buy more time.

Mustache and Brown Eyes, more commonly known as Russ and Cooper, held position near the base of the giant structure, waiting for their cue.

Max spoke first. "Even Steven," he said.

Jace cocked his head in confusion, but Jess understood immediately. She also knew the Erdeans' hearing was excellent. They clearly understood and could speak English, but they would be unlikely to understand such a colloquial phrase. Jess knew that "even Steven" meant that it was now seven on seven. Plus, they had an element of surprise on their side. If they were going to make a move, if they were to have any chance at all, the time was—

"NOW!" Max yelled.

Total chaos broke out.

Jace had already spotted a weapon. It was lying discarded at the edge of the clearing. Pushing his sister in that direction, he found a handgun 10 feet the other way. He scooped it up, took careful aim at the surprised alien leader, and squeezed the trigger.

Click.

He squeezed again. And again. And again.

Click. Click. Click.

Empty

"Here," Max said, tossing him one of the laser weapons the Origin Society had managed to procure.

In turn, Jace pitched him the handgun. In one practiced motion, Max ejected the spent clip and slammed home another as he ran for the cover of the nearby trees.

Several other things were happening at the same time.

Jess had picked up the weapon in her path but had yet to fire a shot. She held the blaster uncertainly. Action and reaction were her brother's specialties, not hers. She rarely played video games, and when she did, it was one of the dancing or karaoke contests. She didn't like watching shoot-em-up games, much less playing them, and now she found herself thrust into the real thing. Too much was at stake. For someone who prided herself on acting logically, she was being illogical now. This could be humanity's one shot. It was no time to be a wall-flower, standing to the side while others got involved. She raised the gun, sought out a target, and was immediately forced to drop to the ground to avoid a blast tracking right at her face.

The Erdean squad leader had reacted faster than the others. Like a cat pouncing on prey, the insect crouched on its inverted rear legs and sprang from the platform to perch atop the outer railing. A slight flutter of wings balanced him perfectly. Highly practiced and well drilled, he squeezed off five quick shots, one at each of the attackers in front of him. None of the shots squarely struck human flesh, but four of the five humans were forced to dive, take cover, and regroup.

Jess felt the heat from the proximity of the shot that had volleyed in her direction. The blast seared a wedge from the trunk of the tree beside her. She could hear the sizzle of the laser beam as it passed and the crackling embers on the tree. There was an unmistakable smell of seared wood. In surprised reaction, she triggered off two quick shots, both fortunately not striking her own people but unfortunately missing their target.

As for the others, Max had reacted most decisively. While making his call to action, he was already lunging for the laser weapon near his feet. Familiar with its operation, he got off one successful blast before the Erdeans could fully react. The bolt of energy struck the alien immediately to the leader's left, hitting it in the junction of its head and thorax. Severed, the two parts of the alien's body were thrown backward into the giant structure, where it fell motionless to the platform.

Seven on six.

It was the only clean shot Max had been able to make. The bulk of the return fire had been aimed to keep him pinned down. He made a mad dash to safety across the clearing, pausing only long enough for his weapons exchange with Jace.

Like Jess, Rick and Aaron had been slower to react. Finally picking up a weapon, Aaron struggled to focus long enough to find cover. He was clipped in the shoulder by the squad leader's blast but barely reacted to the pain. He slumped against the trunk of a particularly large elm and mindlessly rubbed at the wound. He didn't fire a single shot.

It was a different kind of struggle for Rick. After living a couple of days symptom free, thanks to the evil blanket technology, the ALS was now back with a vengeance. The onset of symptoms had originally been so gradual that he hadn't realized how bad it had become. But to go from zero problems back to fully symptomatic in a matter of minutes revealed reality. His suffering went far deeper than a decrease in fine motor control, however. While an Erdean invasion might have been inevitable, he had brought it on more quickly with his determination to find the truth. Not only did he want to uncover a conspiracy, but he had selfishly hoped that revealing the existence of aliens just might usher in a medical revolution born of other worldly advances. It was likely his last chance at survival. Now...this. Unable to stand and fight but incapable of running for cover, Rick crouched behind a pile of brush and shot wildly with shaky hands.

On Max's mark, Mustache and Brown Eyes emerged from their positions and flanked the transporter from the rear. Using conventional rifles, they scored direct hits on the Erdean soldiers standing at each end of their post. The force of the impact threw the alien bodies backward, but the bullets didn't penetrate the hard-shell exoskeleton. Recovering quickly, both Erdeans regained their stance and returned to the fray, sweeping the clearing with their weapons, searching for their attackers. By this time, Mustache and Brown Eyes had secured positions under the elevated platform. They emerged at random intervals to fire off rounds, ducking in and out of sight before their enemies could draw a bead on them.

Unable to find the proper angle to thwart the attack from the platform, the Erdeans unveiled their next surprise. The thin wings on their backs weren't just for show or maintaining balance. As their leader had done earlier, the pair hopped onto the safety railing, but they didn't stop there. Using it as a springboard, they simultaneously leapt off the rail into the air, unfurling second, sturdier pairs of wings that carried them across the clearing into high branches of nearby trees. From there, they began engaging the humans with crossfire.

Although a lot had happened from all corners of the clearing, only mere seconds had passed since the battle began. Jace hadn't run for cover or sought shelter behind brush. Instead, he allowed his gaming instincts to guide him. While not yet having been able to take out one of the enemy combatants, he was still acting strategically, timing shots to disrupt the aim of any Erdean who seemed to be drawing a bead on his people. His weapon was growing hot from firing off so many blasts in succession, but he kept going, moving forward slowly. He wanted to stare. He wanted to take a moment and drink in the unique situation. Jess was right. He *had* done this in a video game. But this was for real. He was literally standing in a faceoff with creatures from another planet. Despite the fear, despite the danger, this was unquestionably the coolest moment of his life. He'd had a bunch of those the last couple of days, each new experience exceeding the awesomeness of the last.

There was still a small chance to stop the Erdeans. If they could finish off this scout team and destroy the receiver, it might buy them enough time to warn others and prepare for the large-scale invasion that was no doubt coming. Unfortunately, they had severely overestimated their odds. Despite having the same number of bodies in the battle, it was never "even Steven." They had yet to lose anyone, but despite Max taking out one of the aliens early on, they were still a rag-tag group taking on a trained alien squad with superior firepower and a physiology capable of withstanding all but the luckiest of shots.

Jace managed one more blow for the good guys, scoring a direct hit to the side of the head of the leader. The alien fell off his perch on the railing and crashed to the platform on his back. It wasn't a kill shot, however. An EncephaLink hovered over the creature, quickly repairing the damage. He was getting back on his legs before anyone else could manage a shot to finish him off.

Aaron remained frozen in place, and Rick was doing his best, but his efforts were largely ineffective. He just couldn't steady himself enough to aim properly or fire straight.

Jess was keeping one of the aliens engaged one on one but was making little progress.

Understanding where the real threats lay, the Erdeans were effectively forcing Max to stay under cover. From its perch in one of the bordering trees, an Erdean there got off a clean shot, blasting Mustache in the arm, severing it from his shoulder. Mustache—Russ—crumpled to the ground in an excruciating heap.

Closest to him, Brown Eyes dropped his weapon and rushed over to his partner with the intent of pulling him to safety, out of the line of fire.

Seeing them disarmed, the two Erdeans took flight from their post in the trees and dove headlong, straight at the humans, their wings tucked until the very last second to maintain a high speed of attack.

All other action in the clearing stopped.

Jess turned her head, not wanting to see.

If Aaron and Rick were feeling any better about themselves and the role they had played in the unfolding drama, such progress was snuffed out as they watched in horror. Max was desperate to fire into the pile, but the risk of hitting his friends and partners was too high.

Sensing victory and smelling blood, three of the other Erdeans hopped off the platform and joined in, leaving only the leader to stand guard above.

Screams—human screams—emerged from the center of the grouping.

Jace moved another step closer, paying no mind to the leader taking aim from the platform, his own weapon dangling forgotten at his fingertips. He watched with fear and disgust. His mind raced, struggling to process what he was seeing. He thought, *Do insects even eat...* But he stopped that thought short. It didn't matter. What he had learned about insects in science class had no bearing on what was happening here. While these creatures might've resembled giant Earthly insects, they were anything but. Who knew what creatures from another world ate? It wasn't a question he even wanted to spend time pondering. He had a feeling, however, that he would be revisiting the query in his nightmares for days to come. This was no longer a video game. It was no longer fun. He stood still and stared, an easy target for the alien leader taking aim from above.

Rick provided a distraction, coming to his senses enough to see his son's dangerous exposure. He rose on shaky legs from his hiding place and fired shot after shot toward the platform, forcing the Erdean's attention temporarily away from the exposed Jace.

"GO!" Rick yelled, his voice nearly as shaky as his aim. "While they're distracted, GO! I'll keep the leader busy, buy you some time."

Jace paid no attention to the shouts and reacted with surprise when he saw his father stumble into the open, wildly firing shot after shot.

"Dad, NO!" he yelled, moving in that direction.

Jess, too, moved away from her protected hiding spot.

Despite all the action still taking place, the battle was over. They had lost. Max saw that. He also understood the sacrifice his friend had already committed to making. There was no turning back. The choice was easy: freeze and let Rick's heroics go for naught, or get out of here and live to fight another day. He didn't even need to think about it.

"Aaron, get Jess and go!" Max commanded.

Surprisingly, Aaron didn't hesitate. He grabbed Jess by the arm and pulled her firmly out of the clearing.

Max made a mad dash across the expanse and grabbed a screaming Jace around the waist, tossing the boy with ease over his shoulder.

Before disappearing into the forest, before moving out of sight, Jace caught one more glance of his father. Rick had stopped shooting. It was his turn to stand and watch. He locked eyes with Jace and smiled. Jace's last glimpse was of a laser bolt striking Rick in the thigh and his father falling to the ground.

The shooting stopped. The silence returned.

CHAPTER 3
Regrouping

A drenaline carried them so far, but the fatigue soon set in. Max managed nearly a half mile with a screaming and kicking Jace slung over his shoulder. He reached a point, though, where he couldn't go on. He was exhausted, dripping sweat and blood through the forest like Hansel and Gretel dropping breadcrumbs. If the Erdeans chose to pursue, the trail would be fresh and easy to follow. He didn't believe that would happen.

Jace was still struggling physically but had calmed down enough to use words.

"Let. Me. Down," he cried, pounding on Max's back. "We've got to go back for Dad. We've got to go back. I can't believe you let him get captured again. We've got to go back."

"Jace, calm down," Jess said, breaking a silence she had held since the clearing. "We can't go back."

Max came to a stop and allowed Jace to slide off his shoulder. Still in a panic, though, the boy struggled to go back the way they had come.

"Jace, NO!" Jess said sternly.

Jace stopped in his tracks, shooting a furious glare in her direction, and demanded, "What do you mean, no? Dad is back there. We've got to save him. I'm not giving up."

"Jace, listen," Jess said, her voice now calm and measured despite the pain evident on her face. She had had a few minutes during the escape to settle her nerves and think things through. "We can't go back. There's nothing we can do now. We were beat, and Dad stayed behind to make sure we could get away."

Jess paused to wipe a tear off her cheek. Her hair hung in limp, damp strands down her face.

"They shot him," Jace said, the fight beginning to go out of his voice. "We have to go back."

"That's right," Jess said. "They did shoot him. And he's either dead or they've captured him. If we go back, the same thing will happen to us. It was a fight we couldn't win."

Max slumped to the ground, breathing heavily from the trek. Aaron was leaning against a tree, noticeably favoring the shoulder that had been grazed with a laser bolt. He seemed to just now be coming back to his senses. With that, though, came the realization of pain.

The forest was stifling hot. Rays of sunlight cascaded through breaks in the overhead foliage, adding heat to the humidity. So thick and heavy was the air that it felt more like they had been swimming than running. The rustling of squirrels scurrying along the ground and the twitter of birds overhead proved they had exited the Erdeans' sphere of influence.

Still wrapped up in panic, Jace paced back and forth but no longer seemed like he'd make a mad dash back to the clearing.

"He can't be dead, Lexy," he said, his eyes pleading for agreement. "He just can't be."

"I don't think he is, Lys," she said, responding in kind to his use of her nickname.

"How can you know?"

"There were no more shots after the one that hit him in the leg," she said.

"But what if...what if...they...what if they...you know..." Jace stammered.

Jess did know. She knew exactly what he meant. She had seen the way the Erdeans had swarmed Mustache and Brown Eyes. That wasn't battle. That wasn't war. It was hunger. She feared for the OS operatives but chose to believe the same fate hadn't befallen their father.

Aaron spoke up for the first time. "We better get going. They could catch up any second now, and we're in no condition to fight."

A panicked look returned to Jace's face, and he turned, staring back toward where they'd been as if expecting the aliens to come crashing through or flying over the undergrowth at that moment.

Jess had thought that through, as well.

"They won't be coming after us," she said confidently. "We're safe for now."

"How can you be sure?" Aaron asked.

"They're on a mission far more important than us," she explained. "We interrupted it. Nothing more. I don't think they ever really saw us as a threat. Now that we're gone, they'll be more concerned about securing the transporter and getting back to business."

"What business?" Jace asked. "The kids are gone. No thanks to me, they're long gone by now."

"Those kids were just a start," Jess said, recalling the portions of the mission she'd been allowed to see while under the influence of the EncephaLink. "They'll bring in reinforcements and start the search for victims themselves this time."

"You...you...you think more of them are c-c-coming?"

"I would bet on it," she said.

As if to confirm her suspicions, the serenity of the forest was broken by a bright flash of red light that was visible through the gaps overhead, and a mighty, ground-shaking WHOOMP sounded as the latest transmission was received in the distant clearing. The group solemnly looked at each other. A succession of blasts trumpeted the arrival of more aliens on the planet.

"That was sooner than I had hoped," Max said, detaching a canteen from his shoulder pack and passing it around. "Everybody, take a drink, and let's go. We have to reach the command center and put in the call for help."

Pulling themselves together, the group trudged on. They focused on their destination. Anything to take their minds off the blinding flashes and repeated thumps shaking the world behind them.

Jess mulled over what she'd left unsaid. She was confident the Erdeans would leave them alone. For now. But the leader had used their given names. Lysander and Axelia. He *knew* who they were. The aliens *would* come after them eventually.

Jace was restless, and Jess remained quietly contemplative. Neither could get a read on Aaron, who seemed to be in a downward spiral of self-reflection over his role in the events taking place. If they could have put the day behind them and stopped thinking about what the future was sure to bring, the setting might have been serene.

The Origin Society's command center RV was humming with electronic activity, but the sound was largely drowned out by the calls of nature. Parked alongside the lake, where they could get a signal out by satellite, the air was full of bird calls, scurrying mammals flitting to and fro in the nearby forest, the steady croak of frogs along the shore, and the occasional splash of a fish jumping for its dinner. The setting sun behind them cast a soft but fading glow on the scene.

In the distance, the flashes of red light and muffled thumps could've been a summer storm far off on the horizon or fireworks on the fourth of July being experienced from miles away. In another time, another place, it might've been peaceful. But they knew better. It was a storm brewing, sure enough, but not of the meteorological variety.

They felt helpless. Every minute sitting here, every flash of red light racing from the sky to a distant point in the forest, meant another enemy to deal with.

It was all Jace could do to sit still. He was ready to go back and fight, ready to find and rescue his father. His skin literally itched with impatience. He ran stubs of broken fingernails up and down his forearms.

The door to the command center opened, bathing them in light, and Max stepped out, closed the door, and took a seat.

"I've sent the message," he said wearily. "It should be seen soon enough. All we can do now is wait on the cavalry to arrive."

Jace blared his eyes in astonishment and said incredulously, "What do you mean, wait? It could take hours, or even days, for help to come. We have to go now."

"Jace—" Max started, but Jace interrupted.

"You see that?" he said, pointing out the latest flash over the tree line. "That's another grasshopper with a weapon that we have to kill. I've lost count of how many that is. We can't wait. We have to go now. It's dark, and we'll have the element of surprise with us. We can take them."

"We had the element of surprise last time, Jace," Jess said. "And we were lucky to get out alive."

"Did we get out alive, Jess?" Jace snapped back. "Did we all? It seems we're missing some."

"Exactly, Jace," Max said. "Your sister is right. We did have the element of surprise. We could launch an attack now, but you can bet they'll be ready for it. They'll have a protective perimeter set up. Even with our night vision technology, we'd be at a disadvantage. If they have compound eyes like Earth insects, they'll still be able to see better than us. They're hearing is superior. We'd be marching to our deaths, and that doesn't do anyone any good."

That stumped Jace, but he still wasn't ready to give in, sit back, and do nothing. He paced around the chairs, mind racing.

Max looked around the circle, settling his gaze on the only other adult, and asked, "How's the wound, Aaron?"

"The salve seems to be helping," Aaron said, nodding positively. "Luckily, I don't think it was a direct hit. Must've only grazed me."

"Or a proximity burn," Max said. "If the bolt had actually hit you, I don't think you woulda come out of it so lucky. Those lasers are concentrated beams of extraordinary heat and intensity. A shot that comes close enough can still leave a burn. I'm guessing that's what happened." Max continued around the circle. "Jess, you're awfully quiet. What're you thinking about?"

"I think Jace is right," she said. "The longer we wait, the worse our odds. I know we can't go trampling back through the forest in the middle of the night, but we should get a start first thing in the morning. We can scout the area, see just how bad it's gotten, and have a plan ready for when the rest of your team arrives."

Max nodded, impressed.

In the distance, the flow of the red blasts reversed, this time heading from the ground and disappearing far into the sky. Jess strained to see where it was headed. She knew a little about astronomy and constellations and was curious to see what grouping of stars the blast was directed at, but the moon was bright and blocking the view of what lay beyond.

"They're sending and receiving," Jace said, exhibiting his ability to observe what was going on around him while being seemingly obsessed or self-absorbed.

"What do you think that means?" Jess asked, intending the question for Max, but Jace was ready.

"I think Dad was one of them," he said.

"In a way, I hope so, Jace," Jess said softly. "That would mean he's not—"

"He's not dead, Jess," Jace replied forcefully. "We can't think that way. Those...those...things knew about us. They knew about our dreams. We're part of something bigger—"

"The prophecy," Jess and Max said at the same time.

"Yeah, whatever," Jace said, annoyed at being interrupted. They had tried to fill him in on the story of the prophecy on their walk to the command center, but Jace's mind had been elsewhere at the time. "They need us for something. They had plenty of chances to shoot me in the clearing. I was just standing there, but the shots they fired at me seemed more defensive. If they wanted me dead, I would've been dead. But something else is going on. If we are that important to them, they'll keep Dad alive until they have us. So, if that means shipping him off to Pluto, that's what they'll do."

The group went silent, contemplating Jace's analysis.

After a while, and following a long internal debate on whether to bring it up, Max spoke. "I didn't...don't...know Rick as well as I knew his father, but I do know they are cut from the same cloth," he began, picking up the threads of the story he had begun telling Jess the day before in the very vehicle parked behind them now. "Luther Grisham, your grandfather, had a top-secret job. He couldn't tell anyone about it. Not even his wife. He worked for the Alien Taskforce during the time when we made first official contact—or I should say when the Mondeans visited us in Roswell—and when the Erdeans and Mondeans fought their little battle in the skies over Ridgeport. There was a lot of debate on how it should be handled, but they decided the general public would panic if they knew a superior and aggressive species was not only aware of Earth but had arrived. They kept it all secret.

"Like myself, however, Luther was also a member of the Origin Society. He was already aware. He also knew the significance of that little battle. He did his duty to both organizations but was uncomfortable leaving this world without passing along a bit of the knowledge to his son. I think he was in contact with the Mondeans at the time, that communication was taking place between them after the incident, but I can't prove it. Some of the records from that timeframe are missing. Anyway, that's how you ended up with the names you have. The Planetary Council had interpreted the prophecy and gave Luther just enough information to fulfill it. In turn, he passed along what he could to his son, your dad, with the hopes that Rick would follow through with naming you in case the prophecy was true, but also with the hope of keeping your father from getting too involved if there was nothing to it. Obviously, the Erdeans at least know of the prophecy and believe you two are the ones to fulfill it. So yes, Jace, I think you are right. If your father survived the initial shot, I imagine they kept him alive. And to protect their asset, they could very well have transported him off the planet."

"Planetary Council?" Jess asked, homing in on the key part of Max's speech she hadn't known about.

Max paused. He hadn't intended to say that much. It was can of worms he didn't want to get into.

"Yes, but that's a story for another day," he said finally. Both kids started to protest. You couldn't bring up something like that and expect there not to be questions, but Max headed them off. "I forget there's so much you don't know, but don't worry. If we get out of this, I'll tell you everything. At least all that I know. But for now, I agree with Jess. Tomorrow morning, we need to scout out that has happened in that forest overnight. And to do that, we need sleep. Let's call it a night."

Despite the expected barrage of questions, Max was able to corral the group into the command center and the bunks prepared for just such an occasion. Once they got still, the kids fell asleep with surprising quickness.

Deep in the forest, however, activity continued unabated. The coming storm continued to brew with blast after blast.

CHAPTER 4
Forest Transformed

For Jess and Jace, the journey back into the forest was like a sickening form of déjà vu. One of their father's favorite movies was *Groundhog Day*, where comedian Bill Murray relived the same day over and over again until he got everything just right. This felt the same. The twins were determined to get it right this time.

Max had awakened everyone just before dawn and laid out a very specific plan for what he wanted them to accomplish. In Jace's opinion, their new goal was very light on action. He nodded in agreement with everything that was being said, but internally he was playing out a different scenario, one he felt was more likely to unfold. This new world, he thought, was turning out to be more and more like the video games he mastered. He was going to be prepared to do things his way.

Jess had agreed, as well, but her nods were more sincere. As much as she might not like the reality they were now living in, it *was* reality. She would do anything to rescue their father and go back home. She wanted her normal life back. Sadly, though, there wasn't much normal about home now, either. That world consisted of parents who were divorced and a father who was living with a terminal illness.

She was beginning to see the allure her father saw in tracking down the aliens. Sure, the Erdeans had turned out to be big, bad, and a threat to the future of all life on Earth, but what about the Mondeans Max had mentioned? Another advanced race so close to humans that they hid themselves among our ancestors a long time ago. Maybe they could help. Maybe they had the advances in medicine that could save her dad. Jess chastised herself for that thought. It was selfish for her desires to be about saving her father when the entire planet was facing the possibility of mass extinction.

It was a lot to process, and she was trying, but the internal struggle was making her feel sick. So she made herself focus on the mission. They would go back into the forest and get as close to the clearing as they could. They would analyze the progress made by the Erdeans overnight, try to get a count on how many of them there were, try to determine the strength of their forces and commitment to a perimeter, and try to determine the best method of attack once the rest of the OS team arrived.

"What about the Alien Taskforce?" Jess had asked during their briefing. "They had a lot of fire and manpower. Why not get them to come help, too?"

Max had been impressed by her reasoning but was ready to counter the question, saying, "The Taskforce has worked for half a century with the primary objective of keeping all of this a secret. With the exception of a couple members I secretly recruited to our side, they have no idea what's really happening. They're trained to deal with humans—Earthlings—not Erdeans. The OS has been preparing for this moment for millennia. Our team is stationed all over the world and ready to respond at a moment's notice. My message last night will bring them running."

Jess had nodded acceptance and understanding, but Max wasn't finished. He pulled away from the group and walked with her around the command center. The lake, sparkling and calm, lay beyond.

"Still, even with all the OS, there are not enough of us to fight off a big alien force," he said, talking quietly as they walked. "But we have more than just trained soldiers on our team. We've recruited politicians, too. Hopefully, conversations are taking place with every major world leader as we speak, them being briefed on the threat and hopefully making preparations for a full-scale military operation. If it comes to that, it won't be a world war. It'll be a war *for* the world.

"I don't want to scare you. I couldn't imagine being 11 and having to deal with something like this, but I wanted...no, I needed to make you understand the seriousness of what we're facing. I'm worried about Jace. He has unbelievable skills and battle instincts. It comes naturally to him, but I'm afraid he feels invincible. Unfortunately, we really need him, but if he gets a chance out there today, he'll go rogue, especially if Rick is there. More than anything, I need you to keep an eye on him. Can you do that?"

Jess nodded. She *would* keep an eye on him. At the same time, she wondered how *she* would act if her dad *was* there. Would she be able to stick to the plan? Could she *really* walk out of this forest without her father for a third time and leave his fate to a team whose primary goal would be destruction of the enemy at any cost? She just couldn't say for sure.

"Why do you keep looking at me?" Jace said, bringing Jess back to the present.

Jess shrugged. "Just trying to figure out how my twin could possibly be so funny looking."

"Har har," Jace said, making a goofy face.

Distracted, he stumbled and nearly fell over a root, and Jess had to slap a hand over her mouth to keep from laughing out loud.

"Shh! Quiet!" Max hissed.

Jess grimaced in embarrassment and kept moving forward, trying her best to avoid the worst of the undergrowth and find a clear path through. Aaron was alongside, using a large knife to cut his way through the thickest of the brambles. He seemed to be doing much better after having a full night to come to terms with his separation from the EncephaLink and what had happened while he was under its control.

It was going to be another scorcher of a day. Despite the sun still being low on the eastern horizon, it was already stifling hot. Even the wildlife in the forest seemed to recognize it. It was quiet and still, their own footfalls the only sounds.

Jess was the first to first to realize it was a little too quiet. Unnaturally so. On their other journeys, there was still a lot of animal activity this far removed from the clearing. The change could only mean one thing, and it wasn't good. The Erdeans' sphere of influence had grown overnight. She alternated her glances from Jace to the path in front of them but kept finding her attention pulled upward toward the treetops. She was still working out why, having yet to put a finger on the reason.

For his part, Jace appeared singularly focused. He was intent on getting to the clearing. He was okay with the mission in principle. He'd do the reconnaissance. He understood this was a battle that they could not win alone, but he refused to see rescuing their father as a hopeless cause. If their dad was there, if he was being held hostage in the clearing, he would not sit back and wait. He'd find a way. It was just like Operation: Covert Extraction. His mission was to beat the odds, overcome the enemy's superior power, and walk away the hero.

Her gaze increasingly shifting from the ground to the treetops, Jess was the first to notice the rustle of limbs high in branches not too far ahead. She held out her arms to stop the team's progress and pulled them one by one behind a thick cropping of mountain laurel.

"What is it?" Aaron asked.

Jess didn't answer. Instead, she slowly parted branches at the edge of the big bush to see forward.

Max had talked a lot about appreciating Jace's instincts, but he trusted Jess's, as well. If she wanted them to stop and take cover, that's exactly what they'd do. He unstrapped his laser rifle from over his shoulder and held it at the ready.

Jess carefully allowed the limbs from the bush to close into place and turned back to face the group, white as a sheet.

"Jess, wh—" Jace started to ask a little too loudly, but she threw her hand over his mouth to cut him off.

The rustling in the trees stopped.

Max took his turn looking through the branches. What he saw was a worst-case scenario. He suspected that the Erdeans' numbers would have greatly increased overnight, but he had hoped they wouldn't have spread out this far already. They were barely a quarter mile from the command center.

But there it was. Roosted in the upper branches of a sprawling oak was one of the aliens, a small leafy branch dangling from its mouth. Clearly, the thing had heard them. It was scanning the forest in their general direction, looking side to side, searching for the source of the disruption. Its antennae flicked up and down.

Max held completely still and prayed that Aaron and the kids would do so, as well. He couldn't risk voicing a warning.

After a couple of minutes, the giant grasshopper turned its attention back to the leafy canopy, using its front set of arms to pull the branches close enough for its mouth to rip them off. The middle set of arms held a weapon of their own.

Jace took his turn looking. He was careful not to cause too big a commotion, but he needed to see for himself.

"We'll have to go around," he mouthed, taking charge with a determined look in his eye. Using hand motions, he indicated a new route.

The laurel behind which they hid was the first of a long collection growing widely and freely across the forest floor, its thick, broad leaves providing excellent cover. It would take them out of their way and off their direct path to the clearing if they went around, but it would also keep them clear of the Erdean watching from high up above.

Jace insisted on leading the way, followed closely by Jess and then Aaron. Max brought up the rear, his weapon poised for use. The other three had the alien blasters, as well, but kept them slung over their shoulders. Max had been clear: The guns were to be used to cover an escape, not for an offensive.

They were no longer careless about their steps, attempting to stay as quiet as possible. The Erdeans' hearing was far superior, and they couldn't be sure just how far away they'd need to be to exceed its range.

Still, it was *Jace* who noticed *them* first. What had started as a low buzzing, like a gnat hovering close to his ear, had swelled. It was louder now, and less constant, coming from different sources. Jace used his hands to advise everyone to keep down. Peering through the edge of another bush, his jaw dropped at the nightmare scenario unfolding before them.

Several Erdeans, moving too quickly to count, were flying through what was left of the trees. More were huddled around clumps of bushes, tearing leaf and limb with their giant mouths. Everything green for as far as Jace could see behind the creatures had been stripped bare. It was a total deforestation. And the aliens were everywhere. They truly were like a plague of locusts, destroying everything in their path. The forest beyond had been turned into a barren landscape.

Jace moved back behind the bushy wall and was about to tell the others what he had seen when the very azalea they were hiding behind shook violently under the weight of a perching Erdean. The alien had landed and immediately began tearing into one of the few sources of lush greenery remaining in the vicinity.

Jess couldn't help it. The startled scream escaped her lips before she could clamp them shut. Aaron reacted more quickly, wrapping Jess in a bear hug, his hand going across her mouth before more than just a squeak could escape. But the damage was done. The Erdean froze on its perch, its head emerging from the foliage on their side of the bush. Alert, the creature looked left and right, searching for the source of the noise, but its downward vision was blocked by the shape of its head, and its forward stare was out over the four huddled humans. Just as it was about to tilt its head to the side to get a look at what was below, another noise shattered the calm. A shrill sound, loud to begin with but growing in intensity, filled the woods. Its curiosity forgotten, the Erdean withdrew into the branches and took off toward the source of the new noise.

Jace and Jess had heard a version of this sound before, and both instantly knew from where. When they had first visited the clearing and were hiding as Max and his group of Alien Taskforce soldiers captured and hauled their father away, the trunk Rick had found in the plane wreckage had begun emitting this same ear-piercing siren.

Finally confident any noise he might make would be drowned out, Jace parted the branches and looked around again. The Erdeans in the trees and on the ground were converging at a single point, where a larger emerald green version of their light green and beige selves was standing on the forest floor. The creature balanced on its front two pair of legs, leaning forward with its abdomen section raised high in the air. The rear legs were rubbing against the very tip of its rear segment so fast that Jace could barely tell what it was. The piercing sound was coming from there. Like a homing beacon, the Erdeans were converging on their leader, piling into a massive ball, crawling all over each other as they tried to get closer to the center, like a swarm of bees surrounding their queen. Grasshoppers didn't behave that way, and locusts were a type of grasshopper, Jace knew, but he again realized that trying to compare these things to Earthly creatures was foolish. It was fascinating to watch, and terrifying at the same time. Certainly not a sight for the squeamish. The bright green leader emerged from the swarm and took flight to the west. The rest of the Erdeans unfurled their wings and followed.

"I guess breakfast break is over and it's time to go back to work," Jace said, falling into a seated position on the ground.

Despite the lump of horror twisting in her gut, Jess was trying to think strategically about what she had just seen, asking, "How many to you think? 20? 30?"

"Too many," Aaron said, his legs wobbling like he might fall at any second. "We have to go back."

Max was about to agree, but Jace rose again to his feet and started forward.

"No way," Jace said. "We have to get to the clearing and see if Dad is there. We have to find out what they're doing. This group is all gone now. The way is clear. Let's go before they come back."

He didn't wait around for debate. He emerged from the laurel and moved quickly through the stripped bare trees and ground. With no undergrowth to go through or around, the journey toward their destination was quick and easy. On two other occasions, from far off in different directions, they heard a repeat of the shrill call echoing through the forest.

If it was a repeat of what they had witnessed, it meant there were at least three squadrons of the things patrolling the forest. If Jess's estimate had been on the low side, there were possibly as many as 100 of the monsters here now.

Or more.

The call came again, this time from their right. Max was the first to recognize the building buzz for what it was, and he pulled the other three to the ground, pressing against a particularly large trunk. There was nowhere else to hide. The buzz increased, like the buildup of a helicopter passing by at low altitude. A swarm of Erdeans streaked past, weaving in and out of the stripped tree branches on their way somewhere else, their shadows sweeping by like puffy clouds on a windy day.

Max heaved a sigh of relief at the close call and urged the kids to turn back, but Jace was not to be deterred. Now that they were this close to the clearing, Jess was on board, too. Lead by the kids, the group pressed forward.

With no foliage left to block the view, they soon came into sight of the giant transporter. The ground and branches were covered in crawling aliens. Even Jace realized this was as close to ground zero as they could risk traveling. With no other real options for cover, each of them picked a tree trunk to hide behind, watching in awed fascination at what was happening in and around the clearing.

The first thing they noticed were the arms of the huge machine. They were angled up, meaning they were preparing to send rather than receive. There were other creatures in the clearing, as well, working under the close observation of armed and attentive Erdeans. The new creatures were oddly familiar yet just as alien as the Erdeans themselves. They resembled monkeys, much smaller in stature than their guards and adult humans, but were completely hairless, their skin the healthy pink of a naked human. Their heads were slightly too large for their frames, but they were too far away to make out features. What they could see, however, were the shackles around their legs and the chains linking them together. They were tied in groups of five, moving dirt with some kind of scoop. They were working around a large mound of freshly dug soil. From the top emerged several Erdeans, entering the clearing on all six legs from tunnels they were digging below the surface. From their mouths, they unloaded a glob of wet dirt and went back down for more. The chained group scooped up the dirt and moved on.

Jess was horrified. She knew exactly what she was seeing.

Slaves.

Whether from Erdea or another planet out there somewhere, these creatures had been rounded up and forced into service.

Jess couldn't help it. She threw up. Beside them, Aaron lost his breakfast, as well.

Worse was still to come.

More Erdeans were coming into view. Some were holding leashes, controlling large furry animals that vaguely resembled what might result if a mad scientist crossed a vicious dog with an alligator. The creatures were lunging against their restraints, trying to get at the chained workers.

All activity stopped for a moment as the biggest Erdean they'd seen yet emerged from a crowd and lowered herself backward into the excavation. Erdean guards, not slaves, formed a protective ring.

From around the giant structure in the center of the clearing, another chained group emerged. Four of the creatures looked the same as the others. But the fifth, the one in the rear, was a human girl maybe two years younger than Jace and Jess. Ashamed, she was trying to cover her naked body, but they were being forced to move too quickly, to work too hard. She stumbled and fell, only to be drug on her knees to the base of the mound.

Jace didn't even have to think about it. He pulled his weapon from over his shoulder and was starting to take aim when something else caught his eye. From a thick branch in the middle of a nearby tree, the Erdeans were detaching what looked like two slabs of beef. Jace lowered the gun and watched.

Jess followed his gaze and tried to make sense of what she was seeing. She had seen butterflies cocoon themselves and hang from underneath branches. This looked a little like that. Whatever the aliens were pulling free under the branch looked to be wrapped in some opaque shell. With an Erdean carrying from each end, they transported the cocoon-like objects to the platform circling the middle of the transporter. Using their strong jaws, they ripped and tore at the outer covering, revealing what was inside. Jess understood first. She recognized the shirt. It was their father and another man. Brown Eyes.

Wasting no time, the attending Erdeans pulled the two men to their feet and unceremoniously shoved them through the dark opening into the center of the transporter. In a blast of light and a ground-shaking *WHOOMP*, they were gone.

CHAPTER 5
Betrayed

Max reacted before Jace could. The OS operative grabbed Jace from behind, one arm around his waist and another clamped over his mouth. The scream died in Max's palm as he dragged the boy away. He didn't let Jace down until they were well out of view of the clearing.

Jess stood trembling in place, staring at the machine that had just shot her father off the planet. The weapon she held flittered up and down, side to side. Aaron cautiously approached, not wanting to startle her into accidentally firing off a shot and giving away their presence. Slowly and deliberately, he eased her finger off the trigger and hooked his arm in hers, guiding her back the way they had come.

When they were confident they had escaped notice and were free to talk, Max took his hand off Jace's mouth.

Jace had a wild look in his eyes but made no move to return to the clearing. There was nothing he could do for his father at this point, and they were hopelessly outnumbered. He understood their best course of action was to get back, spread the word, and formulate a full-scale plan of attack to exterminate these bugs. Another plot was tickling the back of his mind, though. Things had just gotten more complicated. It wasn't going to be enough to just win the battle here. Now he also had to figure out how to get himself in that machine, rescue his father from wherever it led him, and get back. And somehow manage to accomplish this with the understanding that the OS's primary mission would be to destroy the transporter as soon as possible.

Max seemed to read his mind but had no way to comfort him. It wasn't in his personality to dish out false hope.

"We'll do everything we can to get him back, Jace," he said. "But you know we have to protect the planet first, right?"

Jace's eyes were still blared wide open as he continued to process what he'd just seen. The reality of the situation was bleak, and deep down he knew it. Max had just pretty much confirmed that he might never see his dad again. He *knew* but couldn't say it. To agree would be to accept it.

Tears rolled down Jess's face, and sobs wracked her body. All Aaron could do was hold her to his chest. Max's words were a blow to him, as well. Rick had been his best friend for years. They had gotten into this mess together, and now he'd have to live forever knowing his role in it. Loss had become a way of life for him, and he didn't know how much more he could take. So he held Jess for as long as she let him, because once that bond was broken, he wasn't sure he'd be able to go on.

"It's not over, Uncle Urn," Jess said, breaking her silence. "As long as we're still fighting and that machine is still standing, we have hope."

Hope wasn't an emotion he was very in tune with at the moment, but Aaron knew if this 11-year-old girl could keep a fighting spirit after everything she'd seen and been through, then so could he. With his shirttail, he wiped Jess's eyes and stood tall.

Jess grabbed Jace's hand, and without another word, they led the way out. Time had ceased to have meaning, so they had no idea how long it took to get out of the stripped bare part of the forest and back into the undergrowth and leafy overhead canopy. Max kept his weapon at the ready, but they didn't run into more aliens. The swarms seemed to be out stripping another part of the land.

The sun was high overhead when they stopped behind the giant wall of laurels for water and a power bar. Neither kid felt like eating, but they both forced down a couple of bites.

"I'm going to get him back," Jace said, speaking for the first time.

"I don't care what it takes."

"I do," Jess said thoughtfully.

Jace tried to avoid eye contact with her, but she kept moving when he moved, and he finally looked at her.

"Do what?" he said.

"I do care about what it takes to get him back."

Jace's eyes flared again, flashing with anger, as he asked, "So you don't care about getting him back? Is that what you're saying?"

"Of course I do," Jess said, trying to be understanding but determined to stay on point. "If there's any chance, we'll take it, but remember everything else you saw in that clearing, Jace. That girl chained up with those other...other..."

She couldn't come up with a word to describe them.

"People, Jess," Aaron said, filling in the gap. "They might not have been human, and they certainly weren't from this world, but they were people all the same."

Jess nodded. "Okay, people. They certainly weren't there because they wanted to be. Our number one priority HAS to be making sure we defeat the Erdeans. They're evil, and we have to make sure they can't do this to our planet."

"Or any other planet," Aaron said. "Their reign of tyranny ends here."

"So you're willing to just give up on Dad?" Jace snapped back, stubbornly refusing to concede.

"No. Of course not," she said, then paused, not sure if she wanted to say out loud what she was really thinking. This was a time for honesty, though. They couldn't really move forward unless everything was out on the table. "Jace, Dad is sick, and he's not going to get better. I want more time with him as badly as you do, but we can't risk *every-thing* else to try to save him."

Jace's face dropped like he'd been punched in the gut. He knew what his sister said was true, but he wasn't ready to let it go that easily.

"You may be willing to give up on him, but I'm not."

"Nobody is giving up on Rick, Jace," Aaron said. "Not Jess and certainly not me, either. We'll do everything we can, won't we, Max?"

But Max's attention was elsewhere. He was staring off in the direction of the lake and their command center RV.

"Max?"

Max put his fingers to his lips and crouched low, trying to see through the brushy outcropping to the opposite side. The other three were instantly on guard, their conversation not forgotten but on hold until they dealt with whatever new threat had arisen. Jace, Jess, and Aaron pulled their weapons, ready to fight, but Max motioned for them to put the guns away. His own blaster was slung over his shoulder.

Whistles, like bird calls, reverberated through the forest. Jess cocked her head in recognition. She started to speak, but Max hissed at her to shut up and stay low. After another minute, he gathered them close and whispered a command, a different look in his eye.

"Get under those bushes and stay there. Do NOT come out and do NOT make a sound."

"What's—"

"NOW!" he demanded, forcing as much power into a whisper as he could.

They obeyed, sliding under the thick, lush branches, earning deep scrapes down their backs for the effort. Max whipped the laser weapon off his back and tossed it under the bush near where they crouched.

Jess looked at Jace and asked the question with her eyes: What's going on?

Jace shook his head.

"FREEZE!" the voice yelled, booming through the forest, but the kids couldn't see the source.

Methodically, Max took his conventional handgun out of the holster on his hip and slowly set it on the ground by his feet.

Max kept his voice low and even. "I'm Lieutenant Max—"

"I know who you are, traitor."

Max cringed at the volume but otherwise didn't move. From the forest in front of him, several camouflage-garbed soldiers emerged, seemingly out of thin air. All had military issue rifles trained on Max. He recognized a couple of the men moving in to surround him and said, "Johnson. Hodges. What's the meaning of this? What's going on here?"

Another man, this one dressed in fatigues, emerged from behind the cover of a tree and moved into the middle of the circle.

"I'm Colonel Dan Briggs, lieutenant. We intercepted your message last night. I don't know what the OS is exactly, but I suspect you're going to have a lot of time in a cell to think about telling us."

Jace and Jess could see Max's head was spinning side to side, taking it all in and trying to get a grasp on what was happening.

"Briggs?" Max said questioningly. "Aren't you with the Army? What are you doing out here?"

"I could ask you the same thing," the man said. "In fact, I think I will. How does a special operations lieutenant like yourself go AWOL from his unit? And how does a decorated soldier like yourself end up in this patch of trees, sending coded messages to some unknown enemy organization about some alien nonsense?"

Max went silent for several moments, then did the last thing Jess and Jace expected him to do.

"Sir, since you are here and know who I am, I assume you are aware of the Alien Taskforce and my role in it?"

Colonel Briggs crossed his arms, raised his chin, and looked down on Max.

"I was briefed on the matter," he said finally.

"Then you'll be aware that we've been in pursuit of Rick Grisham, who, as you no doubt know, was threatening to go public with top secret, highly classified information."

Jess looked at Jace again and mouthed, *Where is he going with this?*

Jace shrugged his shoulders, but his look said it all. He was afraid they weren't going to like how this turned out.

In front of them, the conversation continued.

Briggs spoke next, saying, "I know Grisham was captured at a nearby area of interest only to escape from your custody. That was along about the same time you pulled a Houdini act and vanished."

"I got a tip about the location of Grisham's kids," Max said. "Twins. *Age* 11. They had knowledge of their father's whereabouts and were in contact with a group called the Origin Society. I went undercover, infiltrated the group, and tracked Grisham back to this forest, sir."

Briggs looked doubtful as he asked, "And where is Mr. Grisham and this group—the Origin Society, I think you called them—now?"

Max glanced around the circle at the men who had him surrounded. Jace was certain that at any moment, he would make his move. To say more now would blow their whole operation and crush any hopes they had of rescuing their father.

Jess had the same thoughts going through her mind. Max had mentioned that members of the Alien Taskforce were also members of the OS. Maybe one of the men in this group was, too. That would explain why Max was looking around, studying each of them closely. Her heart dropped, though, when Max's gaze paused between the two closest to their hiding spot. She felt his gaze burn right through her. There was no warmth, no trust, no compassion, and no sense of "us against them." Max was in this for himself.

"We've got to get out of here," Jess whispered to Jace, realizing the danger they were in was greater than the risk of being overheard. "We've got to go now."

She was scooting backward on her belly, trying to get out from under the giant bush. Aaron, not understanding what was going on, grabbed her arm to hold her still. Jace knew something was amiss, as well, but didn't know what to do.

Max faced the colonel again and answered, "Grisham was terminally ill. Finding the...um...location was his last hoorah. He had no intention of getting captured again. He committed suicide this morning when I caught up to him. Took the coward's way out rather than facing the consequences."

Jess was convinced she must've misunderstood. Jace's jaw dropped. He grabbed Max's discarded weapon and started crawling forward, but Jess caught his ankle and pulled him back. They were starting to cause a commotion. One of the nearby soldiers tilted his head their way. Another looked over his shoulder to see what was going on, but the hidden trio went still again.

What was Max playing at? What was he hoping to accomplish with that lie about their father? They had been through such an emotional wringer over the past few days that both of their minds were having trouble seeing where this was going. For good or bad, it didn't take long to find out.

"I see," said Briggs dubiously. "And what about the rest of this so-called Society? Did they off themselves, too, like some kind of religious cult?"

Max took a deep breath and finished driving the nail in the coffin.

"No, sir. There was no secret group. It was just Grisham, his kids, and his closest confidant, Aaron Bellamy," Max said with a sneer. He then turned and pointed toward the thick laurels. "They are hiding under those bushes."

PART 2
HQ

INTERLUDE, PART 2

1,000,000 Years Ago

The Mondean miner called Darner shut off his mechanical drill and exited his comfortable seat. A sensor on the drill bit had picked up the presence of a foreign object in the salt vein and had automatically shut off. It was a common development in the mining business. Seldom did you run across a pure vein of any resource. There were always rocks and other materials mixed in, and if the big drill hit one of those objects, the ensuing damage could throw the entire operation off schedule for the week.

The drilling machine itself looked a lot like a forklift, the heavy-duty drill out front of a cage large enough to house a full-grown Mondean man. Knobs and levers inside the cage controlled the drill. The whole apparatus sat on a pair of tank treads that looked just like those that would eventually be used to propel military tanks on Earth. In fact, the first tanks were built from leaked Mondean designs, but Darner knew nothing of that.

Out of his control cabin, he squeezed his body against the narrow tunnel to the rear of the machine. He stretched his cramped muscles and scratched his butt before digging through the toolbox attached to the rear bumper.

"I really need to organize these tools," Darner thought aloud, sorting through the clutter before finally finding the chisel and hammer he was looking for.

Squeezing himself past the machine in the other direction, he reached the front, crawling waist deep in the dark hole that had just been opened by the drill. He began the laborious task of chipping away at the rich vein of salt, trying to find the obstruction. Because his body was blocking the light from his drill, he switched on his head lamp to illuminate the leading edge of the newly excavated hole. The shadows were deeper and flitted to and fro with every movement he made, but he could see well enough.

The obstruction should be no more than a couple of inches through the salt. Using the chisel, he began manually scrapping his way forward. His progress stopped with a few taps of the hammer. Whatever it was blocking the way was going to need more force to remove. That wasn't unusual. Some of the rock this deep down was nearly as hard as diamonds.

No problem, Darner thought. He squirmed back out of the hole and slid back to the rear of the drilling machine. From a different compartment, he pulled out the blaster. The general size and shape of a chainsaw, the blaster was a sonic device that created vibrations so intense that its use required the same steady stream of water to cool it. Darner switched on the device, redirected the stream of water, and inserted the sonic probe into the hole.

The resulting explosion was powerful enough to collapse the tunnel Darner had spent the entire week digging. The shaking ground triggered earthquake warnings on the surface, and a rescue team was dispatched immediately.

In an amazing stroke of luck, Darner's life was spared when his body was blown back into the cage of the drill. Equipped with a supply of air, a mask to breathe it through, and a frame strong enough to withstand the weight of the world falling on top of it, Darner miraculously survived the ordeal. Although he remembered very little of the accident, his brain held on to one small but vital detail. In the process, he likely gave humanity a chance to evolve on a small blue-green planet lightyears away.

The first order of business for the rescue team was to scan the ground for signs of life. Second, they used highly specialized sensors to search out the cause of the explosion and see if there was risk of secondary blasts. Only then could excavating commence. During their scans, the sensors picked up two unexpected signals.

Life. And blulex.

There's no blulex in this region, the supervisor thought to himself. But the signature in the scan was unmistakable. Using the scan to map the best possible route to the surviving miner, the digging began. When they reached Darner's collapsed tunnel, however, they also tapped into a well of salt water that gushed forward, filling in every crevice.

They searched and searched for signs of the blulex but eventually wrote it off as a faulty reading. When Darner was interviewed about the incident a week later by the safety committee, he insisted he had, in fact, seen a sparkle of blue rock milliseconds before the blast.

Research was done. Experiments were conducted. And an amazing property of the very powerful but normally stable blulex was discovered.

The Council had to be informed.

"You're certain of this?" the head of The Supreme Planetary Council queried.

"Yes, sir, absolutely," the Mondean representative confirmed. "And in our quest to prove it, we encountered something else. Something far more substantial."

"More substantial than the masking properties of the most valuable energy source in the galaxy?" the head asked, incredulous.

"Well...yes," the Mondean said.

"Explain."

"Yes, sir. As you know, sir, Mondea has no natural reserves of blulex. We mine and import all of our stores from two small moons orbiting the sixth planet in our system."

"Yes, yes, I'm aware," the head said impatiently.

"During an investigation of an accident at a salt-mining facility on our planet, scans revealed the presence of a small sum of blulex."

"A meteor, most likely," the head said, trying to move the story along.

"Yes, most likely. Except when we reached the spot, there was no blulex. Only a massive quantity of salt water."

"You think..." the head said, trailing off.

"Yes, but there's more."

"Go on."

"Not wanting to experiment on our main supply of blulex, we performed a deep space scan in an attempt to find another small supply on which to run our tests. We found a very small piece, likely another meteorite fragment, two star systems away. We ran our tests and replicated the results. Our theory was proven. But during our scans, we uncovered something astounding. Truly amazing. We picked up the unmistakable signature of blulex on another planet out in the far reaches of the galaxy's arm. If our scanners were correct—and we checked many, many times—it is the largest deposit ever found. More in one location than the collective sum of what's been discovered across the entire universe. The entire planet might be made of it."

The head sat down in his chair, his eyes wide. This was big news. Huge. Blulex was the most valuable commodity in existence. A pure chunk no larger than the desk at which he sat would power an entire planet for a year. Wars had been fought over barren moons that contained no more than one or two blulex boulders. His mouth gaped open.

"Sir, there's more," the Mondean rep said, his tone suddenly somber. "For every ray of light, there's a shadow of darkness. News of this magnitude couldn't possibly come without a downside."

The head grasped the armrest of his chair and prepared himself, saying, "Go on."

"During our search, we detected signs of other scans, also directed at this planet."

"Don't tell me..." the head said, dreading confirmation of what he knew in his sunken heart.

"I'm afraid so, sir," the Mondean said. "Erdeans. They've found it, too."

CHAPTER 6
Out of Pocket

For the 100th time in the last hour, Jace grabbed the bars of the cell door and shook them as hard as he could. The door came no closer to opening than it had the first 99 times. He continually paced the confined space, muttering to himself. Only a few words were audible, but it was a repeated combination of jerk, Max, betrayed, Dad, and escape.

It was just him, Jess, and Aaron in the small cell. Three walls were made of painted cinderblocks, with only a barred window on the back wall to break the monotony. Night had fallen, and the only things visible through the small hole were a sliver of moon and a few bright stars. The front wall was nothing but thick steel bars, broken only by the metal frame of a lone door. Beyond was a smaller room with a single plain desk, a basic chair, and another cinderblock barrier.

Jace shook the door again, the wild look in his eye not easing.

"Jace, please," Aaron said from the lower of two bunk beds, pleading with his young charge to settle down.

On the upper bunk, Jess lay flat, staring at the ceiling. She had barely uttered two words since being dragged out from under the bushes back in the forest.

Colonel Briggs had questioned them for what felt like hours at the scene. His attempts continued in the back of the windowless panel van as they drove until the sun had set. He tried again after locking them in this cell, sitting patiently in the solitary chair and calmly asking his questions. He professionally ignored Jace's queries of where they were and demands to let them go. During it all, Aaron and Jess had remained silent.

They had no idea where they were, only that the drive to get here had taken hours. Once in the van, they had seen nothing until they'd parked and the sliding door had opened to reveal a dark garage. They had taken an elevator up, had been led down a long beige hallway, and had been locked in this room. From the time they'd stepped out of the van until the cell door had slammed, four heavily armored soldiers had had military style rifles pointed directly at them. Even Jace had known not to try anything rash. His mouth, however, hadn't been able to help itself.

"LET US OUT!" he yelled, ignoring Aaron and yanking the bars with his most ferocious effort yet.

Jace's rage, if anything, was ticking upward. Spit flew from the corners of his mouth as he continued in vain to push and pull on the locked door and yell for someone—anyone—to come free them. Still, his frustration and anger prevented him from forming complete sentences.

After another five minutes, Jess slid off the bunk, wiped away her own tears of frustration, and wrapped her arms around Jace from behind, embracing him with sisterly love. Resting her head between his tense shoulder blades, she said nothing, just squeezed tighter.

It had the desired effect. Jace's storm gradually blew out, leaving him red eyed and exhausted. It had been a long few days.

"He can't be gone, Jess," he said quietly.

Jess, still holding tightly, nodded. "He *is* gone, Jace. We saw it happen. But that doesn't mean we can't get him back. I don't know how, but we won't quit until we do."

Jace broke free of his sister's embrace and turned to face her. "What if they kill him before we find a way to get him back?" he said, his voice cracking. "What if he...if he..."

He couldn't finish the thought. They had lived the past year knowing that their father's days were numbered. That one day, sooner rather than later, the ravages of the ALS would be more than his body could sustain. It had always been out there in the "one day," though, and until then they had time to spend with him. Now he was somewhere in space, hostage to a horde of super-intelligent insects whose sole mission was to take over their planet and enslave its inhabitants. How long could he possibly survive?

"They won't kill him, and he won't die," Jess said definitively. She believed it, too. Before he could ask, she explained. "Remember the blankets? Remember when Dad was under their influence? He was fine. Same for Mr. Hammonds. And Maggie Karst. The blankets healed them. It's what Dad wanted to begin with. He believed that if he could find proof the aliens existed, if he could make contact, maybe he could find a cure. Well, he did."

Jess shrugged her shoulders and smiled as she said it. Things had certainly not gone the way their father had hoped or expected, but he *had* found the cure.

"You saw what happened when the blankets were taken away, though," Jace said. "They d-d-died."

"If the Erdeans wanted him dead, they would have killed him in the clearing," she said, determined to find the silver lining. "Obviously, in the condition he's in, he won't be of much use to them. They know about the prophecy. They know about us. Maybe that's why they transported him instead of killing him."

Jace's mind was slowly starting to engage again, and he asked, "You think they'll use him as bait to get to us?"

"I hope so," Jess said.

At that, Aaron finally broke his silence. He swung his feet onto the floor and moved his head out of the shadows, saying, "You *hope*?"

"Yes," Jess said with resolve. "As long as they're using him to get to us, that means he's alive. It means we have a chance."

"I think your overestimate us ever breathing free air again," Aaron said, waving his arms to indicate the impenetrable walls of the jail cell.

To hear Aaron speak as if he'd lost all hope spoke to the desperate nature of their current predicament. Jace, however, was perking up, his anger and frustration transforming into a renewed determination. He took the three steps needed to cover the width of the cell and stood on tiptoes to look out through the window. He stared at the moon and stars beyond. The view stood for something different now. Flashes of lightning lit up the sky on the horizon, signaling a coming storm, but the sky overhead was still clear.

"It won't be easy, but as long as we're alive, there's a chance," Jess insisted.

"It would've been easier if Max hadn't turned out to be a traitor," Jace said, his gaze still focused on the heavens.

"It's true. He seemed to know a lot about what's going on, the history between Earth and the Erdeans," Jess admitted. "But there are others like him out there. They'll all be coming out of hiding now. Maybe we can find one of them."

"Maybe," Jace admitted. "I'd sure like to run into Max again, though, and—"

He broke off and tilted his head to the side, continuing to look at the small slice of the night sky visible through the window.

"What?" Jess asked. "What is it?"

She edged in to look out herself but didn't notice anything out of the ordinary. Jace said nothing, but he tried to get his face closer to the window.

"Jace?" Jess asked, concern creeping into her voice.

"Wait," Jace said after a moment. He kept his eyes locked on the sky but used his hand to gently push his sister out of his way. "I saw something."

Aaron got up from his bunk and joined the other two at the window. Being much taller, he knelt low to get the same angle. All he could see was the sliver of the waning moon.

"THERE!" Jace yelled, pointing. "There it was again!"

"What? I was blinking," Jess cried. "What did you see?"

But Jace's mind was racing. His eyes were wide, and the desperation to get out of the jail cell was creeping back in.

"We have to get out of here. We have to get out of here," Jace repeated, leaving the window and starting to pace.

"Jace, tell me what you saw," Jess demanded.

"I saw it," Aaron said, his voice calm and level.

"What? What did you see?" Despite the calm she wanted to portray, Jess was starting to lose it.

"We've got to get out of here," Jace repeated.

Aaron, still staring outside, urged Jess to keep looking.

A moment later, it happened again. There was a faint flash of red, followed by the sudden appearance of an oddly shaped mass nearly as large as the moon itself. Then just as quickly, nothing.

"Did you see it?"

"We have to get out of here," Jace said. He'd returned to the barred door, shaking it again with all his might.

"Was that..."

"A giant spaceship being transported in? Yes. I think it was," Aaron said.

"Where'd it go?" Jess asked.

"Nowhere," Jace responded, knuckles white from grasping the bars so tightly. "They're hiding behind the moon, maybe even cloaking the ships."

Jace shook the bars again, and Jess's face went as white as her brother's knuckles as she asked, "Why are they transporting in giant ships?" It was a rhetorical question. Jess knew the answer. She wasn't a science fiction fan. She didn't watch *Star Trek* and didn't really care one way or another about *Star Wars*, but she didn't need to be that kind of geek to put the pieces of the puzzle together. "Invasion."

Jace nodded. "They're after more than just a few kids."

"They want something else," Aaron agreed.

"We have to get out of here," Jess cried, joining her brother at the door.

Jace suddenly slapped the palm of his hand against his forehead and stepped away from the bars.

"I know how to get out," he said. "Of this room, anyway, but it's a start."

During all of the interrogation they had faced, the soldiers had never once searched the trio. It had been question after question, but not once had they been asked to do so much as turn out their pockets. They'd been locked up and left in this room.

Jace patted his pocket, smiled mischievously, and reached in. Palming something, he instructed Jess and Aaron to go stand by the cell door. Reluctantly, they followed his instructions. Jace himself backed into the far corner of the small cell, squeezing himself between the bunks and wall. He needed to ensure he stayed outside the boundary.

"Jace, what are you—" Jess started to ask, but Jace waved her off, surveying the space.

Satisfied his calculations were correct, he unclenched his palm, revealing a small blue cube. Without a word, he tossed it in the direction of Jess and Aaron. Just as it hit the ground, it expanded, filling most of the jail cell and outer room with blue plasma-like walls. Jace just barely remained outside of the containment field.

He grinned. "Perfect."

The heavy steel bars of the cell, including the door, never stood a chance against the alien technology. The crackling blue box sliced through them like a hot knife through butter. Aaron pushed against the cell door, and it tumbled forward against the blue barrier, crumbling into sparkling silver dust as it fell.

Jace edged himself out of the gap near the bunks, then stooped to touch the lower corner of the transparent box, causing it to contract back into a pocket-sized cube.

No longer confined behind bars, they rushed forward, opened the room's outer door, and stepped out into a long, deserted corridor.

Step one of the escape was complete.

But as Jess took in the long hallway and tried to survey their surroundings, she couldn't help but feel that had been the easy part.

CHAPTER 7

Spies and Traitors

The trio stepped out into the hallway, Aaron closing the door behind them. They froze, trying to determine which way to go. In both directions, the empty hallway didn't appear to end, only angling away slightly far off in both directions. Doors in regularly spaced intervals were all that broke the monotony of the concrete corridor. Each looked just like the one from where they had just emerged. They looked at one another as if expecting someone else to take the lead and make a suggestion.

Jace broke the stalemate. "This way," he said, turning to their right and moving forward with confidence.

"It feels like they brought us in the other way," Jess said, hesitating. "Are you sure?"

Jace shrugged his shoulders. "No," he said honestly, though he didn't slow down.

In video games, uncertainty got you captured. His gamer persona lived by the motto "Fake it till you make it." Besides, with the way the hallway shifted far ahead at a slight angle, he had the feeling both directions ended up at the same place. If so, this building was massive.

There were no defining markings on the doors other than a small black plate affixed to the frame with a letter and three numbers.

"B137," Jess said, reading one.

"B248 over here," Aaron said, pointing out the next door in line on the opposite side.

"How does anyone find their way around here?" Jace asked. "It all looks the same, and the numbers don't appear to be in any particular order. And where is everyone?"

"It's the middle of the night, silly," Jess said.

"But this is obviously a huge government facility. Even if all these rooms are just jail cells like the one we were in, there has to be guards," Jace insisted.

"Jace is right," Aaron said. "We need to get out of sight quickly."

There had to be elevators or a stairwell somewhere, but they'd not come across anything different yet. They randomly checked doors every few steps, but so far all had been locked.

"Here," Aaron whispered, holding a finger to his lips to keep the twins quiet.

The latest doorknob he tried had turned in his hands. Tiptoeing over and staying as silent as they could in case someone was inside, Jace and Jess huddled behind Aaron as he inched the door open just a crack. There was nothing but a sliver of darkness inside, but as Aaron opened the door just a little more, lights suddenly turned on within. Jess let out an involuntary squeal of panic, and Aaron let his hand slip from the door, which closed on its own.

Aaron held his other hand to his chest as if trying to settle his thumping heart, but he understood what had happened.

"Automatic lights. They turn on when you open the door," he said, pulling the door all the way open. "There'll be a motion sensor in the room. If it doesn't detect movement after so long, the lights turn off. It's an energy saver."

Confident now that the room was empty, they slid inside to find a space very different than the one from which they had escaped. The first thing they noticed was the unmistakable smell of stale coffee and old paper. Next, it was much larger. There were desks all over, placed in short office cubicles. The desks were in varying states of messiness, some with stacks of paper threatening to topple over with the slightest breeze, others very neat and tidy. Computer monitors and keyboards were the only consistent feature. Along the edges of the space were glassed-in rooms. Inside those were windows to the outside world, but the reflection of the interior lights off the glass prevented them from making out any details in the darkness beyond.

"Looks like the newsroom at the Daily Sun," Jess said, recalling their class field trip to Ridgeport's newspaper offices two years ago.

"Something like that," Aaron said, scanning the space until he found what he was looking for. "There!" He pointed.

In the far-left corner were three doors unlike all the others. Two were instantly recognizable, even without the familiar "Men's" and "Women's" signs that marked every bathroom everywhere. The third had a plaque that simply said "SUPPLIES." Aaron opened that door and peaked in. The room was full of exactly what you'd expect to find inside such an office space. Behind a very large copy machine were shelves loaded with reams of paper. Pens, pencils, paperclips, staplers, folders of every color, coffee cans, labels, and more lined all of the other shelves. In the corner, though, hung three neatly pressed security guard uniforms.

A plan quickly forming in his mind, Aaron quickly surveyed the uniforms, selected the one he believed would come closest to fitting his large frame, and took it into the men's room. A minute later, he was back out. The top was a little too tight, and the legs were about two inches too short. The hiking boots he'd been wearing since leaving Ridgeport were completely wrong, but it just might be good enough to get them out of there.

Jace couldn't help but take one jab, however, saying, "You look like 15 pounds of potatoes in a 10-pound bag."

That brought a smile to Jess's face. Their father had once said that about an old professional baseball player he'd seen on TV. The memory was bittersweet, but it brought focus back to the task at hand.

"It'll have to do," Aaron said through gritted teeth. "Now, let's find a way out of here."

They made their first mistake of the escape attempt when they barged back into the hallway without first checking that the coast was clear. The door almost slammed into a harried-looking man in an untucked, blue, button-down shirt. Fortunately, the man was absorbed in a report he was holding and barely looked up. He trudged on without paying them any mind.

Jace, Jess, and Aaron quickly turned and went in the opposite direction before the man realized just how out of place two kids and man in an ill-fitting security uniform were in a building like this. The next person they ran into, however, seemed just as anxious to avoid them as they were him. He looked quite guilty about something, like he was sneaking around somewhere he did not belong, as he slid through a slightly opened door. Beyond, Jace was just able to catch a glimpse of a closing elevator. The man was big, taller and wider than Aaron, but seemed to be trying to conceal himself under a large black hoodie that masked his face in shadows.

Before Jace could look closer at the man or the elevator room, a voice boomed out from behind them.

"Hold it right there!" the voice commanded. "Let me see some ID."

Jace whimpered and actually took the first step in an attempt to run away, but Jess grabbed his arm to hold him in place. Turning to look, Aaron backed into them, but Jess put her other hand on his back to hold him still.

It was the stranger who had just emerged suspiciously from the elevator room who made the first move. He didn't run. Instead, he walked directly at the real security guard, his face still deeply shadowed under his hood.

The security officer took a guarded step backward, watching carefully as the strange man approached and reached into the front pocket of the hoodie. The guard's hand reached automatically for the butt of the gun on his right hip.

Making sure they were well clear of the guard and newcomer, Jess, Jace, and Aaron backed away, taking baby steps in the opposite direction until they'd reached the wall. Seeing how a real security guard was supposed to look, they came to the simultaneous realization that Aaron's portrayal was quite ridiculous. But the real guard had fallen for the ruse long enough to turn his attention on the other person. It bought them a second, and now they had to take advantage.

Jace started to pull them toward the door where the elevators lay beyond. He couldn't help but take one glance back. From ahead, Jace couldn't tell what it was, but he knew the stranger had pulled something from his pocket and was handing it to the wary guard. Instantly, the look on the uniformed man's face changed. His eyes lit up, and a smile spread across his face.

"Is that..." he said, wonderment pouring from every syllable. "I haven't...not since...my favorite when I was a boy."

Jace's stomach dropped. He didn't have to see what the stranger had handed the guard to know. Jess's tightening grip on his wrist told him his sister knew, too. Aaron stepped to the front of their little pack and spread his long arms protectively in front of the twins.

The security guard took a step back, and they had a clear view of the pure white scrap of cloth cradled gently in his arms. Forgotten, as if they were never noticed, he lazily spun around and walked off from the small group, his eyes never leaving the EncephaLink that was no doubt masking itself as something comforting from his childhood.

Jess's jaw worked up and down, but no words came out. Jace's mind raced as he tried to work out just how this stranger managed to get his hands on alien technology. Before either could connect all the dots, the hooded stranger turned back to face them and stepped forward. Even Jace's bravado faltered as he tried to shrink farther behind Aaron. The man's features remained hidden in the shadows, but his head tilted sideways, like a curious dog, as he turned from Jace to Jess and back again.

Certain their luck had run out, Jess's legs threatened to give out from under her. They had backed all the way against the door from which the stranger had initially emerged. They had nowhere to go.

The man took another step closer and stooped over to eye level.

From within the shadows, a scratchy, high-pitched voice spoke what seemed to be words, but they were those of a language they didn't recognize. He was so close now, and the twins could smell the putrid stench of his breath. Like some sort of realization had dawned on him, the man rose to full height and took a step back.

"The two," he said, his English perfect.

And with that, he was gone.

Their backs sliding down the wall, Jace and Jess crumbled to the floor, the fingers of their hands entwined. Even Aaron sighed heavily in relief.

"An...an...an Erdean spy," Jace said, finally recovering his ability to speak.

Jess's mind was going somewhere else, and she said, "He...he knew who we were."

"We've got to get out of here," Aaron said, grasping for the kids' arms to pull them to their feet.

Jace stood and made as if to follow the stranger, who was nearly out of view around the distant corner of the long corridor.

"No," Aaron insisted, holding him back. "We have to go. We have to find a way out."

Jace started to argue but knew getting far away from this building was probably best.

"There are elevators in here," Jace said, pointing to the door behind them. "I saw them when the Erdean dude opened the door."

"Great," Aaron said, helping Jess to her feet.

"Let's get out of here," she agreed.

In the elevator room—for that's truly what it was—they pressed the down button and waited impatiently. Finally, with a warbled DING, the elevator door slid open, and they came face to face with the last person they wanted to see.

"Well, imagine that," Max said, shaking his head in disbelief.

CHAPTER 8
Infiltrated

Somehow with only two hands, Max hauled, with one frantic motion, the three escapees into the elevator car. The door closed, and Max used a special key pulled from his pocket to hold the lift in place.

"What do you think you're doing?" Max hissed, fear and panic etched like an advertisement on his chiseled face.

Jace reacted first, twisting to pull free from Max's grip, using the momentum to launch himself back into the OS operative's midsection. The move caught Max off guard, and air escaped his lungs with an explosive *oomph!* A trained special forces agent, Max could've handled two kids and one out-of-shape adult with one hand tied behind his back, but Jace's attack had caught him off guard.

Taking advantage, Aaron rushed forward, slid his arms through Max's, and jerked them behind his body, locking him in place. It was a wrestling move called "a full nelson," and it gave the smaller person control and power over a larger, stronger foe.

Jess smoothly slid Max's holstered weapon from his shoulder harness and pointed it squarely at Max's nose like she'd been handling weapons all of her life.

"You double-crossing, self-serving traitor," Jace yelled, his arm cocked like he was about to deliver a punch at any second.

"*Double-crossing?*" Jess said in amazement. The gun bobbed up and down as her nerves caught up to her actions. "Double? Just two? I've lost track of how many people he's crossed."

Max lowered his head, not ready to refute her claim. Instead, he slowly and deliberately turned his head to look over his shoulder in Aaron's direction, then said, "Take the gun before she accidentally shoots someone," an eerie calmness settling into his voice.

"Shooting you won't be an accident," Jace said, his cheeks glowing a furious red. "Our dad is gone because of you. I could've saved him in the clearing, but you dragged us out of there and then sold us out to your military buddies!"

The gun shook harder than ever in Jess's hands, but she didn't lower it.

"Please," Max said, his voice still level, his eyes still trying to find Aaron's. "You take the gun, and I'll explain."

Aaron moved as quickly as Jace had earlier. He jammed a knee into the back of Max's leg, causing the knee to buckle. Moving more quickly than the twins thought possible, Aaron carried his big body around Max's, carefully grabbed the handgun by the barrel, and lifted it up and out of Jess's fingers, which were bone white from gripping the handle so hard. He moved to one corner and leveled the weapon at Max, who retreated calmly to the opposite corner. Jess and Jace took refuge at Aaron's side. Jace kept looking at the gun as if he wanted to take charge of the weapon.

"We don't want your explanations," Aaron said. "We just want out of here. You're going to help us."

Max sighed, his head still hanging low, and said, "You have every reason not to trust me, but you need to. Things are moving quickly. Too quickly. If we—and by we, I mean the full strength and might of the United States military—don't act immediately, the Erdean presence in the forest of North Carolina will spread too far and too fast for us to contain. I have a video conference with the President in 30 minutes. I need the three of you as witnesses to help our case. I was on my way now to break you out. I don't know how you beat me to it, but I'm glad you did. It saves us time, but we can't waste it here. You *have* to trust me."

Jace laughed out loud. "Trust you? Never!"

Jess was trying to analyze the situation and Max's words, looking for some angle he was trying to play to trick them again.

"We were right there in the forest," she said. "A military squad had shown up. We could've moved then to stop them. Instead, you turned us in."

This time, it was Max who laughed. "Stop them? You're a smart girl. Think about what you had seen. You think Colonel Briggs and his team were enough to even slow down that swarm of Erdeans, much less stop them?"

"You. Turned. Us. In," Jace said, emphasizing each word as he moved across the elevator to poke Max in the chest with a threatening finger.

Jace was letting his anger make him reckless, but Aaron wasn't about to move closer and give up his advantage with the weapon.

"I know it's hard to see, but I turned you in to save you *and* the colonel's team. The Erdeans were swarming the forest. We didn't know where they were or where they were going. Had they shown up, we'd all have been slaughtered. I bought us time. I gave us a chance. But time is out now. I *have* to convince President Taylor to act immediately, and it's going to take your help to convince her."

Max reached into his pocket, a move that forced Aaron forward.

"Uh-uh," Aaron said, brandishing the handgun threateningly.

Slowly, and with two fingers, Max pulled a key ring from his pocket.

"I *was* coming to get you out," he said. "This is a master key to all the cells." He put the keys back in his pocket and pleaded with the trio. "Now, please," he said. "You have the gun. Jace, turn the key on the elevator console beside you and hit the SB button. Sub-basement. That's where the Alien Taskforce headquarters are located. That's where the President will be calling to video conference us in just a few minutes. We can't miss that call. It's our only chance."

They didn't know what to do. Jess looked to Jace for answers. He looked with uncertainty at Aaron, who turned to Jess. The clock was ticking. As usual, Jess thought through the options the quickest, but she was far from confident in her conclusion.

"I don't see how we have another option," she said.

"We can make him show us the way out," Aaron said, proposing a more appealing alternative.

"Dad used to say, 'Fool me once, shame on you. Fool me twice, shame on me,'" Jess continued. "I don't trust him and don't believe he won't try to sacrifice us to save himself again. But we saw it with our own eyes. Those things were all over the forest, with more coming in by the second. There could be thousands by now. You saw the ships by the moon—"

Max jumped forward, his eyes blared. "Ships? What ships?" he asked, voice cracking with concern.

"Shut up!" Jace yelled, and Aaron extended the gun, ready to use it.

Max's attention remained focused, his body taut, but he sank back against the wall, his hands raised to ease Aaron's worry.

Jess kept talking as if Max hadn't spoken at all. "Even if we get out of here, what then? Who do we tell? Who's going to believe us if we run around screaming at the top of our lungs about aliens and UFOs? Maybe he has a call scheduled with the President. Maybe it's another trick. Hoping its true, though, may be our only chance. *Earth's* only chance."

Slightly embarrassed from the display of passion in her speech, Jess looked to Aaron, who shrugged. Jace looked like he couldn't believe they were actually considering trusting the traitor, but he didn't seem to have a better idea. Grudgingly settled, Jess turned the control key on the elevator and pushed the SB button.

The car jolted under their feet and began a slow descent, and Jace stared Max in the eye, his face leaving no room to doubt whom he blamed for his dad's abduction.

Never blinking, his teeth gritted, Jace spoke to Aaron. "Uncle Urn," he said. "If he even blinks funny, shoot him."

The foursome emerged into a hallway that looked exactly like the one they had just left. If they were truly underground, as the sub-basement level suggested, there was no way to tell. Aaron motioned with a flick of the gun barrel for Max to lead the way. Moving carefully and very deliberately, he did. Aaron followed a few steps behind. In case they ran into others, he slipped the gun into his loose front pocket, but his finger remained curled around the trigger. The twins fell in behind, one to each side of Aaron.

Jace attempted to memorize the doors but gave up after rounding one slight bend. Far, far ahead, another bend was evident. Where were they? Just how big was this building? It had clearly been designed to prevent anyone from doing what Jace was trying to do. It all looked exactly the same, and there seemed to be no rhyme or reason to the door numbering system.

Max, however, seemed to know where he was and exactly where he was going. It took more than a minute, with a steady stride, to reach the next bend in the corridor, but before they got there, Max stopped outside a door that looked no different from any of the others. Their commute had been silent, and they'd not passed a single other person.

Finally, Max spoke. "People come and go here at all hours of the day. It was empty when I left to get you, but that could've changed. If anyone's here, keep your head down, follow me, and do not speak. Aaron, just act like a security guard escorting the kids, the same way you have been."

This directive irked Jace.

"You're not giving the orders here," Jace spat, sounding more like a spoiled 11-year-old than he had at any point over the last few days. "If anyone's here, we'll treat them the same as you."

Max sighed and slightly shook his head in exasperation.

"The Alien Taskforce was formed to keep buried proof that we've been visited by beings from another world, right?" Jess asked.

"Among other things, yes," Max admitted.

"What other things?" she questioned.

Max impatiently checked his watch and muttered, "We're cutting it close."

"*What other things?*" Jess pushed.

"The Taskforce's role has always been to run down any credible leads or reports about alien visitations. We investigate the claims. We easily debunk most of them as airplanes, hoaxes, or just people who had had too much to drink and were seeing things. If we can't disprove the sighting, we discredit the people making the claim. Either way, we cover it all up. That's the policy. Above all else, the job of the Taskforce has been to keep the public in the dark."

This wasn't the answer Jess wanted.

"So now that something bad has happened, no one is prepared," she said, and it wasn't a question.

"Well...no," Max admitted. "But we didn't think it would come to this."

"You're a member of the Origin Society," Jace said, his voice rising enough to make Max flinch and look over his shoulder. "You knew for a fact it *could* happen."

Max lowered his head again, then said, "The OS has existed for thousands of years. For generations, we've hoped that our generation would not be the one that had to deal with the Erdeans' return. But it wouldn't have mattered. I don't run the Taskforce, and no one asks my opinion. Even though I'm a squad leader, I'm still a soldier and follow orders. Trying to explain my role with the OS would only get me court martialed for treason and likely put in jail. The best I could do was pass on anything I learned to the rest of the OS and, as a squad leader, subtly point the Taskforce team in the direction I wanted them to go. I've done just that. Right now, all over the world, OS members are coming forward and talking to their national leaders, telling them all we know." He checked his watch again. "And speaking of, it's time."

It was the middle of the night, and the President looked as if she hadn't yet gone to bed. The collar of her white blouse looked tired and wrinkled. Her green eyes were dark, and her skin was blotchy. She had never been one for a lot of makeup. Her election campaign had been largely about her experience and the substance of her message, not about looks. Her joke at every campaign stop had been about not having the time to worry about her looks, except for her lipstick. Because, she said, the deep crimson color that was her favorite made her look fierce. It was a joke, but it had also become her trademark. Above everything else, President Carmen Taylor was fierce. At this hour, though, she just looked tired. There was no sign of lipstick, and the absence of color on her face was striking.

True to reputation, she got right to the point. "Soldier, it's too late at night—or at this point, too early in the morning—for nonsense," she said. "I've been getting a lot of strange reports tonight, each less believable than the one before it. Now I find out that we have some secret... Alien Taskforce...that has been up to something in North Carolina, that there's something happening behind our moon, and that it all ties into something that happened in the 1950s. So, you have five minutes. Please explain to me why I'm still up at this time of night, speaking to you instead of your commanding officer."

Max took a brief second and a deep breath to gather his thoughts. The President's blunt and direct approach had caught him off guard. He was seated at a standard-sized desk in a glassed-in portion of the headquarters. There had been other workers present when they'd barged in, but if anyone was surprised to see Max, a poorly uniformed security guard, and two 11-year-old kids, they didn't show it. Max had led them around a series of cubicles to the office in the back. He pulled the blinds covering the windows and instructed the kids and Aaron to sit off to the side, out of view of the large computer screen already queued up to receive the President's call. The overhead lights were off, and only the glow from the monitor lit the room.

"Yes, ma'am," Max said with a snapped salute, his military training kicking in automatically. "At this point, I'm operating under the assumption that I am the commanding officer. My CO took a squad into the forests of North Carolina for reconnaissance of the enemy and hasn't been heard from since. Having witnessed that enemy myself, I have reason to believe the entire team has been KIA."

President Taylor's expression hardly changed. "When you say 'enemy,' please explain what you mean. Am I to understand that there are agents of a foreign government attacking a team of United States soldiers in North Carolina?"

"With all due respect, ma'am, I suspect you've been told by now that we're not dealing with an enemy of this planet."

She nodded, appreciating Max's direct approach. "As concisely as you can, tell me the story. Have 'little green men' invaded?" Her tone was sarcastic, as if not ready to believe.

From her seat off screen, Jess gave a wry grin. She'd actually *seen* the aliens and still wasn't fully prepared to believe it.

"Ironically, yes, they are green. But they're not little, and there's nothing humanoid about them. Ma'am, for years, there has been an Alien Taskforce whose mission was to misdirect the public about any reports of alien sightings or visitations," Max explained. "It is my understanding that the sitting President has not always been informed of our existence."

"I've recently become aware. Go on," she said.

"In 1954, aircraft of two different alien species engaged each other in combat and crashed near the city of Ridgeport. Not really knowing what had happened, and fearing Russian aggression, the military sent a team to investigate. What they found was clearly not Russian or, for that matter, anything manmade. The area was cordoned off, the contents of the ships were removed, and the crash site was sealed. The contents recovered from the crashed ships were taken to an island in the Pacific where experiments were performed. As you might expect, what was found was unlike anything ever seen before on this planet. It was quite possible that what was found could be turned into the ulti-mate weapon, greater by far than the atomic bomb. In 1964, top-secret orders were issued to bring the materials back to the United States. On the trip, something went horribly wrong, and the two C-130 cargo planes transporting the materials crashed in North Carolina. On the advice of the research team that had been conducting the experiments, the decision was made to cover up the mission. One plane sank to the bottom of a lake, and the other was in forest so thick and remote that nature would do a far better job covering up than man could ever do."

The President's expression remained unchanged, but she leaned forward just a touch to encourage Max to go on.

"Over time, nature did its job, and the secret was buried. But as is often the case, no secret remains buried forever. There were rumors. There were leaks. Conspiracy theories soon sprang up, and the Ridgeport incident became a treasure hunt of sorts. By this time, there were too many people watching. Scrubbing the site was no longer an option. The only thing we could do was misdirect anyone who got too close. Rick Grisham latched on to the conspiracy and didn't let it go. He and his friend Aaron Bellamy pieced together the truth and uncovered the location of the C-130s. Using keyword surveillance, the task force became aware of Grisham's discovery and sought to apprehend and detain him."

Jace became fidgety at these words, moving to the edge of his seat. Max waved him back with a frantic hand gesture just below the camera's angle of view.

"This mission failed, and Grisham reached the crash site in the forest?" the President asked, although her tone indicated she clearly knew the answer.

"Yes, but we caught up with Grisham at the site and detained him," Max continued. "Unfortunately, Bellamy and Grisham's two children also reached the scene. They were able to access the alien technology from the more aggressive and dangerous of the two species."

President Taylor nodded. "I see. And what is this technology? I believe you called it a weapon before."

"It's two things," he explained. "Or I should say, at least two things. First, it's a mind control device. Simply touching the substance gives the aliens a direct link into the mind of the person. The Erdeans were then able to control the kids, get them to do their bidding."

Jess audibly gasped, but the President seemed more concerned over Max's words than what might be happening off camera. Jess looked worriedly at Jace and Aaron, but neither picked up on the mistake. She was certain, however, that President Taylor had. The President's eyes had narrowed, but she didn't interrupt.

"That's the second known function," Max continued. "It's a communication device. The aliens were able to, for lack of a better word, download instructions to the kids."

"What were these instructions?" the President asked.

"The kids were to recruit a team whose job it was to assemble a transporter."

"And I'm to assume they were successful?"

"Yes, ma'am," Max said.

"How'd did two 11-year-old kids convince others to build this transporter?"

Max paused, and Jess caught the corner of his eye. It was the President who had slipped up this time. She clearly knew more than she was letting on, as Max had never mentioned the age of Rick Grisham's kids. She began to appreciate the game of cat and mouse the two were playing.

Max pursed his lips and picked up the thread of his explanation. "The alien substance is almost like cloth, but with entirely different properties than any cloth we have here on Earth. It self-replicates and can be passed to an unknown number of people without diminishing its powers."

This time, it was the President who gasped and said, "That would be quite the powerful weapon indeed."

Max nodded in agreement. "The transporter was built at the sight of the plane crash, and...umm...*transmissions* were sent."

The President's tone notably changed a little. "What were these transmissions?"

"People," Max said. "Or more precisely, children from nearby schools."

President Taylor sank back in her chair and said, "Explain."

"The aliens, while highly advanced, are not made for certain types of labor," Max explained. "They need slave labor for what they're planning next."

"I see," she said. "And what is next?"

Max paused. He looked away from the screen and at the twins. It was almost time to bring them into the conversation, anyway.

"I fear their next step is obvious," he said solemnly. "Invasion."

With pursed lips, the President nodded. "When can we expect this invasion?"

"Sooner rather than later, I'm afraid," Max said. "May I ask you a question, ma'am?"

"Certainly. I can't promise an answer, but you can certainly ask."

"You mentioned something about the moon earlier," he said. "I, uh, heard someone else mention the moon just a few minutes ago. What's happening on the moon?"

The President paused a moment, as if considering how much to tell. It was her turn to look off camera, as if getting advice from her staff. The moment dragged on until she finally answered, saying, "A deep space weather satellite captured an image of unknown activity on the far side of the moon," she said. "It was only a flicker, but it was enough to isolate the image of what might be a giant spaceship hiding behind some cloaking device. We've since lost contact with that satellite."

Max rubbed his jaw, thinking. He looked at Jace, who mouthed silently, *I saw it.*

"I hoped we'd have more time than this," Max said.

"Is there anything we can do to stop it?" the President asked. This time, she wasn't probing for confirmation of information she already possessed. She was genuinely asking.

Max didn't hesitate. He was prepared for this question. It had been the whole reason for his desperation to speak with the President.

"Stop it? No," he said. "I think invasion is inevitable at this point, but maybe we can delay it."

"Go on," President Taylor prodded.

"There are a number of these Erdeans already on the planet," Max said. "Maybe thousands at this point. They will spread quickly and, I believe, serve as the advance guard for the main invasion. If we act decisively and immediately, we can destroy those already on the ground and buy ourselves time."

"There's no chance these aliens are friendly?"

"No, ma'am. They have a history of destroying civilizations and stripping entire planets of their resources."

This time, it was the President who paused and rubbed her chin, and then she asked, "But you think we can defeat them?"

"No, ma'am," Max said without hesitation. "We have no chance."

"Then what good does it do to delay them?" she asked.

"It will buy us time," Max answered.

"Time for what?"

"To find a way to contact the Mondeans," Max said. "That's the species responsible for the second ship over Ridgeport. They have fought the Erdeans all over the galaxy, including here on Earth many millennia ago."

"How, exactly, did you come by this information?" the President asked sternly. "Seems like a lot of knowledge for a simple squad leader to know."

"Honestly," Max said, "that's a story for another time. Suffice it to say, there is a small group of people on Earth who have safeguarded secrets and served to protect the planet for literally longer than there's been indigenous intelligent life here."

"Are you admitting that *you* are an alien, soldier?"

The President was fully at attention now, and the constant activity in the background behind her came to a total stop.

"No," Max said, then after a pause added, "I'm a human of this planet and part of a secret society that has members around the world who are tasked with preventing or protecting against the invasion we're facing now."

The President was silent for a long period. As if sitting at a table surrounded by others, her gaze moved from left to right, pausing at intervals. If anyone there was offering advice, they couldn't hear it.

Finally, she turned her attention back to the screen and said, "I agree that yours is a story for another time, but it is one I am most anxious to hear. But the task at hand seems to be delaying an invasion. To be honest, much of what you've told me tonight, I already knew. I have sent a large military force to North Carolina to contain the aliens there. Do you know how to contact this other alien race?"

Max ignored the question. "Contain?" he said, panicked. "I'm sorry, ma'am, but there is no way to contain them. They are too powerful, too advanced. They will blow through our lines like we're not even there."

"I'm sure our men will be up to the task," the President said.

"I'm sorry, but they won't. It will be a massacre. You have to utterly destroy them. You have to nuke them. It's the only way."

The President's jaw gaped wide open, and a wry laugh escaped. "Are you suggesting that I drop a nuclear weapon on my own country?" She rose from her chair and leaned over the desk, extremely close to the camera. "I don't know who you are really working for, but to even suggest that I do that—"

Jess knew instinctively that this was her moment, the reason why Max had wanted them here for the conference. She rolled her chair into view of the camera atop the monitor. The President showed no surprise at seeing her as she said confidently, "Madam President, my name is Jess Grisham. I've seen these aliens close up. I've fought against them with their own weapons and the element of surprise. We lost horribly. There are hundreds or thousands of them now."

She paused for a second, remembering the giant alien that had backed into the hole. There had been so much going on at the time, so much fear and rage at seeing the chained slaves, that she hadn't taken time to consider what she had seen.

"There's a queen laying eggs in tunnels under the ground," she continued, voicing her new revelation. "They've stripped the forest bare already and are spreading their destruction quickly. We have to destroy the transporter and kill as many of them as we can at one time. It's the only way."

Jace shot forward and screamed, "No! If we destroy the transporter, we can't get to Dad."

"We'll find another way," Jess said. "This is the only chance we have."

President Taylor sank back in her seat. Someone who looked to be a man—an advisor likely—moved in behind her.

The President said, "You and your brother, who I believe I just heard in the background, were the ones who first came into contact with the alien technology. Is that correct?"

Jess couldn't believe it. The President of the United States had just asked her a question. Before she could answer, though, Jace shouldered his way into the picture.

"Yeah," Jace said loudly. "We're supposed to be part of some prophecy to save the universe."

Max, Jess, and Aaron all cringed at the same time. The President, however, glossed over Jace's comment. There was audible shuffling taking place behind the scenes, though. The advisor leaned in closer to the screen, but with an annoyed wave of her hand, President Taylor shooed him back.

"I have to think about this. It would be unconscionable for a President to use a weapon of that magnitude in her own country."

Max spoke again. "Honestly, ma'am, it would be worse to not act. This way, you'd at least give us a chance."

"You have some way of getting in touch with this other species? What'd you call them?"

"The Mondeans," Max answered. "There's a way. But it'll take time."

"I can't believe I'm even considering this," she said while trying and failing to hold back a sneeze.

The advisor standing behind her pulled something from his inside jacket pocket and, with a gloved hand, handed her a handkerchief. The President took the cloth and used it to wipe her nose. Instantly, her expression changed. She transformed from worried determination to a blank slate in the blink of an eye.

Jess moved closer to the monitor. A gloved hand, a white handkerchief, a hypnotized expression. She shot a quick glance at Jace to see if he'd seen. He had. Aaron, too.

In a flat tone, void of the tired but passionate voice from before, the President spoke to the camera, her voice an eerie monotone as she said, "I'd like the three of you to stay right there. There are Secret Service members in the building where you are. I'd like them to escort all of you to the White House so we can talk about strategy and prophecies and how to contact the Mondeans. I have some friends who would be most interested."

Not knowing which button to push to end the conference, Jace reached behind the computer and unplugged it. The monitor went black, and a whirring sound confirmed the device was powering down.

"We have to get out of here," Jess said, already pulling Jace toward the door. "Now!"

CHAPTER 9

Archives

J ess, Jace, and Aaron made a beeline for the office door, but Max sat still, a shocked look on his face as he stared at the now blank computer monitor.

"The President of the United States has been compromised," Max said in disbelief. "She's under Erdean control."

He put his face in his hands.

"Come on," Jess urged. "We have to get out of here."

Max still didn't move as he said, "If they have the President, it won't be long until they have our entire government. If they infiltrate this building, we won't be able to slow them down long enough for it to matter if we contact the Mondeans."

Jace was bouncing from foot to foot, anxious to get on the move.

"It's too late to worry about that," he said. "They're already in this building, too."

This got a reaction from Max, who exclaimed, "What? What do you mean?"

Jess explained, "When we were escaping the jail, right before we ran into you, we saw a man take control of a real security guard with an EncephaLink."

"There's an Erdean on the third floor," Max said, finally popping out of his seat.

"Yes, or a human under their control," Aaron said.

"Which way did he go?" Max asked.

Jace stammered, trying to answer. The building was basically a maze. How could you describe direction when everything looked the same? Then he remembered the elevator.

"He came out of the same elevator you did," he said. "The real security guard had walked up at the same time, but the Erdean went directly to him, handed him the cloth, and took off to the right."

Max looked panicked.

"Is that bad?" Jess asked. "I-I mean...worse. Or is that—"

"It's bad," Max said, heading to a metal cabinet at the back of the room. He opened the door with a small key, revealing a cache of handguns. He ran his finger down the selection, looking for one in particular. "The archives for the Alien Taskforce are on that floor, in that direction. If they find the Sparker before us, we've lost. There's no hope."

"The Sparker," Jess repeated. "What's that?"

Max found the handgun he was looking for. It rested on a hook on the right side, same as all of the others. Surprisingly, he reached in and pulled the trigger. Instead of firing, this triggered a catch on the cabinet. The back wall sprang open, revealing a hidden space behind. There were two weapons that most people on Earth had never seen. Jess and Jace had, though. These were the laser weapons the OS team had used in the forest. Max strapped one into his shoulder holster and looked at the three innocent civilians standing with him. Two kids and Aaron. Making a quick decision, Max handed the second weapon to Jace with the stern warning, "Use this only if I'm dead. Use it to get out of here."

"How do we get out?" Jess cried. "Where are the doors?"

"All the doors will be covered by now," Max said. He closed the secret compartment in the cabinet. Facing the rack of conventional handguns again, Max counted three over and six down and pointed out a gun that again looked just like all of the others. "If anything goes wrong and we get separated, come back here and pull that trigger. It opens the very back of this cabinet. There's a secret passage behind that leads out. Go all the way to the end and take shelter there."

"What do you mean, come back here?" Jess asked, fear in her voice. "We need to go now."

"We have to get up to the archives. I know what they're after. If we can find it first, we still have a chance."

Jess looked torn between taking the immediate route to safety and rushing straight toward the enemy.

Jace, however, didn't hesitate.

"Let's go," he said, holding the alien weapon like a seasoned soldier.

"One more thing," Max said, searching for yet another handgun on the rack as he spoke. "This one."

He pulled the trigger. This time, it was only a small compartment door that popped open, much like popping the cover of the gas tank on a car. Inside this small space was one thumb-sized button. The button flashed intermittently green. Taking a deep breath, as if contemplating the severity of what he was about to do, he sighed and then pressed it. The result was anti-climactic. The button continued to blink, but the flash had turned red instead of green.

Jess looked at him questioningly.

"It's a doomsday button," Max said solemnly. As he spoke, his watch lit up a bright red and flashed just like the button he pushed. He held it up for all of them to see. "Every member of the Origin Society just got this alert. Code Red, DEFCON ONE, whatever you want to call it. All of the members in the world are going to drop what they're doing and convene at designated locations."

"Then what?" Jess asked.

Max chuckled. "I don't know. We truly didn't think it would happen in our lifetime. That alert has never been used. But now everyone knows the threat is real. That it's here."

"Where do we meet?" Jace asked, leaving no room for doubt that they were coming, too.

"Through there," Max answered, nodding his head toward the cabinet. "But we've got work to do first. Let's go."

As the group exited through the main office, Jess noticed one of the men standing at his desk with a panicked look on his face, a hand covering the face of his watch. With a subtle nod, Max caught his eye and urged him to follow. There were two more in the office now than there were before, but none of the others seemed to know anything unusual was going on. They continued to work at their stations. The panicked man joined them outside in the hallway a second later.

"This is Brooks. He's OS," Max said by way of introduction, giving no indication if that was his first or last name and not bothering to introduce him to the others.

"What's going on?" Brooks said, holding out his arm with the watch. "It's red."

"No time for the full story," Max said, moving at a near run down the corridor. "We've been infiltrated. All the way up to the President. The Erdeans have control, and the invasion could start at any time."

"Why are we going this way?" Brooks asked, looking over his shoulder at the office they'd just left. "Aren't we supposed to...you know..."

"We have to secure the archives," Max said. "They're already there."

"The Sparker?" Brooks asked.

Max nodded, picking up the pace to a jog.

"What is this Sparker thing you keep talking about?" Aaron queried, breaking his long silence.

But Max had stopped, opened another of the random doors, and urged the others inside. It was a stairwell.

"Five floors up. Let's go."

Already out of breath, the others followed.

Emerging back on the third floor, Jess looked around, amazed once again that anyone would know one room from the other. There was a difference this time. About 50 yards down the long stretch, two people were standing outside of a door, acting like guards. Even from this distance, they could tell these weren't normal guards. First, they were dressed in long tan cloaks with hoods pulled up over their heads.

There was no visible sign of weapons, but it was a safe bet to assume they had firepower close at hand. Second, they were big. Really big. Far taller than Aaron, who had at least two inches over Max. Jess doubted what stood under the cloaks were human. As they opened the door, the sentries down the way turned to look in their direction but didn't move.

Thinking quickly, Max whispered to the group, "That's the room."

"They've beat us to it," Jess said, concerned.

"No, I don't think so," Max responded. "If they had, they wouldn't still be here. They're still searching. We have a chance."

"I can take them," Jace said, leveling his weapon at the sentries.

Max hurriedly extended his hand, forcing Jace to lower the gun.

"Put that away," he hissed. "Remember. Only if I'm dead."

Jace didn't look happy, but he tucked the gun behind his back.

Jess was trying to process everything but knew the answer was in a story that hadn't yet been told.

"What are they after?" she asked Max.

Max stopped briefly, grabbing her shoulders to make sure he had her attention, and said, "If this goes wrong, you have to get to the Sparker first. It's a communications link with the Mondeans. It's what the Erdeans are after. If they get to it first, we have no chance."

Jess nodded. She had many more questions, but this wasn't the place. She could only hope she'd get a chance once they got out of this building.

"What's the plan?" Brooks asked, nervously eyeing the sentries in their way.

"Walk by like we have somewhere else to be," Max whispered, already on the move. Just standing there was more likely to draw suspicion.

Using hand signals, Max and Brooks formulated a plan that Jace couldn't follow. Itching to be involved, he moved closer to the two OS members.

As they got closer, Max started talking loudly. "Can you believe the budget cuts we're facing this year?"

Brooks played right along. "No kidding. I don't know how they expect us to keep the parks open if they refuse to fund security."

They were 10 steps from the two sentries. The closer they got, the more obvious it was these weren't humans standing guard. Five steps. *How had the Erdeans spread out so far, so quickly?* Jess thought. *Had they had spies lying in wait here all along?*

"We'll just have to do what we've always done," Max said, continuing the fake conversation. "Make the most with less."

The sentries were watching now. Their hooded heads turned in their direction, but still they made no move to intercept the newcomers. Jess couldn't help but look at them. Jace, too. But with Max and Brooks leading the way, carrying on their conversation like nothing else mattered, the sentries had eyes only for the two soldiers. Their posture remained attentive but unconcerned.

Three steps.

Two.

Max and Brooks pulled even with the closed door. Their next move was so quick and so rehearsed that the sentries had no chance. Like a blur, both soldiers pulled their weapons and fired shots. It was over in the blink of an eye. The shots were aimed just below the sentries' hooded faces, where Jess and Jace knew the Erdeans' Achilles heels were located. The junction of head and thorax was not as heavily armored. Precision combined with the power of the laser weapons meant the sentries were dead before their decapitated heads were fully separated from the rest of their bodies. The tall figures crumbled and fell to the ground. The blasts were loud, but they were not at all like conventional weapons. If they were lucky, other Erdeans inside the thick doors might not have noticed.

Jace had his weapon out front again, waving it around, but there was nothing to shoot at. He actually looked disappointed. Aaron had Max's handgun out but was holding it by his side. Not knowing what they would be facing inside, there was no reason to make a plan.

Instead, they moved quickly, hoping the element of surprise would be enough to win the day. With a quick glance at each other and a simultaneous nod of the heads, Max fired his blaster at the door handle as Brooks slammed his shoulder in the wood. The door gave way, and they were all quickly inside.

The room had been the sight of a bloodbath. People—human people—were lying dead in the most grotesque ways. Jess quickly noticed four bodies and was grateful for the early hour. Just a little later in the day, and the death count would've been much higher.

One lady had been gutted by sharp talons and was stretched in parts and pieces across a desk. Two others, a man and a woman, looked as if they had been thrown hard across the room. Their bodies were physically lodged in the plaster wall, their necks turned at such an angle that there was little doubt of their status. The worst, though—the one that Jess was sure would give her nightmares for the rest of her life—was the one straight ahead. An Erdean, no longer bothering to hide beneath a cloak and hood, was standing atop another body. Pinning the person down with its legs, the alien was in the act of using its middle set of arms to feed itself a bloody lump of flesh torn from its victim. The Erdean looked up just in time to see Max's blast slam it through the window and into the lightening sky outside.

Two other Erdeans were to the right and reacted quickly enough to return fire with laser weapons of their own. One of the shots clipped Brooks, who spun into Aaron, taking both men down. Brooks's weapon clattered out of his hands and to the ground at Jess's feet. She scooped it up but pulled her brother down and out of the line of fire. They hid behind a desk.

The second Erdean blast sailed high over Max's head. Max retaliated with two quick bursts that bounced harmlessly off the aliens' armored bodies.

Peeking over the desk, Jess and Jace analyzed the scene. One of the Erdeans was sending blast after blast of laser energy at Max, who was spending more time dodging than returning fire. Currently, he was shooting blindly over the top of a tipped desk that was serving as his refuge. The second Erdean was holding a tablet up to a nearby desktop computer. It looked like the device was wirelessly downloading information. Behind them, a commotion in the hallway caused Brooks to crawl over and close the door. Aaron, who had gotten back to his hands and knees, was trying to barricade the entry with furniture. More Erdeans were trying to force their way in.

They were trapped.

Jace's eyes were wild but alert. His head swung side to side, taking it all in and formulating an escape plot.

The Erdean holding the tablet called out to the others, holding up the device to indicate the completion of its task. He turned his own weapon on the desktop computer and fired two quick bolts into the machine. In a flurry of sparks and a muffled explosion, the computer went dark.

"We need that tablet," Jace said, taking aim with his weapon.

His shot soared harmlessly into the ceiling because just as he squeezed the trigger, Aaron bumped him with a chair he was trying to wedge into the growing collection of furniture at the door.

It was a total melee, but another sound began permeating the air. Like a deep, throbbing, and pulsating bass drum, the sound was rattling the windows and shaking the floor. The two aliens ceased fighting, spread their wings, and took flight across the room, heading toward the window. The first landed and peered outside. Whatever it saw prompted it to use its middle set of arms to create a vibration near its throat. The sound seemed more like screeches and whistles to Jace and Jess, but it meant something to the Erdean holding the tablet and the aliens fighting to get through the door. They all responded with similar sounds.

Taking advantage of the distraction, Max found a clear line of fire and shot at the alien closest to the window. The shot struck just below the junction of head and thorax, but it clearly injured the invader. Struggling, the Erdean used its weapon to break the glass in the window, and it tumbled outside, its wings fluttering in an attempt to prevent it from plunging to the ground at an unknown distance below. The Erdean with the tablet used a free arm to start firing wildly in Max's direction. The volley missed, but the desk that Max was hiding behind was thrown into the air, landing on top of and pinning the OS soldier on the ground. His weapon skidded inches out of his grasp.

"OH NO YOU DON'T!" Jace yelled, rising from his hiding place and firing laser blasts toward the alien trying to escape through the window.

Whether it was blind luck or the highly practiced skill of someone who lived for computer games, one of Jace's shots struck the arm holding the tablet, causing it to fly across the room. The alien made a move to retrieve it, but Jace was already scrambling over the desk. It was a race. Like a TV hero, Jace jumped over one desk and slid across another, sending a pile of paper flying like a whirlwind. He dove for the tablet, scooped it up ahead of the Erdean, and rolled under yet another desk. Controlling his momentum, Jace rose to a crouch and peered over the desk. The Erdean was right there! With an effortless bend of its inverted knees, the alien hopped onto the edge of the desk and peered over at Jace.

For the first time, he got an extremely close-up look. At the end of all six spiny legs were hand-like appendages. There were three long fingers on each, or rather, two long fingers and something resembling an off-set thumb. Moving his eyes up, Jace saw a terrifying face staring back. In two large, very dark eyes, he could see his reflection. There was a nose-like protuberance, but there were no holes through which to breathe. Its mouth was small, but razor-like mandibles clicked open and closed. Jace could hear them snap over the throb of noise growing louder outside. A pair of antennae were aimed forward, right at Jace

In his scramble to get to the tablet, he'd dropped his weapon. He was defenseless.

The Erdean fluttered its wings for balance and leaned over with its middle set of arms, grasping Jace by the shoulders and jerking him violently into a fully upright position, his feet dangling inches above the floor. Jace felt the skin over his shoulder blades break, and blood dripped down his back from the grip of the talon-like hands. Its mouth moved in closer to Jace's face, its breath smelling like rotting cabbage. One of its upper arms reached for the tablet.

Then suddenly, the grip on Jace's shoulders released, and the over-sized bug slumped across the desk before crumpling to the ground.

There stood Jess, smoking weapon in hand.

The explosive sounds of more laser blasts sounded, and the barricaded door threatened to give. Aaron, who had been helping Max out from under the desk, rushed over to throw his body against the chairs, desks, and cabinets that were sliding inward. Injured, Max crawled over to his weapon and picked it up. He was moving slow and shaking his head as if trying to clear the cobwebs of a concussive blow.

Jace scanned the room. It might have been called the archives, but it was an office space no different than the others they'd seen. It was one room. One door. One way in, and one way out. And currently, an unknown number of Erdeans were fighting to get in that door.

They were trapped!

Or were they?

Jace scrambled over to the broken windows and looked down. He guessed they were 30 or 40 feet high. Jumping was out of the question. But sticking his head out, Jace saw a tiny ledge stretching from the base of the window to the next office over.

"Come on," he yelled to the others. "We can get out this way!"

Another surge from outside the door pushed the pile of furniture another few inches. As they tried to brace the barrier with their backs, Aaron's and Max's bottoms scooted forward involuntarily.

"Go!" Aaron yelled. "Go! Get to the tunnel. We'll hold them off and join you!"

The pulsing throb continued to get louder. It was coming from everywhere. That, combined with the commotion at the door, made it impossible to hear what Max said from his spot just across the room.

"What?" Jess yelled, her voice struggling to rise above the din.

"Go!" she saw Aaron mouth, his arms waving frantically. Another surge from behind him, and she could see an opening forming. In a matter of moments, the Erdeans would be in.

Jace was already straddling the windowsill, carefully balancing as he stepped out onto the ledge. He had stuffed the tablet in his waist-band to give him use of both hands. With one, he reached back and helped his sister out the window.

The noise was louder out here. For the first time, Jace looked up and discovered the source. It was so shocking that he nearly lost his balance. At a total loss for words, he blindly tapped his left hand in Jess's direction, trying to get her attention to see if she saw what he was seeing. His hand resting on her shoulder, he tore his eyes away from the scene overhead and looked at his sister.

Jess was still peering through the broken window and into the room. What she saw was just as disturbing.

Seeing the kids make it out, Max had turned his attention toward the struggle at the door. Taking a second to fiddle with something near the trigger, Max grimaced and fired two shots toward the barricade. Both struck their targets full on. Aaron and Brooks collapsed in a heap. The barricade gave way, and the doorway cleared.

Jess screamed, but it was drowned out. The last thing she saw before Jace forced her attention away from the window was Max turning the weapon on himself.

Then the horror of the scene was instantly forgotten. Fully onto the ledge and clear of the archives window, both kids looked up in awe. The morning sun had not yet crested the horizon, but there was enough light to leave no doubt about what they were seeing. A giant spaceship was emerging from the wispy morning clouds as it drifted down out of the sky and toward the ground. It was as big as a city. So large, in fact, that they couldn't see the edges from where they were. The vibrations grew even louder as the ship settled in and hovered just above the rooftop.

Jace recovered from the sight first and edged himself across the narrow ledge, one hand pressed against the wall for balance, the other holding Jess's outstretched hand. As quickly as they dared, they reached the next window and busted their way in before the Erdeans next door could look out and discover them.

The twins had managed to escape again, but the sinking realization that they were alone settled in as Jess tried to process what she had seen. Shocked, they stared out the window at the impressive sight.

They had arrived. All of them. The war for the planet was about to begin.

CHAPTER 10
Safe House

Transfixed by the scene playing out in the skies over their heads, the twins temporarily forgot the aliens barging into the room next door.

With a twinge of shame, Jess snapped to first. How could she be more concerned with what she was seeing than with what she had just seen? Aaron—their father's best friend, the man who had stayed right by their side since this nightmare began—shot down by Max. Had the OS operative done it as an act of mercy? Brooks had been injured, and Aaron had been defenseless in the middle of the room. Maybe Max did what he did to save them from the horrors of the Erdeans. It was possible, but they'd been burned by him before.

"Jace, we've got to go," Jess said meekly. "We have to get back down to the Taskforce office and through the tunnel before they realize where we've gone."

Jace finally turned away from the window, his face etched with concern. He stormed over to the door and opened it just a crack to see down the hallway toward the room from where they'd just escaped. He saw three security guards, all with telltale white bandanas wrapped around their necks, enter the archives office. The rest of the corridor appeared empty.

"Aaron, Brooks, and Max...they're trapped in there," Jace said. "We have to go help. Back out the window. We'll catch them by surprise."

Jace raced back across the room and was partway out onto the ledge when Jess grabbed him by a belt loop and pulled him back in, saying, "They're dead, Jace."

"No way," he said defiantly. "They had weapons and plenty of cover. They might be pinned down, but they'll still be fighting. If we can get back in the windows, we'll catch the aliens in a crossfire."

"Jace..." Jess tried. "Listen. There's no battle going on."

"Maybe the walls are soundproof," he insisted, straining to pull free and get back outside.

"Jace, LISTEN TO ME!" Jess hissed through clenched lips. "I saw Max shoot Aaron and Brooks, then himself. They're gone. We have to get out of here before they figure out where we are. It won't take them long."

Stunned, Jace propped himself against the window seal. To his credit, he accepted the news quickly. Blinking back tears and biting his lip, he gave a slight nod. They moved rapidly out the door and into the hallway. It was still empty, but that could change at any time. The thrum of the ship hovering outside was muted in the center of the building but was still loud enough to cover their footfalls as they took off at a run. The only way they knew to the stairwell led them past the door to the archives room. They had no choice. Not even slowing or turning their heads to look in, they dashed past. Unfortunately, their attempt at escape didn't go unnoticed. Two of the human guards jumped into the hallway behind them.

"Hey, there they are!" one of the guards yelled. "STOP!"

The twins kept going. The slight turn of the hallway was not too far ahead. That would give them some cover. Jess could remember passing eight other doors before making the turn on their way in.

Behind them, a pair of Erdeans acted more decisively, ramming the human security guards out of the way. Laser pulses shot past Jess and Jace, impacting the wall just inches from where they'd been. The bend in the hallway was so close. They were running as hard as they could, but they couldn't outrun the alien weapons. The first shots were too close. Jace knew he couldn't risk giving them another chance. Acting on instinct, he threw his legs out in front of him and slid across the tile floor like he was sliding into second base during a baseball game. Already twisting his body before his momentum came to a stop, he squared off against the Erdeans, firing two quick shots of his own. One of the blasts struck true, knocking the lead alien into the second. The energy bounced harmlessly off its armored mid-section, but the impact knocked both off balance. Jace was instantly back on his feet and running to catch his sister.

Jess had already rounded the slight corner and was counting doors. It was going to be close. She counted breathlessly as she ran.

"Six...seven...eight. This one!"

Jess pulled open the door and barged into an office much like all the others. She'd miscounted. She froze, confused.

Jace, however, was in video game mode. Keep moving. Never stand still. Think quickly.

"You started counting from the first door we came to," he said. "You didn't count the one we came out of. It's one more down."

She slapped her forehead and turned back into the corridor. A laser beam missed her head by inches.

Taking the low ground again, Jace crouched in the doorframe and squeezed off three quick blasts. The pursuing Erdeans had to take cover. They had reached the bend in the hall, gaining ground with scary quickness.

Jess didn't waste a moment. She dashed to the next door, pulled it open, and nodded back to Jace, who was still kneeling behind the first doorframe.

One Erdean spread its wings and took flight, covering ground at twice the speed. Jace fired again, forcing the alien back to the ground. Luckily, it landed in the line of fire of the other one, giving Jace a chance to cover the short distance to the stairwell door. He hit the steps at a run, using the railing to propel him all the way down to the first landing. Jess was already rounding the corner and heading down the next flight. Not having legs designed for steps, and not having room to fly, the Erdeans' pursuit was slowed.

The twins reached the sub-basement level well ahead of their pursuers and raced down yet another similar corridor. They had rounded the corner and were out of sight by the time the aliens barged through the door themselves. The throb of the massive ship outside was still evident, even below ground. There was a clear vibration in the walls. But it was soon drowned out by the screeching wail of an alarm. Red lights flashed from small boxes set in the wall near the ceiling. A door burst open not too far in front of the twins. Two soldiers, dressed in the same black ops uniforms Jess and Jace had come across so many times in the last two weeks, emerged and raced past the kids like they didn't even see them. They were quickly engaged in a firefight with the approaching Erdeans.

It was the break Jace and Jess needed to get away. Not having to search for the right room, they slipped into the Alien Taskforce headquarters before the door even closed. Hopefully, the soldiers who had emerged would slow the aliens down just enough. They ran into Max's office and pulled open the cabinet, and Jace ran his fingers down the stockpile of handguns, counting under his breath. He reached in to pull the trigger, but Jess's hand caught his wrist.

"One more down," she huffed, gasping for breath.

Trusting her, Jace pulled the next trigger, and the back of the cabinet swung open. Fluorescent lights popped on one at a time, revealing a long tunnel stretching out before them. Not wasting time, they jumped through the opening and closed the secret door behind them.

They were safe. For now. But a crushing reality sank into Jess as she breathed heavily on the pristine tiled floor of the well-lit tunnel: They were also completely alone.

The tunnel was long and far from flat. Except for the elevation changes, it was very monotonous. Without a watch or a phone to check, time seemed to have no meaning. They walked slightly downhill for a long time. Then walked uphill for a long time. It was stifling hot, then cool and comfortable. It didn't take long for the complaining to begin.

"I'm hungry," Jace said.

"You're always hungry," Jess answered.

"We missed breakfast," he pouted.

Jess wasn't sympathetic. She was hungry, too. Complaining wasn't going to help.

"I'm tired," Jace said, changing his complaint.

"I'm tired, too," Jess said with no emotion whatsoever.

"It's been like 100 hours since we slept."

"Feels like it," Jess agreed.

"I'm tired of tunnels," Jace continued.

"Me, too," Jess sighed. It was easier to just go along with him. "Find something else to think about to occupy your mind."

On they walked. Jace pulled the tablet they had taken from the Erdeans out from the back of his shorts. The screen was dark except for a flashing red, outlined box in the middle. Within the box was what appeared to be words, but it was in a language neither of them recognized. For all Jace could interpret, it was nothing more than an incoherent jumble of dots, dashes, and squiggly lines. Who could possibly make heads or tails of such craziness?

"Think about English," Jess said when Jace voiced his opinion.

"What about it? English makes perfect sense," Jace said, cranky. Being tired and hungry did not bring out the best in him.

"It makes perfect sense to us because that's what we were raised on," she said.

"We have letters, letters make words, and words make sentences," Jace insisted.

"Yes, and think about our letters," she said patiently. "Think about the lowercase i. It's a dot and a dash. Same with j, but it has a little curve. All of our letters are just combinations of lines put together."

In his current state, Jace would never admit she was right, but he went silent and studied the screen more intently.

After another long stretch, the tunnel turned upward so sharply that steps had been built into the floor. Straining her neck to gaze up the climb, Jess thought she could see the end. At least at some point up ahead, the lights lining the wall-ceiling junction ended.

As they started up the steep steps, Jace put the tablet away and concentrated on climbing. They were definitely reaching the end. Several hundred steps later, they finally reached the top. It wasn't the end of the tunnel, but it was close. Only a few yards ahead of them was a door set into a concrete wall. It was a normal door, like one you'd find in any house. They looked at each other, and Jace shrugged. He turned the knob, and the door opened into a garage. Two cars, covered in an inch of dust, were parked side by side. They didn't look like they'd been moved for years, but the hoods were propped open, and power cords dangling down from the center were plugged into the batteries.

"Keeping them charged," Jace said, putting voice to what he was seeing.

"In case they need transportation in a hurry," Jess said, puzzling it together. "This is the safehouse. Origin Society members might come here to hide, but if they needed to get away, they'd have cars."

Jace nodded appreciatively and said, "That means they'll have food here."

He scanned the garage and quickly found a set of three steps leading to a small landing and another door. Just like every garage he'd ever been in.

Moving forward, the entrance into the tunnel closed behind them. With a glance back, Jess noticed the door disappearing, seamlessly becoming part of the wall. A variety of tools hung from hooks on a giant peg board, not so different at all from the way the handguns hung on hooks in the cabinet on the other end. She was willing to bet that squeezing the trigger on the electric drill hanging about where a handle should be would open the door. She didn't get to try it, however, as Jace was pulling her forward.

The house looked just as unused as the garage. There wasn't a layer of dust—someone obviously came in to clean—but there was just a feel about the place that no one spent time there. Still, Jace was right. There was food. A lot of it. The pantry was stocked. Jace grabbed a bag of potato chips, opened it, and stuffed his mouth full as he searched for something else. He groaned from the pleasure only barbecue chips could provide.

Jess opened the refrigerator and found it was fully stocked, as well. Recently, by the looks. If nothing else, the OS had someone come by on at least a weekly basis to clean and stock. There appeared to be enough food and supplies to keep a small army for a month. She didn't want to be like her brother, but Jess had to admit she was starving, and seeing all of this food was making her mouth water. She opened a package of sandwich meat and munched on thin slices of turkey as she walked around the rest of the house.

Except for the light Jace had turned on in the kitchen, it was very dark. Only a small outline of sunlight penetrated the heavy blackout curtains over every window. She couldn't help but look at the couch and imagine herself stretching out for a long nap. She was exhausted. Any thought of sleep was quickly chased away, however, when she slowly opened one of the curtains.

The world outside had changed.

The safehouse sat atop a high hill, with a clear view across a broad river and a big city beyond. To the right and left, there were other houses. They were in a neighborhood. Every back porch along the bluff was packed with people who were gazing out at the scene. High above, massive alien ships were lining up. It reminded Jess of driving past an airport at dusk, the planes with their landing lights on forming a trail as far as the eye could see.

Except these weren't airplanes. Six, eight, 12 of the ships were drifting in the air, heading east toward the ocean, each larger than the large city below them. Smaller ships—hundreds of them—buzzed around the larger ones like bees around a nest. The smaller ships at least resembled the shape you'd expect from a flying machine. They were sleek and silver. What appeared to be a cockpit area tapered into an aerodynamic point near the front. Jess racked her brain, trying to come up with a way to describe the larger ships. Although not a huge fan, she'd seen many science fiction shows where the mother ships were round disks, or wedge-shaped battle machines. This, however, was like nothing she'd ever seen. These were giant blocks that had no business hovering in the sky. The constant rumble she'd felt since before escaping the Taskforce headquarters must've been some kind of anti-gravity drive, but she could see no source of power or propulsion. The entire lower half of the ships and the majority of the back portion looked like giant gas tanks. The top and front half were black and dark gray and looked to be metal of some kind. The tanks were opaque, a tan color.

Jess had a horrifying thought. Never mind that she'd seen and actually had a hand in building the transporter that delivered real life aliens to Earth. Never mind the amazing technology that allowed those aliens to control minds of those holding a scrap of cloth. Forget about the laser weapons and all of the other gadgets she'd seen. Witnessing these ships fill the skies over her planet allowed reality to sink in, and she turned to Jace and said, "We're in trouble."

"Whut?" Jace said through a mouth of chips.

He was still holding the bag, walking around the room. He hadn't yet noticed the view through the window. Jess caught his arm and pulled him over to the glass. He dropped the bag, his mouth gaping. A steady stream of the smaller ships were darting up and down from one of the enormous tankers, forming a highway in the sky from the ship to the city below. The twins watched in horror as a pair of fighter jets raced to the scene at near subsonic speeds. Before they could engage the smaller alien ships, however, sudden streaks of cobalt blue energy beams shot from the tanker ships. The beams tracked across the sky before impacting the fighter jets. They were vaporized in a blinding flash of light.

"Th-th-those were F-35s," Jace said, struggling to form the words. "Th-th-the most advanced jets in the world. Gone in a second."

"We're in trouble," Jess said again, her shocked expression unchanged.

She pulled the curtains closed again and dropped onto a nearby couch. Seeing a remote on the end table, she picked it up and looked for the TV. It was mounted on the wall, overtop a stone fireplace. The first few channels she tried were nothing but static. She finally settled on a news channel that was showing disturbing images from around the globe. An anchor was talking off screen while image after image of the giant ships dominated the screen. It wasn't just in America. It was Brazil, England, France, Beijing, Sydney, Hong Kong. They were everywhere. Hundreds of the ships hovering over major cities. More images were pouring in of failed attempts to attack the invaders. Ground-to-air and air-to-air missiles either shot down or impacting harmlessly against an unseen protective shield around the ships. Pilots daring enough to engage directly were easily erased from existence. The efforts at defending the airspace, though, seemed surprisingly sparse.

"Why are we not attacking?" Jace said.

He had plopped on the couch beside Jess. He had also recovered the bag of chips and resumed eating.

"How can you eat at a time like this?" Jess said, disgusted.

"What?" he said defensively. "I'm hungry. Can't save the world on an empty stomach."

Jess shook her head. Her own stomach was threatening to expel the little bit of food she'd eaten a few minutes ago. The thought of eating more was unthinkable. Instead, she turned her mind to her brother's first question.

"They are already in control of the government," she said. "We saw the President herself fall under the control of the EncephaLink. I bet that's happened all over the world. There's no one to give the order for a full-scale attack."

Was it possible for the entire planet to fall this quickly? Was there not someone who could save the day, mount a counterattack?

Helplessly, the twins watched the broadcast. There was little more to report at the moment. Both kids fell into a long overdue and well-deserved sleep.

CHAPTER 11

Dasher

J ess was startled awake, and she saw a young man sitting in a chair across from her. She let out a scream, causing Jace to snap awake and jump off the couch, comically looking left and right, the forgotten bag of chips scattering across the floor. The man never flinched. He was hunkered over, his elbows on his knees, his chin resting on a flattened palm, studying the two of them. He was wearing a camouflage tank top. Dog tags swung from his neck. Jess was terrible at guessing ages but knew he couldn't be older than 20.

"I knew the recruits were getting younger, but seriously?" the young man said, raising his thick, dark eyebrows.

The voice surprised Jace, who was still trying to figure out where he was. The nap had been quick, and the sleep he'd fallen into had been deep. They'd been running on adrenaline since Team Creepy had crashed into their house days ago. He'd lost track of just how long ago it had been. Now he stumbled backward, the back of his legs buckling against the couch. He collapsed into a seated position beside his sister. His blurry eyes found the newcomer.

"You're OS?" Jess asked.

"Obviously," he answered. "I'm Mitchell. Call me Mitch. Who are you?"

Jess was nervous about giving away too much about themselves, but if the guy was here, he must belong. Just to be on the safe side, though...

"What's OS stand for?" she asked.

"Origin Society," he answered without hesitation. "Again, who are you?"

"I'm Jess. This is my brother, Jace," she said. "We—"

"You're the two!" Mitch said, interrupting. He sat back in his chair, his jaw gaping. "Aren't you?"

"That's what Max says," Jace added, finally shaking loose the cobwebs. "But other than being two super, alien butt-kicking 11-year-olds, there's nothing special about us."

Mitch laughed. "There aren't many alien, butt-kicking 11-year-olds out there. I'd say that makes you pretty special." He looked around the room as if he'd missed something. "Where is Max?"

The truth was evident in Jess's eyes before she spoke, saying bluntly, "He's dead. He shot our friends, then himself."

"No way!" Mitchell yelled, popping out of his seat. "He wouldn't!"

"He did," Jess said, her voice barely above a whisper. "I saw it."

Mitch rubbed both hands over his closely cropped scalp, his expression one of panic. He rose, started pacing, and mumbled something over and over. He went to the large bay window and pulled back the curtain. The scene outside hadn't changed. The ships were still hanging there, the smaller crafts continuing to stream back and forth in a steady flow to and from the city across the river. Sunlight flooded the dark room, but its warmth didn't quite break the chill in those witnessing the seemingly impossible activity. The steady thrum of the ships' anti-gravity drive had become a background noise so constant that they had stopped noticing. Another sound, however, was present in the room. Static from the TV signaled the loss of another station.

"What's going on out there?" Jess asked. "We've not been outside in two days. Are people panicked? Are the Erdeans attacking?"

Mitch was lost in his own mind, however, continuing to pace and mumble.

Jess stood and cut him off, snapping her fingers in his face. "Hey!"

"What? Oh... Sorry," Mitch said. "Did you say something?" But instead of giving Jess a chance to repeat her questions, he continued on. "If Max is dead, this is bad," he said. "Really bad."

He pulled the curtain, and the room plunged back into semi-darkness. Without another word, he raced into the hallway that led to the front room. On the left was a big table neither Jess nor Jace had noticed before. It held one item: a giant book. A single spotlight inset in the ceiling illuminated the gold-embossed cover. On the wall over the table were three rows of framed pictures. Jess scanned them as she stumbled after Mitch. The picture on the lower right-hand side—the last in the sequence—was of Max. Next to it, on the left, was a picture of a boy not much older than the twins themselves. To the left of that was an older woman with a stern smile and curly white hair. The pictures were obviously a timeline. The pictures on the top left, however, weren't photos at all. The images of the person represented were drawings, detailed sketches.

Mitch, though, wasn't looking at the pictures. "No, no, no," he said, flipping through the pages of the book at a blurry pace. He couldn't possibly be reading anything. He was almost in a panic.

Jess could relate. It was understandable to be panicked over what was happening all around the planet. But as she watched, it dawned on her to be curious about what exactly he was looking for and what this giant book was, anyway. It was overly large, almost like a decorative Bible in a church foyer. It was eight to 10 inches thick and two feet tall. From what little she could see from Mitch's frantic page flipping, it looked like journal entries.

"What is this?" she asked, moving in beside the young soldier for a better look.

"This is a book," he said simply, as if that was the most obvious answer to a silly question. He wasn't being a smart aleck, though. "This is the OS—"

Before he could explain further, Jace jumped in excitedly. "Hey! It's me!" he yelled.

He was jumping up and down and pointing at the next to last picture hanging on the wall, the one to the left of Max. Jess had only glanced at the picture earlier. It was different than the others. The rest were portraits—if not taken in a studio, then at least with the purpose of being a headshot. This one was not. It was a side angle, and as if the subject were trying to avoid being photographed at all, a hand was raised, trying unsuccessfully to block the profile view. On closer inspection, it *did* look like Jace. Not exactly, but enough for eerie familiarity. She had to look close to see the difference.

Something else was odd. The frame housing the picture didn't fit the discoloration of the wall behind. Studying closer, Jess moved other frames slightly and saw a purer shade of paint perfectly squared behind. The photo of Jace's lookalike had replaced another. Leaning closer still, Jess read the small nameplate affixed to the bottom of the frame.

"Liam Dasher," she read.

"Big mystery," Mitch said, turning his attention away from the book. "No one knows who he is. Or what happened to him."

"Who are these people?" Jess asked, waving her arm at the wall of photos.

"That's what makes it really strange," he said. "These are all the heads of the United States chapter of the Origin Society. They predate the country itself. Max was named head a couple of years ago, right before I was recruited. You can see the date beside his name. Dasher took over in the forties, and until Max, there hasn't been another one."

"This Dasher guy took over in the forties?" Jace asked.

"Yes. But look closer. Does that look like a picture taken in the 1940s?"

The subject had, for the moment, brought Mitch back to the present, his panic from before temporarily halted.

It didn't. In fact, it looked suspiciously like a cell phone photo. Jess scratched her head in confusion. The boy looked their age. That presented numerous questions. How could he have taken over the OS at such a young age? That was one. But perhaps more pressing than that, how could he take over the organization in the 1940s but look 11 in a picture that had to have been taken recently?

"There's nothing about him in the book," Mitch said. "But there's a bunch of pages torn out. See?"

He opened the book from the back and showed the kids tears near the spine, where pages had obviously been. As if struck with an idea, Mitch slammed the book shut and raced again into the back room. He picked up the remote and clicked obsessively through channel after channel of static. After going through the entire selection of channel options three times, he slapped his forehead. Reaching into a backpack beside the chair in which he'd been sitting before, he removed what looked like an iPad. He swiped sideways at the screen and tapped the app he was looking for. He typed a password using the touchscreen keyboard and turned the device toward the kids.

"Satellite's been knocked out," he explained. "First rule of engagement. Disrupt communications. We were ready for that. This is a ground-based broadcast. They'll find the signal eventually, but it's deeply encoded."

What they saw on the screen wasn't much different than the news broadcast on the TV earlier. What appeared to be video shot from a drone hovering near the treetops of a shoreline showed more of the giant alien ships. There was activity this time. One of the tankers was firing its laser weapon into the ocean, close to the breaking waves. The water froze. Or at least that appeared to be what happened. The water now looked like it had been transformed into crystal blue blocks. A line of smaller vessels was scooping the blocks and taking them to the larger ships. As the blocks were scooped, liquid water rushed in to fill the void, until the ship fired its laser again and the process continued.

The camera on the drone rotated to a scene farther up the shore. Another ship was hanging very low, close to the water. Several clear tubes extended from its underside into the ocean. The water was being sucked into the ship. The mammoth tanks were darker from the bottom to about the halfway point. Jess couldn't fathom how much seawater had been taken in. Judging by the size of the ship, enough to fill the lake back home.

"They're here for the water," she said, understanding dawning.

"That's not water," Mitch said.

Before he could explain, or Jess could ask what he meant, the camera moved again. The view this time was frightening beyond words. Spaceships—tankers—lined up as far as they could see, hovered over the ocean, tubes extended into the water. Many, many more were lined up above, awaiting their turn. It already looked like low tide on the beach. Something blurry moved in front of the drone's camera. Adjusting automatically, the camera focused on the closer object. It was one of the smaller ships hovering directly in front of the drone. It swayed from side to side in the air. There was a flash of red, and the picture went black.

Stunned, Mitch lowered the iPad and stared off at nothing. Suddenly, he scooped up his backpack and took off at a run, through the hall and into the front room. He opened the door, leapt off the small stoop that served as a porch, and took off across the yard and down the road.

Without knowing why, Jace started to give chase. He made it as far as the stoop before Jess caught him and pulled him back.

The OS operative was gone, and Jess doubted they'd see him again.

CHAPTER 12
A Welcome Return

J ess stepped to the edge of the porch and took in her surroundings. Mitch had disappeared around a bend in the road, never breaking stride. They weren't alone, however, at least not in a physical sense. All down the block, people—adults and children alike—were out on porches or in their yards. Almost all were staring at the sky, staring at the impossibilities hanging unsupported in the air, unlike anything they'd ever seen in real life.

Turning, Jess took notice of the porch and the front of the house. Unlike the rear, which dropped off the side of a big hill, like a cliff, the front was flat. The porch was covered. Ceiling fans dangled motionless. A painted white railing lined the outer edge, separating the porch from the row of trimmed hedges. Beyond that, a yard like any other you'd expect to find in a suburban neighborhood.

"This could be our house with Mom," Jace said, noticing the same things as Jess.

"They designed it to blend in," Jess said. "It's supposed to be a safehouse, somewhere the OS can go and not be noticed."

"Well, I'm still hungry," Jace said, going back in.

Jess stayed out, however. She didn't have Jace's ability to just accept. She had questions. A million of them. She wanted to know more. The answers she sought wouldn't be found with the neighbors, but she was still curious. She stepped off the porch and moved cautiously toward the road. She kept her head turned skyward, like everyone else, but from the corner of her eyes, she was watching. Next door, a man had an arm wrapped around a woman. Her whole body was visibly shaking. She was trying to rest her trembling head on his shoulder while he patted her on the back. At their feet sat a little girl, no more than two, wearing a short, striped dress and a diaper. She was reaching for a bright yellow dandelion. Her brother, at least a couple of years older, was running around the yard holding a toy gun.

"Pew-pew-pew," he said, pretending to fire the weapon at Jess. "Are you an alien? I'm shooting aliens."

Jess smiled, but there was something profoundly sad about the scene. Up and down the street was more of the same. On this road alone, dozens of lives had been permanently disrupted. From what Jess herself had experienced over the last few days, she knew their lives would never be the same. What made her heart drop was the realization that this was happening in every neighborhood in every city, state, and country across the world.

A species with no regard for human life had come to rob this world of all of its resources. She flashed to the dream, or vision, where she and Jace were standing on a dying world that was stripped bare. The Erdeans has miscalculated. Their intent had been to make Jess feel sorry for them, to show how desperate their need was. Instead, she now realized they were scavengers. Locusts who took what they needed and moved on, without regard to the devastation left behind.

"Are you alone, dear?" a cracking voice asked. An older woman was hobbling on a cane toward Jess from the house across the street.

Seeing the cane send a jolt of pain all through Jess's body. She'd been so wrapped up in the escape and the journey to the safehouse that she hadn't thought about her dad in hours.

"Are you okay?" the woman asked, drawing closer. She was looking Jess up and down, motherly worry etched in her eyes.

Jess realized how she must look and suddenly felt very dirty. She hadn't washed or changed clothes since the beach house, long before the big battle in the forest. A lot had happened since then. Suddenly, showering was the most important thing she could think of. If she could wash away the dirt and sweat and grime of the last few days, maybe she could wash away everything else, as well, make it all normal again.

Looking at the woman, Jess thought quickly.

"No," she said, trying to keep her voice calm and measured. "But I better go. My parents will be looking for me. They worry."

Without giving the woman a chance to respond, Jess quickly moved back up the porch and into the safehouse, locking the door behind her. She moved directly to the back of the house, toward the bedrooms and bathrooms.

Jace heard his sister come back inside and then the running water of the shower a minute later. He briefly considered bathing himself. He sniffed his underarms and curled his nose at the stench.

"Wow, I stink," he said out loud, then grinned from ear to ear. "Awesome!"

He gave his right pit another sniff, nearly gagged, laughed, and went back to his sandwich. The food was helping clear his mind.

Unlike his sister, Jace's mind had never left his father. Everything had been about getting him back. He looked at the alien tablet again and started tinkering. He was certain the answer was here. He just had to break the code. The device remained as stubborn as ever. He searched the back and sides over and over, looking for any sign of a button or knob, anything that would help activate and adjust the settings. There was nothing but a smooth shell of some metal-like substance. He tried to pry the cover off in case what he held was only a protective device, but there was no give. That left the screen itself. He tapped, pushed, slid. He even licked. Nothing changed. In frustration, he gripped the edges of the tablet firmly and shook it with all of his frustration.

"WHY WON'T YOU SHOW ME ENGLISH!" he hissed through gritted teeth.

"Showing English," a smooth, monotone, electronic voice said.

Jace dropped the tablet in surprise. Scrambling to pick it back up,

THE ORIGIN SOCIETY: US

he saw that the box on the screen had words he recognized.

DOWNLOAD COMPLETE. TO ACCESS MAP, SAY "MAP."

Jace blinked rapidly. In his excitement, he had to try twice to get the word out. The screen instantly changed into a map very similar to what was on his cell phone. The view was of the entire country. Two blinking dots, so close together it would have been impossible to discern the difference had they not been different colors, one red and one blue, were flashing on the lower right side of the map.

He sat down at the kitchen table and went to work. Using his thumb and forefinger, he tried to zoom his view like he would on his iPad. Nothing happened. Stumped, he rubbed his chin and thought. He could do this.

"Zoom," he spoke simply.

The tablet responded, and the view of the map zoomed in, but from the center. He was getting a close-up look at Middle America. The blinking dots disappeared off the screen.

"Move right," he said. Nothing happened. "Hmm," he sighed, totally engrossed in the challenge. "Show me the East Coast." Nothing. "Expand view," he tried.

The map returned to its original size. The blinking dots were back. Out of habit, he tried again with his fingers. Again, nothing happened.

"Enable touch screen," Jess said from over his shoulder.

Jace jumped so hard that his knees slammed into the underside of the table.

"Mable's bloomers! Don't sneak up on me like that!" he snapped, pretending to pound his chest to restart his heart.

Jess, a large fluffy towel wrapped around her body and a smaller towel tying up her hair, had moved in behind him to watch his progress.

"Touch screen enabled," the computerized voice said.

With a smirk of success, she reached over his shoulder and swiped her fingers across the screen. The map moved in response. Jace slapped her hand away and did it himself, zooming in closer and closer on the blinking dots. It didn't take long for the targeted location to become clear.

The twins looked at each other, equal expressions of shock on their faces. The blinking dots were hovering right over Ridgeport, their hometown.

"Home," Jess whispered.

Jace was thinking furiously. What could possibly be so important in Ridgeport that the aliens had gone to the trouble of breaking into a secure government building to download this map?

He zoomed in closer, down to street level, and his breath caught in his chest. For a moment, he thought the dots were hovering over their dad's house, but as he got closer still, the street view came into focus, the dots shifting slightly west of their home. The map was blank under the dots. There were no streets, no train tracks, no creeks, and no rivers. Just empty land.

Jess gasped as understanding dawned, but at that very moment, a familiar voice emanated from the television in the next room, replacing the static-filled screen they hadn't bothered to turn off.

"Ladies and gentlemen, citizens of the United States and the world," the President of the United States said in a dull, almost sleepy voice, "today is a monumental day in the history of our planet. As you can see, Earth is playing host to beings from another planet."

"Duh," Jace said, rolling his eyes.

"Shh," Jess hissed, elbowing him to be quiet as they exited the kitchen and moved closer to the TV screen hanging on the wall, just above the fireplace.

The President was sitting behind the famous Resolute desk in the Oval Office. The legs and torsos of other people were visible, standing behind and around her, but the camera was focused tightly on her face.

"I assure you and our guests that there is nothing to fear. These visitors have a great need, and we will help them. We *must* help them."

Jess's heart fluttered at the familiar words. The memory was foggy, as if a dream, but she remembered speaking similar words herself while under the control of the EncephaLink.

"Look around her neck," Jace said, pointing.

What at first appeared to be a scarf was clearly the pure white technology that was controlling every word the President spoke and every action she made. That answered the question of how the TV signal was getting through. The Erdeans *wanted* the people of Earth to hear it.

"Our obligation as humanity is to assist our guests in any way, including protecting them from those who wish to do harm," she continued. "Unfortunately, already, we have identified segments who are plotting against our peaceful mission."

On the screen, the President's face was replaced by two very familiar pictures. It was Jace and Jess, photos taken directly from last year's school yearbook, their names printed clearly beneath.

"As a matter of national security, and for their own safety, we are desperately looking for these two young Americans. Anyone with information on their whereabouts is urged to call this number immediately."

A 1-800 number flashed on the screen.

Jess tensed. Everyone in the country—in the world, for that matter—would be on the lookout for them now. The damage may have already been done. In her mind, she pictured the worried look on the old lady's face, the one she had met outside just minutes ago. The lady could be picking up her phone and dialing at that very second.

"Jace, we have to go," she muttered, trembling. "We have to get out of here."

Jace didn't understand. "Are you crazy? This is a safehouse. No one knows we're here. Plus, there's food. There may be more OS members on the way. We *have* to stay here."

Jess told him about the encounter outside. His face fell. He actually looked longingly back at the kitchen and the refrigerator before agreeing. Scrambling around, they found a cooler and a couple of plastic bags. They hit the pantry and fridge and packed as much as they could.

"Where can we go?" Jess asked with a sigh. "Everyone will be looking for us. We can't call a cab, we don't have Aaron to take us anywhere, and we can't go back to the Taskforce office because we don't know who has been compromised. Maybe the neighbor lady won't turn us in. Maybe she didn't see the broadcast, or even if she did, maybe she won't recognize me in the pictures."

"We can't take that chance," Jace said, nervously peeking through the curtains. He wasn't searching the skies for alien crafts this time. He was back to looking for black vans and special ops soldiers closing in to surround and take them into custody. He saw nothing but the skyward-gazing neighbors. For now.

"But where will we go?" Jess asked again.

The answer was easy for Jace. He held up the tablet with the blinking dots.

"Home," he said.

"Home?" Jess said incredulously. "That's hundreds of miles away, and we don't have a driver."

"I'll drive us," Jace said confidently. "No problem."

Jess shook her head nervously. "I don't think that's a good idea."

The steady and almost forgotten thrum of the hovering spaceships above was drowned out by the screeching of tires on the road. Shaking, Jace opened the curtains and looked again. An old, souped-up hot rod was squealing around the turn down the way. It wasn't Team Creepy this time, but it served as a lesson to Jess of how quickly their luck could change.

If she needed another reminder of the urgency, the TV behind them came to life once again. It was a repeat of the President's message. They watched again, looking for clues they might have missed the first time around. They had missed something. They'd both been so stunned to see their own faces on the screen that they hadn't paid attention to what came next. After the 1-800 number flashed, the screen returned to a wide shot of the President and the people standing around her before returning to a close-up of her face.

Horrorstruck, Jess and Jace looked at each other and said at the same time, "Did you see that?"

Jace hurried to the remote and hit the rewind button, hoping the TV was equipped with DVR capabilities. It was. He zipped back to the moment his own face disappeared from the screen. On the far-right side of the gathered supporters stood a man who couldn't possibly be there. He hit the pause button, and they both moved closer to the screen. There was no doubt.

"Impossible," Jess breathed. "I saw it. I saw him shoot himself."

Regardless of what she thought she saw, however, there could be no mistaking the identity of the person standing behind the President.

Max was very much alive.

Their clock was ticking. If Max was with the President, there was no doubt she now knew about the safehouse. Team Creepy—or worse, Erdean soldiers—would be racing their way now. They had no choice; they'd have to put their trust in Jace's ability to drive.

Gathering their bags of food and the weapons, they quickly exited the kitchen and went into the garage. Searching both cars, they saw no sign of the keys that would start them.

"They have to be here somewhere," Jace said. "Search drawers and cabinets."

Frantically, they opened every drawer and every door but came up empty.

"I could try to hotwire it," Jace suggested.

"Do you know how to do that?" Jess asked hopefully.

Jace shrugged and shook his head. Somehow, he didn't think pushing the right sequence of buttons on a video controller would work in this case. He wouldn't even know where to start.

Jess, however, slapped her forehead as she remembered something. She dashed back up the steps into the house. Beside the door was a cabinet. Opening it, she found more than just the keys to the two cars in the garage. There were many more key fobs, each labeled.

"Surveillance van one, van two, comms truck, cargo van," she read. "What are these doing here?"

"There's another garage," Jace said certainly. "If these are like the Team Creepy vans, we can blend in. I bet there will be a bunch of those on the road now."

"Where's the other garage, though?" Jess asked, but she stopped before finishing the question.

She flashed back to their trip through the tunnel. She grinned. It had to be! Grabbing a couple of the keys, Jess dashed back into the garage and to the tool board on the back wall. Jace followed right behind. Guessing the drill was the lock release, Jess gave the trigger a squeeze. Instantly, a seal broke and the door popped open. They slipped back into the tunnel. Jess knew they couldn't risk going all the way back down the steps but didn't think they'd have to. There was something about this landing between the garage and the stairwell down that seemed odd. There was something else nagging her about this section of tunnel, too, but she couldn't think about that now. If they successfully got out of here, she'd have plenty of time to sort through her thoughts.

Because she knew what she was looking for, she noticed it right away. It was so subtle that it would've been easy to overlook otherwise, but there was a slight discoloration in the wall. Looking closer, almost imperceptible, she could see the smallest of seams.

"Found it," she said triumphantly.

"Shh," Jace said, slapping his hand over her mouth.

The unmistakable sound of footsteps trudging up the long stairway echoed its way to their ears. They were coming.

Panicking, Jess ran her hands all over the wall, looking for a door release. Other than the carefully concealed seam, there was nothing. She pushed in every spot she could reach. Nothing.

The footsteps were getting closer. Jace set his bag of groceries down and pulled out his weapon, aiming it at the top of the steep stairway.

Frantic, Jess leaned her shoulder into the wall.

"Help me," she pleaded.

Holding the gun with one hand, Jace leaned in, too, but the

wall remained firmly in place. Could she be wrong? Was this not the hidden garage?

They were out of time. The echoes from down the hall were so close now that they expected to see a head emerge at any second. Even Jess had pulled her weapon. They were backing up toward the main door and the house beyond. With no other option, they'd have to take one of the plain cars there. They wouldn't make it without a fight, though. Over their own held breath, they could hear the noisy huffs of the person climbing the long stairwell. Fortunately, it sounded like one person. With both of them armed, Jace was confident they could dispose of this enemy and get away. Copying the stance of snipers he'd seen on TV and in video games, he lay down on the floor of the tunnel and stretched the weapon out in front of him. He urged Jess to get behind him. It would make them as small a target as possible. Their chaser rose into view, and Jace nearly fired by mistake out of surprise.

"Don't shoot," the familiar voice called. "I've been shot enough for one day."

"AARON!" Jess screamed, dropping her weapon and taking off at a run. She leapt into his arms, wrapping her father's best friend in a bear hug.

"Wh-wh-what?" Jace stammered. "How?"

"I'll explain later," Aaron said. He'd set Jess down and was bent over at the waist, trying to catch his breath from the long climb. "I don't think my escape went unnoticed. You can bet they're on their way."

Jess tried to explain their dilemma as best as she could. "There's cars in the garage of the safehouse, but we think there's a hidden garage here, with vans like Team Creepy used. We thought being in one of those might help us stay unnoticed."

She held up one of the key fobs, and Aaron took it and studied the key closely. Shrugging, he pressed the unlock button. A section of the tunnel, right where Jess had found the seams, retracted smoothly until the door was clear of the rock wall. Once clear, it slid to the left, revealing a brightly lit space beyond. The room was loaded with the vans and other vehicles. Aaron hit the unlock button again to identify the vehicle the key belonged to. Lights flashed on a van to their right.

Jess dashed out into the tunnel to retrieve the food bags. Back down the steps, she heard an unmistakable commotion. It was clearly more than one person. At a run, she bounded back into the hidden garage and jumped in the running van.

"They're coming," she said, her voice anxious. "It sounded like a bunch of them."

Aaron put the van in gear and started rolling toward the back of the manmade opening.

With a flash of inspiration, Jace grabbed one of the extra key fobs and hit the lock button. The door to the hidden room slid closed behind them.

"That should slow them down," he said, earning a pat on the back from Jess.

The exit to the secret garage was hidden by a rocky outcropping and fake bushes toward the back side of the neighborhood, not far from the edge of the cliffs. They emerged on an empty road far from the safehouse. At least for now, they were safe.

"Where to?" Aaron asked.

The twins looked at each other and spoke the same word at the same time: "Home."

PART 3

CAVES

INTERLUDE, PART 3
1,000,000 Years Ago

Panic erupted all across the council. Despite millennia on probation, the Erdean delegation had only recently been removed from the council, and nerves were still raw. There was no doubt the entire race of scavengers had gone rogue and instigated attacks on sovereign societies for their own gain. Still, though, some representatives on the council had fought to keep the Erdeans as members. Their argument was that allowing them to maintain a seat would, at the very least, keep the channels of communication open.

In the end, the Terragoddrians granted the request of those opposed to the Erdeans and severed their membership. The Erdeans had a history of independent action, anyway. They treated their own planet with disregard and gave little thought to others as they sought out and overwhelmed other inhabited worlds. Their capabilities and sheer numbers had grown tremendously over a very short period of time, and they gave little consideration to what any council—or for that matter, their makers—had to say. For them, it was a matter of survival.

The new planet, the one overrunning with unheard-of quantities of blulex, was far too distant, at least for now, for mass invasion, but if they if they were to obtain those amounts of the substance, they would shortly have the capability to wipe out everyone standing in their way. The entire universe would be at their fingertips. The homes of the council members would surely fall. No inhabitable planet would be out of their reach with the capabilities provided by that much blulex. The sovereignty of the entire galaxy would fall.

It was not overlooked that the Terragoddrians had taken special interest in this matter. It was largely suspected that the new planet was not, in fact, new to them. Had it already been seeded? Would it be the home of the next wave of experimental intelligence? It often took years, sometimes decades or centuries, for the Terragoddrians to respond to the council. Either they had been monitoring the Erdean aggression themselves and were ready to cross that species off the list, or their tendency for destruction was a threat to something else. Maybe it was both. Regardless, they were quick to respond and wasted little time before both supporting the removal of Erdea from the Supreme Planetary Council and sending a massive fleet to protect and hide the new planet they called Earth.

Because of the newly discovered properties of the blulex and the quick actions of the Terragoddrians, an advance scout team, comprised primarily of Mondeans, was able to reach Earth ahead of the aggressors. The blulex was transformed into tremendous oceans of salt water, a substance that would still show as blulex on long-range scans but would fade as the scanners drew near.

The Mondeans discovered something else on the planet. The indigenous dominant species had evolved into an animal not so different from themselves. Mass quantities of blulex or not, this planet was rich in many things that would interest the Erdeans. The new planet was rife with burgeoning civilization. The land masses were separated by huge expanses of the unusable salt water, but there was more fresh water than the Mondean team had ever seen. Lush forests, fertile fields, protective mountains, and air so pure they didn't need the lung filters necessary on so many other planets. The inhabitants were humanoid. They walked mostly on two feet but utilized their upper limbs to propel them when speed was necessary. Long black hair draped most of their bodies, rendering clothing mostly unnecessary. They were different, but in these new creatures, the Mondeans sensed a kindred spirit.

Similar to the Mondeans' own history of evolution, and that of all the other represented cultures in the Supreme Planetary Council, the Earthlings were advancing. It wouldn't be long before they achieved space travel and devised means of communication capable of reaching beyond their own system of planets.

That chance would never come. The Erdeans arrived ready to fight. Small though their scout team was, they never traveled without a fighting force.

Frustrated by not finding the precious resource they had traveled so far to harvest, the Erdeans were determined not to leave empty-handed. They had harvested and transported most of the Earthlings before the Mondeans were finally able to gain the upper hand and drive them away.

The planet had been devastated by the war, but it would recover. Going against their instructions to mask the blulex but otherwise not interfere, the Mondeans left a small delegation behind.

The Erdeans would not forget about this planet. The bugs would continue to monitor. When the population grew again, they'd be back. And there was still the matter of the blulex showing up on long range scans.

First, the Mondeans constructed communication arrays around the planet that could be used to signal for help. Then, they disguised these arrays, covered them in a manner where their true intent could never be discerned or uncovered until needed the most. They knew that to truly protect and ensure a future for these Earthlings, there had to be no indication of civilization. That would only attract the Erdeans sooner. So they erased all signs of advancement, dismantled cities, removed all technology, and resettled the few remaining Earthlings around the planet.

When the Mondean fleet pulled out, they left a few behind. Finding volunteers was easy. They had formed such a bond with the newly discovered species that they couldn't just walk away. The origins of this society needed protected. They would rise again, but the Mondeans would be there to monitor and restrain the progress. The Terragoddrians might not approve of the interference, but it was a risk they were willing to take. They'd stay on the sidelines and monitor the regrowth of the species. If necessary, they would hold them back enough to keep from drawing the attention of the Erdeans for as long as they could.

CHAPTER 13

Going Home

Jace and Jess had seen so much over the last couple of weeks that the alien invasion had just become part of their lives. They didn't simply accept it, and they didn't see it as normal, but it had become a reality they had to deal with on a minute-by-minute basis. Determination had become their mindset.

It wasn't until they neared Ridgeport that fear of what they were truly facing set in.

The trip home from their narrow escape at the safehouse had been largely uneventful. Despite being in a Team Creepy black SUV, they had stuck mainly to backroads. As they traveled farther and farther from the coast, they drove through towns where the invasion was just something seen on TVs—before the signals were lost—or gossiped about over white picket fences with neighbors.

In other places, especially as they neared the general area of the crash site where it had all begun, quaint rural towns looked more like third world war zones. Long stretches were little more than ghost towns, the land stripped bare by the spreading Erdean presence on the ground. Despite being the middle of summer, the trees were as bare as they were in the dead of winter. It was nothing more or nothing less than the twins had expected to see on their journey.

When they saw the giant structure on the outskirts of Ridgeport, however, that all changed.

Although it hardly resembled the one they had constructed in the forest, there was no doubt this behemoth was the Erdeans' own version of a transport. It was easily five times larger than the one made of scrap metal, stolen ladders, and pieces of downed airplane. It towered over the landscape like a New York City skyscraper. Currently set to send rather than receive, near continuous red blasts fired from its tip, likely sending enslaved humans off this planet. The transporter itself was sleek and seamless, perfectly melding a steel-like substance with the white cloth. The entire structure crackled with blue energy. Like bees zipping to and fro from a hive, the transporter was being swarmed by smaller Erdean ships.

The twins were speechless.

Aaron broke the silence. "I think we need to detour," he said, taking the next road, which led away from the horizon-dominating tower.

"We have to get into town," Jace said, speaking up.

Jace was clutching the tablet tightly in his clenched fists. He'd spent the entirety of the trip alternating between staring out the window and studying the map with the two blinking dots.

"We need to get home, Uncle Urn," Jess added.

The pinpoint location of the two dots wasn't over their house, or even their neighborhood; it was over an unmarked patch of empty land close by. Jess had a really good idea of where and why, but she wanted to see for herself before sharing. The house would be the perfect place to start.

"I'll get you there," Aaron said, "but I think we'd better go around that giant ray gun."

He found a route through empty side streets, and they were soon out of view of the transporter. Aaron had been trying to get information from the kids since they'd escaped the safehouse, but both seemed lost in their own worlds, and conversation was scarce. He understood. It had been a long, grueling experience, and they were tired. He was tired. As they got closer to home, however, the energy had returned. The twins had perked up, ready for a fight.

"We should go find your mother," Aaron said, trying again to

THE ORIGIN SOCIETY: US

redirect the kids. "She'll be worried sick."

"No," Jess said adamantly. "The dots are here in Ridgeport. The aliens were trying to find this location, so it must be important. Why else would they risk breaking into a government facility? Why else would they build one of their transporters near Ridgeport? Something important is there, and we need to get to it first. Besides, Mom is probably trapped on her trip. She wouldn't have been able to get home."

"Would it do any good for me to ask you to drop this?" Aaron said, knowing full well what the answer would be. "Let the military handle it. They're trained for these kinds of things."

Jace laughed. "You think our military trains for an invasion of giant, intelligent grasshoppers? And besides, the President controls the military, and we all know who controls her now. No, Jess is right. We have to get to those dots. It might be a way to save Dad."

Aaron nodded. He expected nothing less. They were close enough to home that he knew the roads. He was confident he could bring them in from here.

That confidence evaporated as they neared their neighborhood. The small alien ships, about the size of American fighter jets, were swarming the area. They were rocketing around in every direction at blurring speed. Some fired their laser weapons at unseen targets on the ground. Others circled slightly larger ships. The action in the air seemed to be tracking something happening on the ground and was collectively moving in their direction.

Instinctively deciding to get off the road as quickly as possible, Aaron backed the SUV into the carport of an empty-looking house. He estimated that they were no more than a mile away from the Grisham home. He had just turned the engine off when the sounds of another car approached, its engine screaming in protest and tires squealing madly as it turned on their road. An alien jet dropped out of the sky right in front of their hiding place, hovering just above the pavement. The racing car screeched to a fishtailing stop, as its way forward was blocked. A second fighter dropped into position behind them, blocking off any possibility of retreat. The passenger and rear doors of the trapped car popped open, and five men carrying a variety of guns tumbled out. They fired at the ships, which floated above the ground like a fishing float bobbing in water. The gunfire ricocheted harmlessly off the craft. The men, not ready to give up, made a mad dash for the house where Aaron and the twins were parked. They sank down low in their seats to stay out of site but stayed barely high enough to peek out the window. It was important to see what was happening.

A larger craft, one that the smaller ones seemed to be protecting, hovered into view overhead. From a gun-like appendage attached to the underbelly of the ship, a blue pulse shot out toward the frantically running men. When the pulse reached them, it expanded into a plasma cage similar to the one Jace now carried in his pocket. The cage expanded around all five men, trapping them inside. Once secured, the cage was pulled toward the ship like it was caught in a tractor beam. Bay doors opened underneath, and the cage was swallowed whole. The ship rose and broke off in the direction of the transporter.

Jess hung her head. She didn't want to think about the fate of those men.

Back on the ground, the action in front of them had not yet reached a conclusion. The driver had remained in the trapped car. Witnessing what had just happened to the rest of his group, he began revving his engine. Smoke billowed from the back tires as the driver prepared to launch himself toward the fighter in a desperate bid for freedom. He never got a chance to attack. Understanding his intent, the Erdean pilot acted first. A red blast issued from the front nose cone of the alien jet, and the car simply incinerated. There was no explosion, no burst of flame or scattering of parts. The car simply ceased to exist.

Aaron and the kids dropped all the way out of view. They could only hope the alien fighter jets didn't have scanners capable of detecting signatures of nearby life. Just in case, Jace had dropped the tablet on the seat and gripped his alien pulse weapon. Reluctantly, Jess had hers out, as well, though she was shaking far too hard to have any actual hope of hitting a target. Their blasters might not cause much damage to the ships, but it might give them a better chance than those men had with their conventional Earth guns. Typically anxious to try out his video game reflexes in the real world, Jace was quite content to hide and wait this one out.

The two ships lifted slightly and, with cockpits riding low, drifted around the street, searching for any others looking for a fight. They clearly didn't have scanners capable of picking up the trio hiding under their noses, because the ships soon lifted above the streets and shot off to rejoin the hive of activity overhead.

Inside the SUV, there were three sighs of relief. The fear welling up inside them was threatening to bubble over, however.

Jace was turning that fear into determination. After a couple of quiet minutes, he was getting antsy to get back into the action.

"Let's go," he said impatiently.

Aaron sighed, nodded, took the keys from the ignition, and opened the door.

"Where are you going? What are you doing?" Jace asked, his voice rising in agitation.

"You saw what just happened," Aaron said. "I'm not about to risk driving any farther. We're pretty close to your house, no more than a mile. We'll walk from here."

From the back of the SUV, they made sandwiches to eat while they walked. It was Jess's idea. Sure, they were headed toward their home, but those blinking dots were not exactly there. Who knew what they'd run into or when they'd get another chance to eat. Better safe than sorry.

For most of their journey on foot, the only action they saw was in the skies above. One of the giant mother ships drifted by overhead, its gravity drive so loud that it shook their teeth and made it impossible to hear. The fighter ships and the slightly larger transporters zoomed here and there, but the trio was able to keep moving, seemingly unnoticed. As they got into town, about a block away from their house, that changed. Erdean troops were everywhere. Swarms marched on the ground. Others flew low through the air. Dozens of ships raced to and fro overhead. To the east, they could see the very top of the transporter. It was sending "transmissions" into space so frequently that it looked like one steady blast of red streaking through the atmosphere. All were sent in the general direction of the waxing moon, barely visible in the bright blue sky.

Aaron, Jace, and Jess took shelter under trees at an overlook near the river that snaked through town. From there, they had a good view of what was happening. Through trees stripped bare by the invading bugs, Jess was sure she could see their house across the way, but there was no way to get there. The bridge across the river was swarming with Erdeans. Watching the skies, she saw transporter ships firing their blue cages toward the ground. The air was full of the cracks and bangs of shotguns, rifles, and pistols being fired. The human resistance didn't seem to be doing anything more than calling attention to their hiding places.

Jace elbowed Jess in the ribs and nodded his head toward the bridge. It wasn't just Erdeans. The center of the span was crowded with people—humans—being corralled into a tight group. Aliens with laser weapons were advancing from both ends, squeezing the group even tighter. Others were crawling on the concrete sides and the bottom of the structure. When they had the group where they wanted them, a soldier tossed a blue cube like Jace's into the middle. The box expanded until it had encompassed all of the humans. Screams of fear from those trapped inside the crackling blue walls were audible over all of the other activity. A transport ship hovered into position overhead. The bay doors beneath opened, and the cell, holding at least 100 humans, was lifted into the cargo hold. The doors closed, and the ship moved on. Most of the Erdeans left the bridge, scattering in different directions to continue their hunt. Others remained to guard the river crossing.

"Well, we can't go that way," Jace said. "How are we going to get home?"

"We're not going home," Jess answered. "Not really."

"Then where?" Aaron asked.

Jess looked at Jace. Jace held up the tablet and enlarged the map. There was nothing listed underneath the blinking dots. At first, that had been odd. Then he had realized where it was and what it meant. Jess had figured it out, too.

"Five Caves," they said together.

Aaron's eyes widened. Of course. The site of the air battle between two alien crafts more than 50 years ago. But that area had been quarantined and cleared out. Why would that be the targeted location on Jace's map?

Looking out from their spot on the banks of the river, they could see that the bulk of aerial Erdean activity was centered over the area where the caves were located.

"They're already there," Jace said. "We're too late."

Jess was thinking hard. The Erdean fighter jets were buzzing to and fro, swarming the area of the caves. Their troops on the ground and in the transport ships were moving out from the center of the city, rounding up all of the people they could find. Maybe they weren't taking these people as slaves. Yet. Maybe they were taking them for questioning. That would mean they hadn't found what they were looking for. How was that possible? But then something clicked in her head, and her eyes widened. How could she have not thought of this before?

"Where are the ships?" she asked.

"Huh?" Jace said, looking at his sister like she'd lost her mind. "They're, um, buzzing all around."

"No, not those ships," Jess said, feeling the excitement that came with solving a mystery. "The ships that crashed here in 1954?"

"They were—" Aaron started, but he stopped mid-sentence. He'd been about to say that they had been taken to the island in the South Pacific for testing and brought back, but that wasn't true. The *contents* of the ships had been removed from the crash site, but what about the ships themselves? They were never mentioned.

"They're still there," Jess said, really ramping up now. "The government didn't remove them. They buried them. They sealed off the caves and...and..."

Jess stood up suddenly and started to traipse along the wooded riverbank, headed toward downtown.

"Jess," Aaron said, concerned. "Come back here. What? Why? Where are you going?"

Jess barely slowed down as she said, "They sealed off the caves and created a secret entrance."

Jace's face lit up. He, too, rose and took off.

Aaron struggled to his feet, his mind not quite catching up with the twins.

"The tunnel," Jace said. "Our grandfather was part of the Origin Society. His house was *right there*. The house was the secret entrance at one end of the tunnel. The other is hidden in an alley downtown. That's how Jess and I escaped the house when Team Creepy came to get Dad. Remember?"

"You think The Sparker is there?" Aaron asked.

"It has to be," Jess said, swatting branches away from her face as she emerged onto the river road. It was a straight shot from here into town, and most of the alien activity had moved out closer to the caves.

Jess's mind was still racing. When she'd been in the tunnel at the safehouse, something had seemed so familiar, like a thought she couldn't grasp or a word stuck on the tip of her tongue. She had a feeling that the secret door to the hidden caves would be harder to find than the garage door, but she was equally certain it was there. They would find it.

They snuck into town without issue, but as they neared the alley with the hidden tunnel entrance, another swarm of ground troops blocked the way. The Erdeans were flitting around, using their wings to fly up to rooftops and cling to light poles. The few trees in the area had already been stripped bare.

The trio huddled between a dumpster and the Waffle House where their adventure together had started. So much had changed in so little time. The scene was hardly recognizable. The hedges that separated the busy commercial street from the sheltered neighborhood were gone.

Aaron looked longingly in that direction. Jess was first to realize he was looking toward his home. It was eerie to reflect on all that had happened in such a short period. Last time they were here, they were escaping the tunnel, on the run from Team Creepy. Now they were trying to find a way back in.

"We need a distraction," Jace said.

Aaron sank back against the brick wall and closed his eyes.

"Uncle Urn," Jess said, concerned. "Are you okay?"

Aaron sighed and slowly opened his eyes, taking in each twin like he might not see them again.

"Do you believe in this prophecy?" he asked.

Jess looked at him suspiciously.

Jace answered quickly. "Of course," he said. "We've seen too much not to."

Aaron nodded. "Then fate will protect you more than I ever could. I got you here, and I feel like that was my role."

Jess didn't like where this was going. "Uncle Urn..."

Aaron waved her off, shutting her up. "You'll get in. You'll find the Sparker and contact the Mondeans."

"We need you to get into that alley," Jess said, her voice starting to crack with emotion as she sensed what Aaron had in mind. "We can't do it alone."

Aaron was shaking his head. "You can. You *will*. I'm going to cause a distraction. It should clear the way, buy you enough time to get into the alley unnoticed."

"No!" Jace cried, louder than he'd intended.

"Yes," Aaron whispered, lovingly putting his large hand on Jace's shoulder. "You've got this. But this trip, coming back here to Ridge-port... I think my role has changed. I'll distract the Erdeans, and if everything goes right, I should be able to sneak back out of town."

"But where will you go?" Jess asked, trying and failing to blink back tears.

"To find your mom," he said. "It's what your dad would want."

Jess tried different ways to argue but couldn't put voice to any of her objections. Jace was silent, gritting his teeth and biting the inside of his cheek to keep himself from crying. The moment was interrupted when an alien fighter jet tore across the sky, lasers blazing toward an unseen target. It was a reminder that the Erdeans were all over. They did need a distraction.

Jess wrapped her arms around Aaron and sobbed.

Jace stood straight and nodded, saying, "Go find Mom. Keep her safe until this is over."

Aaron gently pulled free from Jess's embrace and said, "Wait for my signal. You'll know it when you see it. Find the Sparker. Call the Mondeans. Save us all."

Without another word, Aaron raced off toward his home.

They didn't have to wait long. Only minutes later, a shrill whistle sounded out. It was a catcall whistle, the kind made by sticking your fingers in the corners of your mouth and blowing hard.

Jace pulled Jess up off the ground and moved them toward the corner of the restaurant. The alley was in view, but a dozen or more Erdeans were crawling over the street. More were on top of the buildings overhead. At the whistle, their movement stopped, and their attention was drawn down the road toward where the unexpected sound had originated.

The whistle repeated. The Erdeans began moving that way.

"On the third one, be ready to run," Jace whispered. "Don't look back. Whatever he's planning will be big, but we'll only get one chance."

Jess nodded, understanding.

As predicted, the third whistle cut through the bustle of activity, followed quickly by a BANG and the twilling sound like that of a firework being launched into the sky.

The Erdeans' attention was fully on the gas station opposite the Waffle House.

Jace grabbed his sister's hand and took off running in the other direction. He glanced back once, just in time to see the fiery streak of a flare impact with a gas pump. The handle at the end of the hose, which was connected to the pump, was lying on the ground, spilling gas into a large pool.

The explosion was massive.

It went against his every instinct, but Jace turned away from the sight and ran as hard as he could. Jess had never slowed. She reached the mouth of the alley first and disappeared around the corner. Jace was right on her heels. They didn't even pause to see if their mad dash been noticed.

Breaking through the fence at the unmarked gate in the alley, both worked together to pry up the manhole cover, then dropped down into the darkness. They had safely reached the secret tunnel.

Next mission: Save the world.

CHAPTER 14

Guardians

The first half of the trip through the tunnel went quickly. They'd found a flashlight discarded on the floor, right where the rungs led up to the manhole. Jace replaced the light's dying batteries with fresh ones he had pulled from his backpack.

Jess looked at him curiously. How did he just happen to be carrying batteries?

"What?" he said. "They were in the SUV. Batteries are always useful."

They had raced through the hollowed-out space, and their best guess told them they were nearing the area where Five Caves might be located. From there, the going was slow and tedious. Jess constantly checked the walls of one side of the tunnel while Jace closely studied the other. He alternated the flashlight from side to side. As Jess expected, this search was much harder. Unlike the tunnel back at the safehouse, this one was carved out of the earth itself. The walls, floor, and ceiling, while perfectly leveled and squared off at every corner, were packed dirt and chiseled rock. There were cracks and seams everywhere, none of which seemed to be the frame of a secret door.

The search wasn't helped by the fact that there seemed to be countdown clock ticking away in the back of their minds. Somewhere above them, a swarm of Erdeans were searching for the very same prize. They had a head start, but their advantage was dwindling by the second.

"I'm hungry," Jace said after an hour of fruitless searching. "Let's go to the house and get some food."

He looked longingly down the tunnel, where somewhere, just beyond the reach of their light, a hidden door in a discarded pantry opened into their basement.

Jess rolled her eyes. "You can't be serious."

"Do I ever kid about food?" her brother said, his mouth hanging open, as the thought of eating had him nearly to the point of drooling.

She sighed and shook her head. "You're always hungry, Lys. That's why we brought food from the safehouse."

She nodded her head toward the backpack slung over Jace's shoulder. It didn't escape his attention that she'd reverted to using her nickname for him. Lys, short for Lysander.

"Oh yeah," he said, grinning stupidly. He pulled a pack of crackers and a bottled water from the pack and started munching. "Thanks, Lexy."

Agreeing to rest just long enough to eat, they sat down in the tunnel and rested against the dirt wall.

"I think it's because we're close to home," Jess said after a minute of quiet.

"What is?" Jace said, spraying cracker crumbs as he spoke.

"I just called you Lys. You called my Lexy. We've barely used those names since we left here. But we're back. This is Dad's territory. Subconsciously, I think we feel that."

"We're going to get him back," Jace said, his voice suddenly steely with determination.

Jess took a sip of water and rested her head against the wall, staring up at the perfectly packed ceiling. Except the spot right above them wasn't quite as perfect as the rest of the walls. A dense patch of cobwebs stretched over a small section. She grabbed the flashlight and shined it directly on the spot.

His mouth still full, Jace joked, "We need to have a word with the maid."

"Have you seen any other cobwebs in this tunnel?" Jess asked.

"Haven't been looking," Jace admitted.

Jess stood up and looked closer, saying "I haven't, either, but I'm sure we would have noticed."

She stepped directly under the white patch of spun silk. It almost looked more like a caterpillar cocoon than a cobweb. The ceiling of the tunnel was barely within reach of Jess's outstretched fingers. She reached up and ran her fingers through the webbing. It peeled away easily from one side, revealing a small, plastic bulb. Grasping the bulb, she tugged, and a thin chain pulled free. With a slightly more force-ful jerk, Jess pulled on the bulb again. A shower of dirt fell from the ceiling.

She gasped.

"Don't!" Jace screamed, louder than he'd meant to. "You'll cause a cave-in."

But it wasn't a cascade of the ground above them that descended from the ceiling. It was a hidden stairway.

"Like the ladder into our attic," Jace said, now on his feet.

Without wasting another second, the twins ascended, emerging into a space no person had entered in over half a century.

They didn't really know what to expect as they rose through the ceiling of the tunnel and through the ground above, but what they saw certainly wasn't it.

They were in the corner of a cave. They'd gotten that much correct. Light, without a discernible source, spread out across the ceiling, illu-minating the space in a pale-yellow glow. The cave was large, about the size of Aaron's backyard garage. And it was totally trashed. The ground was littered with pieces of shredded metal and chunks of rock. It looked like a stalactite had exploded. To their right, a large chunk of metal twisted into a ball-shaped mound rested against the cavern wall. It was about the size of a small boulder.

Jace and Jess saw all of this in their periphery, for their primary focus was understandably drawn to the center of the room. A gleaming metal spaceship—or what was left of it—took up most of the space. It was basically a larger version of the sleek silver drone that had emerged from the lake by the clearing in the forest. Only this ship was much larger. It was no drone. A cockpit large enough for three, or maybe four, people was open on top of the ship, near the front. The glass cover to the open space had been shattered in many places. The body of the ship itself was dented and cracked. Clearly, it was supposed to be perched on three legs of landing gear, but one of the legs had collapsed.

"No wonder they left it here," Jace said, stepping forward to take a closer look. "This thing belongs in a junk pile."

Careful to avoid the pieces of the ship scattered all over the ground, they walked around the cave, taking a look from all sides.

"This has to be the Mondean ship," Jess said.

She didn't need to explain. They could both see the resemblance to the drone that had saved them in the clearing.

"Look, there's another room," Jace said, pointing.

Across from where they had entered, a smooth, oval-shaped gap revealed an entire other chamber. It, too, was lit from the ceiling. Stepping in, they saw much the same level of wreckage. The ship resting at the center of this space didn't seem quite as damaged, though.

"Erdean," Jess said.

It looked to be a cross between the jet-style fighter ships and the larger transports hovering over Ridgeport. Up close, they could see details in the ship they couldn't make out in the versions zipping through the skies. Jace walked around the ship, his hand extended, touching the smooth, almost-steel surface. There were dents here and there and chunks missing, but overall, this alien vessel seemed to be in better shape that its counterpart in the other room. There were no wings, but folded into slot where the wings should be was a compressed collection of familiar-looking white fabric. Jace didn't dare touch it. It hovered over the ground, its anti-gravity drive still functional, negating the need for landing gear. Unlike the massive mother ships they had seen, this smaller ship floated soundlessly.

They had no sooner noted the silence, though, when a buzzing sound began echoing through the chamber. Jace knew that sound. Something was powering up. A little scared, they looked around, searching for the source.

"There!" Jace yelled, pointing at the jagged ceiling of the cave.

A chunk of rounded metal was lodged in the rock. An internal glow was growing brighter. Unlike the soft golden glow of the ambient lighting, this light was blue-white, almost the color of the sky lightening. Together, the twins began backing up toward the wall to the left of the entrance.

Whistles and squeals began emanating from the lump of metal. Remembering the violent, shrill sound of the trunk in the forest, Jace instinctively put one finger in each ear. Jess cocked her head sideways, trying to remember where she'd heard these sounds before. Despite Jace's fear, it wasn't the same as the ear-splitting siren that had taken out the Team Creepy soldier guarding the clearing. It sounded more like...

"Crickets," she said aloud.

The lump of metal detached from the ceiling and dropped onto the spaceship, unfolding as it fell. When it clanked on the metal, it had assumed a whole new shape. It looked like an all-metallic version of an Erdean soldier. It was crouched on four of its six legs, the back two hinged on knees turned backward in relation to a human's. It was ready to spring forward. Its face was purely robotic. Two eyes glowed the same blue-white as the power source within. Smooth strips of metal wrapped around the head in place of a nose and chin. Its mouth was nothing more than a gap between the strips. The sound was whistles, twills, and chirps, the Erdean language.

"I don't know what its saying," Jace whispered. "But I don't think it's a friendly greeting."

As if trying to confirm Jace's theory, the droid sprung from the top of the ship. As it leapt, however, the body of the robot showed itself to be as damaged as the ship. Its left side's rear leg was clearly broken, hanging limp. As the metal bug jumped, it actually traveled sideways, crashing into the wall of the cave to their left. More twills and chirps. If a robot could curse, Jace thought this one might be.

Moving quickly, they raced toward the oval gap between the chambers. Recovering its balance, the droid leapt again in an attempt to cut them off. It landed feet away and rose to its full height, studying the human intruders like it was trying to determine which one to eat first. It moved a step closer. Metal mandibles extended from the open mouth, clicking and clacking as they opened and closed. Combined with the eerie glow from its eyes, the sight was horrifying. The droid was stalking toward them. There was no better way to describe it. It clanked and popped as it moved, its broken leg popping out of socket and dragging along the ground. The effect was menacing.

With nowhere else to go, they retreated fully into the first chamber. If the droid attacked, they had little chance of making it back to the trap door and the tunnel, but they had to try. The intent of the alien droid was unknowable, but it couldn't be good.

Clink.

Clank.

The droid moved closer. The buzzing of its power source seemed to intensify. Gathering its broken leg under its body, the giant metal bug crouched, preparing for a surging leap that would overtake its prey. It exploded forward with a jump so quick and powerful that the twins barely saw it coming. The Erdean droid launched right at them, then...

...was repelled backward as it slammed into a blue plasma force field that had sprung up in the oval gap between the two caves. The droid slammed into the front nose cone of the spaceship. The broken leg gave way and separated completely from the body. Other small pieces and parts dislodged and scattered across the floor. The strange creature struggled to an upright position and began gathering its pieces, Jess and Jace seemingly forgotten.

The two of them stood weak-kneed and trembling at the close call. They looked around for the source of the sudden protective force field and panicked when they saw another droid standing beside the

Mondean ship, a finger on its human-like hand extended, a thin blue string streaming from it to the entrance between the caves. What they had mistaken for a lump of boulder-sized metal earlier had been another of the droids. This one, however, was significantly different, though no less damaged. What should have been its left arm had clearly been ripped off the metallic frame that served as a shoulder. A bluish glow issued from only one eye socket, the other a darkened hole. Other than that, this droid was more or less human shaped.

"Humans," the droid spoke, breaking the silence and eliciting a scream of shock from Jess.

Jace whimpered and stepped back.

The voice was robotic. Computer-generated. It reminded Jess of Stephen Hawking, a famous scientist she had seen on a TV show. Coincidentally, Hawking had suffered from the same disease—ALS—that had stricken their father. Beating all odds, Hawking had lived with the disease for 55 years. He spent the majority of his life in a wheelchair and had lost the ability to speak, but through great advances, he was able to use an infrared device attached to his glasses to "look" at a keyboard and create words. A computer translated the words to sound. The voice from the droid was very similar.

Unsure of its intentions, they said nothing but continued to back away.

"Ahhh, humans scared," the droid said.

Using the thumb on its glove-covered hand, it "pinched" the blue stream, breaking it off. The plasma field in the gap remained, separating them from the Erdean droid beyond. This freed the droid's arm to make a sweeping, welcoming gesture, as if inviting them into its home.

"ABCs and one, two, threes make the humans easy to please," it said.

Despite the stiff, unmoving metal mouth and electronic eye, Jess could imagine the droid smiling. Feeling it was the right move, instinctually thinking they were safe, she broke free from Jace's grasp and stepped forward.

"Are you a Mondean robot?"

A whirring sound came from inside the droid, like a computer trying to reboot. With its one arm, it slapped the side of its head.

Jess's voice was spoken back at her. "Are you a Mondean robot?"

Several strange sounds rattled around in the droid's mouth before it finally said again, "ABCs and one, two, threes make the humans easy to please."

The light in its one eye flickered and went out. Its head slumped forward, and the whole body went still. Instantly, the plasma field behind them vanished. Fortunately, the Erdean droid was too worried with putting itself back together to mount any kind of attack. With a couple of sputters and false starts, the whirring kicked back into gear, the light returned in its eye, and the droid was back.

Jace pulled free, too, and moved up beside his sister, saying, "Great. Just great. We find a friendly robot, and it's like a senile old man in a recliner falling asleep mid-sentence."

Jess laughed, and the sound surprised her. It felt good to laugh. Jace's description was right on the money.

The droid extended its finger again, and the force field returned. For two solid minutes, sounds that both kids assumed were words in some language they didn't understand poured from the droid.

Jess moved even closer.

"ABCs and one two, threes," she said. "Do you speak English?"

Again, Jess's words and voice were repeated back to her like a recording.

This time, the robotic voice added something different. "A quick brown fox jumps over the lazy dog," it said. "ABCs and one, two, threes."

Jace cackled. "Man, this thing is cuckoo for Coco Puffs."

"No, I don't think so," Jess said, speaking softly while looking curiously at the droid.

"Jess, it's talking about dogs and foxes and silly rhymes," Jace said, twirling his finger around his ear. "Cuckoo."

"No," Jess said forcefully, frowning at her brother's characterization. "A quick brown fox jumps over the lazy dog is a mnemonic device."

Jace cocked his head in her direction. "A what device? Pneumonia? Are you saying this thing has pneumonia?"

Jess shook her head. Her brother could be exasperating sometimes.

"No, silly. A mnemonic device is a trick to help you remember something. A quick brown fox jumps over the lazy dog is the shortest possible sentence that includes every letter in the alphabet. The English language is made up of ABCs and one, two, threes. It's linking us with a language it has programmed. But I think something has gone wrong. Maybe its processor was damaged in the crash."

The droid was staring straight at Jess as she spoke.

"Crash," it repeated, using her voice, then continued on with its synthetic speech. "Warning! Erdean droid ship entering human air space. Warning!"

The droid shut down again. And with it, the shield went out. Jace started to move forward, but Jess hissed for him to stay still. Behind them, the Erdean droid was back on its feet. It was looking around as if trying to locate the source of an intrusion. They stayed completely still until the Mondean droid rebooted.

"Damage diagnostic," it said when the light in its eye returned. "Catastrophic. Phooey."

"Who are you?" Jess asked, trying a different tactic.

"Mondean deep space drone pilot XR737," it answered. "Mission: Shield Earth-bound humanity from Erdean detection. Mission failure. Erdean presence detected. Warning! Warning!"

Suddenly, the droid shot forward past the twins, going through the blue plasma shield and straight at the Erdean droid. A ferocious battled ensued, with metal parts flying everywhere. The clashing of metal was so loud and intense that Jess and Jace actually worried the Erdeans above the ground would be able to hear and would come investigate. After nearly 10 minutes, the Mondean droid seemed to get the upper hand. The Erdean bot curled up on itself and sprang back to the ceiling, where it lodged itself back in the spot where it had been earlier, then powered down.

The Mondean droid returned to its side of the double cavern and said, "Commence recharge and repair. Estimated time: Unknown."

The droid didn't curl back into the same ball shape as before, but the light in its eyes dimmed until it was barely more than a flicker of a candle. Soft clicks and whirrs were audible from deep inside its body.

Jess finally pieced parts of the puzzle together.

"These are robot pilots," she said. "They've been trapped in here together since 1954. All these scraps of metal aren't from the crash, or at least all of them aren't; they're from these two fighting over the years. The Mondean is programmed to scan for Erdean presence and protect us from them. A guardian."

"How do you know that?" Jace asked.

"It just makes sense," she answered. "But I want to ask him questions. I want to ask him about the Sparker. It might be in that ship, but I don't want to risk looking. Messing around with the ship may trigger some defense that will cause the droid to attack us. I wonder how long he'll be in repair mode."

"Hard to tell," Jace said.

Despite everything they'd seen the last few days, it was taking longer for Jace's brain to process all that he was seeing. It was a strange new world.

"How long do we wait?" Jess asked.

"I'm hungry," Jace said.

Jess shook her head and took the backpack from Jace, saying, "All right. Let's eat. Hopefully, Mr. XR737 here will be back with us by the time we're done."

So they ate and waited. Above them, the destruction of the world as they knew it continued.

CHAPTER 15
A Droid's Tale

"ABCs and one, two, threes make the humans easy to please," XR737 said in a sing-song tone, its mechanical voice barely louder than a whisper. It was attempting a soothing tone. "A quick brown fox jumps over the lazy dog."

Jess awoke with a start. Jace's head was resting on her shoulder. They were propped against a cavern wall. She blinked her eyes, trying to remember what had happened. Looking around, it all came back in a rush. While waiting on the droid to power back on, they had eaten. With nothing to do beside sit and wait, and with their bellies full, sleep had overtaken them.

It was amazing how the brain could adapt. Here they were, in a cavern containing two alien space craft with crazy droid pilots, both seemingly intent on destroying the other. Not far over their heads, an alien invasion was in full operation as a species determined to strip Earth of all resources, living and non-living, implemented its plan without resistance. Their terminally ill dad was somewhere in space, having had his body disassembled on a molecular level and blasted off the planet.

Yet sleep had come.

XR737 had returned to what served as consciousness, although there was a constant whirring sound from inside his chest that hadn't been there before. The droid was whispering his two favorite English sayings over and over. He had covered their bodies with what appeared to be fabric removed from the seats of the spaceship. It was trying to comfort them.

Jess's stirring woke Jace. He jerked to attention, ready to fight.

XR737 got right in his face and said, "A quick brown fox—"

"Yeah, yeah," Jace said, physically pushing the droid backward a little. "Foxes, dogs, ABCs. I get it. You have a few screws loose."

"Jace!" Jess snapped. "It's trying to take care of us, and you're being rude."

Jace looked at the tattered seat cover that was draped over his legs and held it up questioningly. "Take care of us?"

"A droid would have no need for blankets," Jess hissed. "It was using what it had."

Jace looked from his sister to the robot, which was still hovering uncomfortably close. Despite having a metal face incapable of moving, he was certain the droid was looking at him with a hopeful expression.

"ABCs?" it asked.

Jace looked to her for help, but Jess laughed and shrugged.

"The human is pleased," Jace said finally. "Umm, thanks, XR737."

With a glance in the other chamber to make sure the Erdean bot was still powered down, Jess began firing questions at the pilot, asking, "Have you been in this cave since the crash? Why did the humans seal you in here? Do you have the Sparker? Can you contact the Mondeans?"

XR737 finally backed away from Jace, picked up a random piece of metal off the cave floor, and tried unsuccessfully to reattach it to the ship. The section stayed in place for a hopeful second before crashing to the floor.

"Communications inoperative," the droid said after a long silence. "XR737 has been abandoned for 34,164,724 Mondean units of time. One, two, threes. One, two, threes. Please. Please."

The internal whirring sound increased. The light in the droid's chest, and the one behind its lone eye, flickered off and on for a few seconds. Jess was scared for a moment that it wasn't going to restore itself, but the light finally flickered back to full glow.

"What do you mean, communications inoperative?" Jace asked,

jumping into the strange conversation.

The droid turned its head toward Jace and paused, as if considering the question. Before it could answer, however, there was a flash of red from its body. It turned and dashed as quickly as its broken parts would allow toward the force-field protected entrance to the second cave. It held up its one hand and wiggled its human-like fingers. The movements activated something on the glove it was wearing. Blue sparks popped and fell toward the floor. Nothing, however, was happening on the other side. The Erdean droid was still powered down and attached to the ceiling.

"Alert malfunction," XR737 said. "Recommendation: Shut down and run diagnostic. Proceed?"

"NO!" Jess and Jace yelled at once.

"Don't shut down again," Jess pleaded. "We need more answers. Please."

"ABCs and one, two, threes make the humans easy to please," the droid said. "Diagnostic postponed."

"Thanks," Jace said with a sigh. "Now, can you tell us about the Sparker? Do you have it? Is it here?"

"Sparker," the droid said. "Mondean communications device designed for remote outposts and foreign civilizations."

"Yes," Jess said excitedly. "Do you have it?"

"Sparker model number 7J64FS21, assigned to Earth organization Origin Society. Delivered Earth year 1947 to replace discontinued model 5H63DB08—"

Jess interrupted. "1947? That was seven years before your ship crashed here in Ridgeport."

Jace deflated. "So you don't have the Sparker?"

The droid paused. There was more whirring inside its body. Jess had the distinct impression that it was accessing memory banks.

"Verbal receipt of Sparker model number 7J64FS21 by human Origin Society representative Luther Grisham accepted Earth, date June 14, 1947."

"Our grandfather!" Jess yelled, grabbing Jace by the arms and shaking. "Our grandfather had the Sparker."

"XR737, do you know where our grandfather is now?"

"Grandfather. Human term referencing parental lineage. Parent once removed. Pleasing to humans. ABCs. One, two, threes."

"Yes," Jess said. "Luther Grisham was our grandfather. He disappeared the day he found out we were going to be born."

The whirring grew louder as the robot said, "Luther Grisham. United States head of Origin Society. Subject of controversial prophecy. Recipient of Sparker model number 7J64F—"

"Yeah, yeah," Jace said impatiently. "He got the sparker in 1947. We get it. Do you know where he is now?"

A small antenna emerged from the droid's head and began to rotate in a circular motion.

"Luther Grisham's presence not detected," XR737 said. "New database file not accessible. Update required."

While Jace was trying his best to get more information on his grandfather and the location of the Sparker, Jess's mind was racing. Their grandfather was a member of the Origin Society? Did their dad know? Is that why he disappeared all those years ago? In her mind, she was seeing the pictures hanging on the wall of the safehouse. Their grandfather's picture wasn't here. Before Max, there was only the picture of the boy who looked like...

"Jace!" she said, interrupting her brother's interrogation of the droid. "The picture that looked like you... Liam Dasher. I think that was our grandfather."

"Liam Dasher," the droid repeated. "File not found. New database file not accessible. Update required."

The words caused Jace to pause, but he was too locked in on finding the Sparker to get lost in his sister's latest theory.

"Umm, not now Lexy. Trying to find the Sparker so we can save Dad, save the world, and then maybe worry about our grandfather."

"But—" Jess started, only to be cut off.

"Can that antenna thing detect the Sparker? Do you know where it is?" Jace asked the droid.

"Sparker must be activated to be detected," XR737 said. "Safety protocol."

Jace deflated. They'd come all this way for nothing. He'd been certain the Sparker would be here. Now they were back to square one, with no idea where to go next. He slumped to the ground.

Jess, however, was just getting ramped up. She was certain she was on to something.

"Jace, I think we need to go back to the safehouse," she said.

Jace laughed. "Are you out of your mind? We were lucky to get here without being sucked up into one of those Erdean ships. The safehouse is probably overrun with Erdeans by now, or humans under their control."

Jess wasn't about to be deterred.

"The picture that looked like you," she said, trying to make him see. "It was covering a spot where another picture used to be. I bet that was our grandfather's picture. Now it's a kid who looks like you. And the book. The history of the OS had a bunch of missing pages. I bet information about the Sparker was there. We have to go back."

Jace was shaking his head. "We can't go back. We're miles away from our SUV, we don't have Aaron to drive us, anyway, and even if we did, I don't think we'd make it. The Erdeans are rounding up everyone they see up there."

"So maybe we don't drive there," Jess said, another plan forming in her head. "Maybe this time, we fly."

She rounded on XR737 with a new batch of questions.

CHAPTER 16
The Sparker

"**W**hy were these ships left behind after the crash?" Jess asked. She had several questions and a plan in mind. XR737 whirred internally and was silent for several seconds. Again, Jess was afraid they'd lost the droid for good.

"The ships have similar protocols programmed in. When disabled, the ships go into lockdown mode until released. It was not possible for the humans to remove the ships themselves. However, I have conducted 7,637 inventory counts and can conclude that some materials were removed."

"Yeah," Jace said, butting in. "We saw those materials. Saved our lives."

"What about you?" Jess asked. "Did you go into lockdown mode, too?"

"Affirmative. Both my Erdean counterpart and I shut down. For me, it was protocol alpha 928-47 zeta. I am unfamiliar with Erdean protocol coding. I am programmed to revive and assess my situation every 1,000 Mondean units of time."

"Can you release the ship from lockdown mode?" she asked.

"Certainly," XR737 replied.

Jace saw where this was going and asked, "So we *can* fly out of here?"

"Negative," the droid said. It walked over and put its lone hand on the cracked hull. "I have conducted 434 damage assessments. This ship is too damaged to fly." Gaging the twins' reaction to this news, the droid sensed they did not like the answer. "ABCs and one, two, threes make the humans easy to please?" he asked hopefully.

"No, XR737," Jess said dejectedly. "The humans aren't pleased. This is bad news. Our planet is being overrun, we can't find the Sparker to call for help, our father has been disintegrated and transported into space, and the only way to get back to where we might find some answers is in a ship that can't fly or an SUV we can't drive."

"The quick brown fox—"

"Jumps over the lazy dog. Yeah. We know," Jace said gruffly, his frustration boiling over. But inspiration struck. "Hey, what about the Erdean ship? Can it fly?"

Jace stepped cautiously around the pieces and parts scattered on the ground and approached the crackling, plasma-like shield separating the two rooms of the cave. He gazed across at the other ship. It was beaten and banged up, too, but maybe not as badly.

"I have not run diagnostics on the Erdean vessel," the droid said.

"You know more about this than we do, XR737," Jess said. "What do you think?"

"Think?" the droid said, confused. "That's outside the scope of my programming. Mondean droid pilot's artificial intelligence capabilities are limited to mission parameters. I do not have authorization to speculate on the state of enemy aircraft."

"Your parameters include pleasing any humans you interact with, correct?" Jess asked.

"Affirmative," XR737 said. "ABCs and—"

"It would please us to know if that ship is capable of flight."

More whirring. This time mixed with worrisome clicks and pauses.

"The Erdean vessel is likely incapacitated," XR737 said at last. "Assessment of all likely scenarios suggest the pilot would have flown away and completed its mission otherwise."

That made sense, unfortunately. Jess hung her head. They'd have to find another way. Catching on to his sister's early enthusiasm, though, Jace wasn't ready to give up.

"Could you take parts from that ship to fix yours? No, wait! The other way around. We'd have a better chance at getting away in an Erdean ship. Can you use parts from your ship to fix the other one?"

"Diagnostic unknown," the droid said. "Analysis required."

"Then analyze it," Jace said, losing patience.

The droid walked over to the shield and stared into the other side. A laser shot from its one operational eye. It wasn't a laser bolt or any kind of weaponized blast. It was a green widefield laser. More like a scanner. It was sweeping across the ship. Instantly, the red light appeared within XR737. This time, it wasn't a malfunction. The Erdean droid awoke, detached from the ceiling, and dropped in front of its ship. It assumed a combative, protective stance.

"Scan disrupted. Proper analysis will require permanent disabling of the enemy pilot," XR737 said.

"Can you do it?" Jess asked doubtfully.

The droid appeared to be in far worse shape than its Erdean opponent. Decades of battles inside this cave didn't appear to have gone the Mondean droid's way. However, the question sparked life in the droid that they had not seen before. It was as if the challenge energized its circuits. It leaned over, and although physically impossible externally, there was no doubt XR737 was smiling on the inside.

"This will get messy. The humans are organic life forms and subject to accidental death. You will need to leave this cave. XR737 will disable the Erdean droid and attempt to repair the enemy ship into proper working condition. Give me one hour."

The droid disappeared around the back side of the ship and could be heard rummaging around in a cargo hold. It came back empty-handed but seemed to focus on Jace's backpack. The laser scan occurred again.

"I will require use of one of your weapons," it said. "And unless potentially excruciating death is an acceptable risk, the time to leave is now."

The twins looked at each other and shrugged. After handing over one of their Mondean laser blasters, they dropped through the trap door and back into the tunnel. One hour seemed like an eternity while the world that had always been their home was being destroyed on the surface.

"I'm hungry," Jace said after two minutes of pacing. He looked down the tunnel in the opposite direction from where they'd arrived. "Let's go home and find more food."

Jess was skeptical of how safe, or smart, it would be to go back to their house. Surely, it was being watched. There might even be Erdeans, or humans under Erdean control, staked out inside. But that familiar tickle in the back of her mind was turning into a full-out itch. She didn't know why, but she was certain they were missing something and that the answer could be found in their dad's house.

"Okay," she said with a resigned sigh. "Let's go home."

* * *

Jess couldn't explain it, but the closer they got to the hidden entrance to their house, the more certain she became that they were headed exactly where they needed to go. It was almost like there was a voice in her head, guiding her, whispering encouragement. She'd never experienced anything like that and wondered if it had anything to do with the prophecy that she and her brother were supposedly the subjects of.

When they first caught sight of the tunnel's end, Jace extinguished the flashlight, plunging them into near total darkness. Ahead, though, there was a faint light. An outline of a door.

The pantry.

Jace raced forward to plunge through, and Jess felt an almost irresistible urge to follow. It truly hadn't been that long since they'd first escaped Team Creepy, but it felt like an eternity. This was home.

Their home.

Their father's house.

The realization brought a pang of hurt and sorrow. It also served as a reminder to Jess of why they were here to begin with. She caught Jace's shirt with the tips of her fingers and pulled him back. She had caught him just in time. He had his arm stretched out to bust through the hidden panel at the back of the pantry door. It was an old kitchen cabinet set that had been placed, for storage purposes, in the basement side of the downstairs area.

Voices came from the other side of the sliding panel.

"We've searched this house 100 times and found nothing," a male voice said. "It's a waste of time."

"Our visitors insist that what they are searching for is nearby." A female this time, her voice speaking in a sing-songy tone the twins both recognized. She was under the hypnotic control of an EncephaLink.

"Then why aren't they in here looking?" the man said gruffly. "I don't understand why they have us doing their dirty work."

"For the last time, our masters' talents and skills are most needed on the surface and in the air," the female said, her tone never wavering.

"Yeah, rounding up humans and blasting them into space to do God knows what. Probably probing their keisters."

"Sacrifices are required," the woman explained patiently. "For the good of Erdea and Earth, servants are needed. You should be pleased you were given an opportunity to serve here and not selected to be one of the bound."

"Don't really have a choice, do I? My son was taken," the man said, a crack in his voice. "He's being held at that giant eyesore of a satellite dish."

"As has been explained, if you cooperate, if you do as I command, and if we find what our masters are looking for, your son will be returned." Her voice never changed tone or inflection, but it was clear she had spoken her last on the matter. "Now come. I do not believe what we are searching for is here. Perhaps we missed something in the yard or in a neighbor's house."

Jace and Jess waited by the hidden door until the sound of retreating footsteps faded completely. Jace's eyes were wide, trying to process what he had heard. His hands were shaking a little from the close call. Had his sister not grabbed him, he might've walked right into their arms.

Jess, on the other hand, was calm and focused, and when the house on the other side of the sliding wooden panel had gone completely silent, she whispered to her brother, "Do you hear the voices?" she asked.

"No," Jace said, misunderstanding. "They're gone. It's safe to go in now."

From the dim light seeping in from around the pantry, Jace could see his sister shaking her head.

"Not *those* voices. In your head. Have you felt like something has been pulling you home, toward this house?"

Jace laughed. "I think you're starting to crack, Lexy," he said.

The only thing speaking to him at the moment was his stomach. On cue, it gargled loudly.

Jess sighed. Now wasn't the time to think about it. She was certain that whoever had been in their basement would come back. They needed to go now. She was confident that whatever was calling to her would reveal itself once they were inside.

Reaching up, Jace put his hands flat against the back of the hidden door at the rear of the pantry and slid it aside. They stepped into the cabinet, paused to listen one more time for any sign of life on the other side, and pushed through the real pantry door. They had been underground so long that they had forgotten the deep bass throbbing noise that had become a constant in the above-ground world. Even in the basement, they could feel it in their guts.

The basement had been ransacked. Cabinet doors were open, and the contents from within—Jace's toys and their father's tools, mostly—had been scattered across the floor. In the finished portion of the basement, furniture had been overturned and sliced open with a knife. The table where their dad had spent countless hours tracking down his

THE ORIGIN SOCIETY: US

conspiracy theories (Were they still theories if they had been proven true?) had been broken in half, papers littering the floor.

Jace looked around, stunned. A furious anger swelled up in him.

Jess, however, had never made it out of the storage side of the basement. She had been drawn immediately to the one thing in the room that look undisturbed. Understanding immediately dawned. *This* is what had been drawing her. *This* is what the voice in her head had been guiding her toward.

The locked plexiglass case rested on top of the cabinet, exactly where it had been for years. Inside, the mannequin head was adorned with the crown and earrings. How many times had Jess been down here daydreaming of wearing the crown? Of slipping those earrings into yet unpierced ears? She had admired the jewels adorning all three pieces of jewelry.

It was so obvious now. Those weren't jewels. These pieces weren't jewelry. Looking closer, she could see. How had she not noticed before?

"Jace!" she called out to her brother in the next room.

"They've trashed the place," he said, anger evident in his voice.

"Lys," Jess said just loud enough to be heard over her brother's building outburst.

At the sound of his nickname, Jace calmed instantly and returned to the unfinished portion of the basement. He saw his sister studying the old mannequin head. It took a second for understanding to dawn.

"Lexy?" he said softly.

But then he understood. They had found it.

The Sparker had been in their basement all along.

CHAPTER 17
Sacrifice

Jess wrapped her hands around the plexiglass case and stared inside as she had so many times in the past. She had daydreamed of wearing the jewelry, of being a princess. This time, though, the vision wasn't of herself looking beautiful and important. It was of saving the world. She was separated from the ability to contact a species from another planet by a quarter inch of plastic.

The case was heavier than she thought, so she fingered the lock instead. It was small and cheap, not much heavier or stronger than the small lock that came on the diary she had bought from her school's book fair last year. That lock had a flimsy key she kept on a necklace. For a second, she considered running upstairs and rummaging through her jewelry box to see if she could find that necklace and key. There was no need, though. Her dad's tools were scattered all over the floor at her feet. Something here would work much better.

Already seeing what was needed, Jace had found a pair of needle-nosed pliers and was edging Jess out of the way. She looked at her brother resentfully. The Sparker had been calling to her. It had *always* called to her. Before she could fight back, however, she looked into her brother's eyes. With steely determination, he was trying to use the pliers to break the lock with one hand while using the other arm to hold her at bay. She had seen that look before. She had *worn* that look before. She flashed back to their reactions over what they thought was Ranger Ron and Baby Molly. Their selfish desires had been an easy target for the Erdeans' EncephaLinks.

Calmly and gently, she put a hand on Jace's arm and smiled at him, saying, "We'll use it together."

He smiled back and winked. He hadn't been in a hypnotic trance, after all.

"The sooner we get this open, the sooner we can call for help," he said. "Then we can get figure out how to get Dad back."

She stepped aside and let him work. The lock was no stronger than it looked. It snapped under the pressure Jace applied and clanked to the cabinet top. A small door on the plastic case popped open, and Jace stood aside to let his sister reach in and grab the piece that looked like a crown, or tiara. Immediately, the blue jewels lit up and crackled with energy. It was pieces of blulex, not sapphires, that adorned the Sparker. That was what powered the communications device. Even the two earpieces glowed with energy.

The ability to talk to aliens had been inches away from Jess for as long as she could remember. No wonder she had been under strict guidelines to look, not touch. But to leave something this powerful where she could see it and want it also spoke of its importance. Her grandfather must've known this day would come.

They were so entranced by the Sparker and what it represented that they almost missed the warning signs. At first, they mistook the increasing buzz and bass-like throb as the activation of the communications device. The sound grew louder and louder, until the whole house was rattling. It was Jace who first realized what it really meant.

"Jess, we gotta go," he said, tugging on his sister's sleeve.

The gradual increase in noise wasn't coming from the Sparker. It was coming from outside. The Erdeans were on their way. When the Sparker had activated, its signal was picked up by the searching aliens. They had an entire squadron in Ridgeport looking for it, and it had probably lit up their scanners like a Christmas tree. XR737 had even told them the Sparker had to be activated to be located.

Jace started dragging Jess toward the pantry and tunnel beyond. The thrumming grew so loud that he was afraid one of the Erdean ships was going crash through their roof. The sound of soldiers entering the house shook the ceiling over their heads.

"Come on," Jace insisted, but Jess resisted.

She pulled out of his grasp and reached for the mannequin head. When she picked it up inside the plexiglass box, a roll of papers fell out of the bottom. One of the pages fluttered free from the rest, and Jess got a good look at the size of the paper. Immediately, she knew what she had found. Frantically, she tried to gather up all of the pages, and then the door at the top of the basement steps exploded inward in a cloud of dust, smoke, and splintered wood.

Jace grabbed the whole box and shoved it into Jess's arms.

It sounded like an entire alien army was descending the steps. The first ones—Erdeans, not hypnotized humans—came into view as Jess stepped through the secret panel behind the pantry. Jace had had just enough time to pull their one remaining laser weapon from his backpack and squeeze off a shot at the leader of the pack. The shot struck the alien soldier squarely in the chest, the spot guaranteed to do the least damage. The Erdean staggered backward, though, throwing the others in his group off balance as they half ran and half flew down the narrow stairwell. It bought enough time for Jace to get through the pantry and into the tunnel, as well. He didn't even bother closing the hidden panel. The Erdeans had seen the opening. They would be coming in full force.

There was only one chance to get out of this. Fortunately, Jace had practiced this exact scenario. There was a scene in his favorite video game, Operation: Covert Extraction, where he was desperately outnumbered. His only chance to escape and save the hostage was to lure the bad guys into a trap. He wasn't certain it would work, but it was their best shot.

"GO GO GO!" he yelled at his stunned sister. Uncertain of what to do, she had stopped near the mouth of the tunnel. "Run as fast as you can. I'll slow them down."

Frozen with fear, it took Jess a moment to react. That was all the time the Erdeans needed to recover. With another blast, the pantry exploded inside the basement. The entrance to the tunnel widened. Dirt from the roof of the ceiling sprinkled down on Jace.

"Not yet," he whispered, firing his own weapon as fast as his fingers could squeeze the trigger.

The air was filled with smoke and dust, making it hard to see and even harder to breathe. Jace began coughing but continued firing at the Erdeans trying to enter the tunnel. Jess finally gathered herself enough to take off, her arms squeezing the plexiglass case tightly to her chest. Jace backpedaled farther down the dark path, bouncing from one wall to the next to make himself a harder target to hit. In these close confines, he was a sitting duck. But he only needed a little luck. Just a few seconds.

All around were the growing sounds of explosions. More dirt poured on Jace's head. He actually smiled. His plan would work. He wasn't sure he'd be around to brag about it, but Jess would at least have a chance to get away. He was a little worried about the other explosions. It probably meant the Erdeans had discovered the tunnel from above and were trying to create their own entrance. If Jace could buy just a little time, they would be under the caves and safe from attack from above.

The Erdeans were in the tunnel now. It was impossible to tell how many, but by the constant barrage of blind laser blasts fired through the smoke and dust in his direction, he figured it was enough. Instead of sending return volleys down the tunnel, he turned his weapon to the roof and squeezed off as many shots as he could.

With a thundering rumble, the ceiling began to cave, and the tunnel started to collapse. Jace turned and ran as fast as he could. The ground over their heads was crashing down on the Erdean soldiers. The laser fire ceased as they were buried under tons of dirt and rock. The collapse wasn't contained to the area over the aliens, however. Like a domino effect, the walls and the top of the tunnel were buckling around the twins. Jace could see it giving way ahead of him. He wasn't going to make it. Like an avalanche, the wall immediately to his right gave way and swept over him. Luckily, he stayed on the leading edge of the racing ground. It pushed him forward, faster than his legs could keep up. He stumbled, fell, and rolled, clods of dirt forcing their way into his mouth and down his throat as his entire body was swallowed by the moving ground.

As suddenly as it started, it stopped. The collapse was complete. He was buried in a landslide. His lungs burning and chest heaving desperately for air, Jace clawed with his hands. He felt his fingers break through into open space. He was close, but his body was screaming for breath. There was no air to breathe, only more dirt to suck down his windpipe.

He felt another hand latch on to his, followed by a second hand grasping his wrist. Jess was pulling as hard she could. Fortunately, they were on the edge of the avalanche. The dirt here was dry and loose. She was able to pull her brother free. He landed with a painful thud on the tunnel floor, beside the plexiglass box.

Coughing and gasping, Jace tried desperately to inhale while, at the same time, expelling the dirt from his mouth and throat. They had reached the part of the tunnel under the caves, where the rock overhead was strong and unmoving. Struggling to his feet, Jace tested all of his body parts. Everything seemed to be working. He was still trying to cough up dirt, but there was no time to waste. The trap door to the cave was close, but farther down the tunnel, toward town, they could hear the unmistakable sound of Erdeans approaching. They'd either exposed the tunnel and entered at some point along the way, or they'd found the hidden entrance under the manhole. Either way, time was running out. They could only hope XR737 had been able to get one of the ships operational.

Lowering the trap door, Jess and Jace climbed back into the cave, closing the entrance behind them. The first cave was empty. The ship still parked there looked greatly diminished. Compared to the ruckus they had just left behind in the tunnel, the cave was eerily quiet. It wasn't completely silent, however. The sounds of mechanical clicks could be heard coming from the second cave.

The twins tiptoed toward the junction, unsure of what they would find. If it was the Erdean droid on the other side, they were defenseless. They had given XR737 one of their weapons, and Jace had lost the other in the tunnel collapse.

As they neared the entrance to the second cave, the clicking stopped and a red light began to pulse, its flash reflecting off the part of the other cave they could see. Their presence had been detected.

"Intruder detected," a broken but familiar voice called from just out of sight. "Identify yourselves."

It was XR737!

"It's us," Jess called, slowly moving through the entrance and into the second cavern, stunned by how much had changed in the short time they'd been gone.

The first thing they noticed was XR737. The droid has suffered significantly more damage. Most noticeable was that the one working eye had now gone dark. The face was severely dented, and the gap in the metal where the mouth was supposed to be had been caved in. That explained the broken voice.

"Motion detected," the droid said. "Scans failed. Maintenance required. Shutdown to commence in 20 Mondean units of time."

The droid tried to move in their direction. That's when Jace noticed the leg. It had clearly been severed from the rest of its body. XR737 had tried to tie it back on with wiring from one of the ships, but the leg was literally hanging by a thread, dragging uselessly behind.

Jess look at the rest of the cave. In the corner, she spotted what remained of the Erdean droid. It was slumped, clearly dead and destroyed. It was missing arms and limbs, as well, but the final blow had clearly been delivered by a laser blast. Scorch marks spread out from a dark hole in the center of the body.

The ship looked completely different, as well. There were patches of mismatched metals where XR737 had repaired holes in the main body, but overall, it looked solid.

"The ship," Jace said, addressing the Mondean droid. "Were you able to fix it?"

XR737's head turned in Jace's direction, and he said, "ABCs and one, two, threes—"

"Yeah, yeah," Jace said, not wanting to go down that road again. "If the ship is fixed, we are pleased."

"The vessel needs one more part to be operational," the droid said. "Once charged, the engine should be fully functional."

"How do we charge it?" Jess said, worried.

She could feel a clock ticking down inside her brain. The Erdeans in the tunnel would find their way in at any moment. She was still holding the box with the Sparker, and as long as the stones were glowing blue, it was activated. That meant it could be tracked. Jace's actions in the tunnel had bought them some time, but not enough.

"There were two active energy sources in this cavern," XR737 said. "Unfortunately, the destruction of the Erdean pilot damaged one beyond repair. Only my power source will charge the engine."

"Then charge it," Jace said, feeling the same sense of desperation Jess was feeling.

Jess moved closer to the droid, understanding dawning, and said, "We'll have to remove your power source to do it, won't we? It will kill you."

"XR737 is a functioning droid, neither living nor dead," the pilot said. "Programming mandates attempting to please any Earthlings. I would gladly give my power source to please the humans, but I cannot both detach the source and properly place it inside the ship's engine."

"You need us to do it," Jace said, understanding.

"Affirmative."

"No," Jess cried. "There has to be another way."

Living or not, XR737 was helping them escape. It wasn't fair that it should suffer an end to its own existence.

"I don't think there's another way, Lexy," Jace said sympathetically. "And even if there was, we're out of time."

Even as he said it, explosions from below rocked the caves. The Erdeans were getting closer.

"But XR737 is the only pilot," Jess said, desperately racking her brain for another solution.

"I can fly it," Jace said confidently, glancing toward the cockpit.

"The ship's functionality is similar to the Mondean vessel," XR737 said. "Its auto-navigational system will respond to the direction of the pilot. Manual control also available."

Another explosion shook the cave, this one so close that they were sure the Erdeans had just breached the cave floor from the tunnel below. The aliens would find them in a matter of seconds.

XR737 hopped on its one good leg to a spot near the rear of the ship. A panel there was open. The droid showed Jess how to detach its power source and where to plug it into the ship.

Jace scooped up the laser weapon from the ground near the destroyed Erdean pilot and took the plexiglass case from Jess's arms. He headed up the ramp that extended from the belly of the ship to the floor of the cave.

The Erdean troops were inside. They would enter the second chamber at any moment.

"Intruders detected," XR737 said. "Hostile signatures."

"How do we get out?" Jess asked, a new panic rising.

They were in a cave. Even if the ship worked, they were still underground.

"The vessel's weapons system is sufficient to blast through the ceiling," XR737 said. "If the human's wish to escape. The time in now."

It was a useless gesture. The droid didn't feel emotion. It was operating on programming, but Jess threw herself on XR737 anyway, giving the pilot a hug.

"Thank you, XR737."

She reached into the chest cavity of the droid and grasped the power source as she had been shown. It was a small chunk of concentrated blulex, no larger than a fingernail, encased in a transferable cube.

"A quick brown fox jumps—"

The droid's voice went silent as Jess removed the source.

"Over the lazy dog," she said, finishing the sentence.

She plugged the power source into the proper spot and closed the panel. A laser bolt slammed into the ship just over her head but was diverted by a glowing blue shield that had just powered on. It had worked! The ship was operational. More blasts followed, but Jess was protected by the ship's defenses. She raced up the ramp and into the cockpit.

Jace was already strapped into the captain's chair, looking over a vast array of blinking buttons. Seeing his sister safely inside the ship, he pushed the most obvious button, a giant green one blinking front and center.

The ship roared to life all around them. The throbbing of the anti-gravitational engine was muted in the mostly soundproof cockpit, but they could feel it in their chests. The walls and floor of the ship turned almost completely transparent. They could still see it faintly, but they also had a clear view of everything in the cave around the ship.

"Cool," Jess said, stealing the word right out of Jace's mouth.

What wasn't cool was the number of Erdean soldiers pouring into the cave around the ship. That it was one of their own vessels kept them from attempting to shoot it down as it hovered above the cave floor. Their shields might block a single blast, but Jace didn't want to find out how they'd fair against an entire legion of enemy troops. He took hold of the steering column that extended from the control bank, suddenly unsure of what to do next.

Jess didn't hesitate, though, confidently saying, "Activate weapons system."

A targeting display showed up on the transparent walls of the ship, the crosshairs moving with Jess's eyes. She locked her gaze on a cluster of Erdeans attempting to fly onto the nose cone of the ship.

"Fire!" she yelled.

A blue blast appeared from over her head, incinerating the alien swarm.

"Whoa!" Jace said, seriously impressed.

Jess shifted her gaze upward, locking her eyes on the widest part of the ceiling.

"Fire!" she shouted again. And again. And again.

This blasts blew apart the top of the cave, revealing sunlit blue skies overhead.

Gripping the handles of the steering column and pulling gently, Jace imagined the ship rising up through the narrow gap. The ship responded immediately, taking them above ground.

Now hovering outside, Jess and Jace became overwhelmed by the scene playing out all around them. The glimmer of sunshine and blue sky they had seen through the ceiling of the cave must've been the only clear sky for miles in any direction. The air was full of dust and smoke. It looked like most of Ridgeport was on fire. Dozens of Erdean ships of all sizes and functions hovered all around, each facing the Five Caves area from where they had just emerged.

They were completely surrounded.

Taking a cue from her brother, Jess wasn't about to go down without a fight. She moved her eyes, searching out the best target, trying to find the weak link.

"No," Jace said, surveying the scene. "Weapons system offline."

The ship's computerized voice responded in perfect English, "Weapons offline."

"What? Why? How?" Jess was confused, and she turned to her brother, ready to argue.

"We're in an Erdean ship, remember?" he said.

Jess's eyes widened, and she nodded her head and asked, "What now?"

"We do what Han told Chewie in 'Return of the Jedi,'" he said, referencing his favorite *Star Wars* movie. "We fly casual."

"Fly casual?" Jess asked, her eyebrows raised.

"Sure," he said with a smile. "We act like we belong until we have a gap to slide through." As he took another look at the firepower assembled around them, the smile vanished. "But just in case," he said before switching to a formal voice, "transfer control to co-pilot. Activate weapons system on my mark." He pointed through the transparent wall of the cockpit at one of the larger cargo ships hovering to their east. "Slowly take us over there. It looks like fewer battleships that way. At the last second, slide under the big one and accelerate with all you've got. Let's hope XR737 got all the screws locked down tight."

"I can't fly this thing!" Jess said in a panic.

"You already are," Jace said. "Just grab the handles on the steering column and think about where you want to go. Give the controls a nudge if it helps. It's easy!"

"Then why don't you drive," she said, still uncertain.

"How many shoot 'em up video games have you played?" Jace asked. "I've been practicing my whole life for this. If we have to fight our way through, I need to be on the guns."

Jess couldn't argue with that. Turning her focus to where Jace had pointed, she willed the controls to move them toward one of the giant Erdean cargo ships. Like her brother said, the ship moved casually in that direction. The other Erdean ships continued to glide nearby, keeping the new ship in sight, and surrounded.

A yellow light on the console began to blink. With a shrug, Jace reached over and touched it. The cabin was filled with the sounds of chirps and whistles and squeaks. It took a moment for him to realize it was the sound of the other Erdean pilots calling their ship, no doubt wondering who they were and where they'd come from.

"I'd guess silence will be just as much of a giveaway as getting on there and asking politely in English for them to let us by," Jace said. "I think we better make our move...NOW!"

Jess pulled back on the steering handles and imagined the ship launching forward at full speed. The ship responded instantly.

166

"WEAPONS SYSTEMS ONLINE," Jace shouted.

Red crosshair targets immediately popped up, following his eyes. Working instinctually now, he focused on a smaller fighter turning to face them. He blinked to engage the weapon, and the target exploded in a massive fireball.

It was a bit of a bumpy ride as Jess gained confidence in her piloting ability, but she managed to avoid crashing into anything. She navigated them around a cargo ship and pointed their nose toward clear skies ahead. Suspicious but not expecting an all-out attack by one of their own ships, the Erdeans were slow to respond. By the time they reacted, Jess had found a clear path and shot them like a rocket toward freedom.

Jace rotated in his seat until he was facing the rear of the ship. He could see just as clearly through the back as he could out the front. He almost wished he couldn't. Dozens of fighters had accelerated and were on their tail. Like the video game expert marksman he was, Jace was looking from side to side to find the next target. By focusing his eyes through the crosshairs, he locked on and blinked. His eyelids were the trigger.

KA-BOOM

Lock on and blink.

KA-BOOM

"Rear shields maximum," he called out just in time.

Dual blasts from pursuing fighters ricocheted harmlessly away from their ship. With increased shields, the view out the back dimmed, but he could still see. Lock and blink. Lock and blink.

For the most part, Jess was letting the ship fly itself. It seemed to bob and weave of its own accord, as if predicting when and from where the next volley of laser beams shot by their pursuers would come.

Off to the side, Jace noticed the giant transporter growing out of the ground like a steel mushroom. It had shifted into receiver mode, its top opened like a satellite dish.

There was a bright flash, and Jess temporarily lost control as a concussive wave of air blew past them. Out of nowhere, another Erdean fighter jet appeared just over the receiver. It engaged its engine and rocketed toward them, getting out of the way just before another blast arrived with another ship.

"Jace," Jess said, her voice quivering.

"I see it," Jace said. "Shields forward."

He rotated his seat and focused on the new incoming fighters. He blew one out of the sky, but the second evaded with a sharp turn left and a steep dive.

Another transmission shook the air around them, and a third ship appeared.

"Take us right at it," Jace called out to his sister.

Banking hard, she guided them toward the transmitter, and Jace focused every ounce of his concentration on the tip of the transmitter, squeezing off shot after shot. The structure had lowered its shields to receive the fighter jets. It was defenseless against the attack. At first, Jace was afraid it had absorbed his shots, but suddenly the whole structure blew in a massive fireball.

Piloting like an expert, Jess swerved the ship around the billowing plume of fire, smoke, and raining debris. Jace angled the shields to deflect the violent expulsion of air pushing away from the blast.

Blocked from view of the other Erdean ships, they had the window of escape they'd been hoping for. Jess closed her eyes, concentrating, and the ship accelerated to thousands of miles per hour. They were gone from sight in the blink of an eye.

Jace was beginning to lose count of how many times they had narrowly escaped, but he licked his finger and made an imaginary mark in the air, sighing with relief. Add one more to the unlikely tally.

PART 4

BATTLES
(PAST, PRESENT, AND FUTURE)

INTERLUDE,
PART 4
1954

Luther Grisham nervously looked around the dark clearing. There was hardly any light, and nobody was around, but this wasn't the type of meeting he was comfortable having out in the open. While this undeveloped piece of land would be ideal for a safehouse, and maybe even a permanent base, it was not the most secure location to meet with an alien, even under the cover of night.

To his left, the capital sprawled out near the banks of the river. Anyone down below could've seen the strange ship glide in and land. Hopefully, it would have been mistaken for a plane landing at the airport located just below, on the banks of the river itself.

The Mondean droid pilot handed over a package, and he shook the robot's hand. Although the AI technology was wondrous, far superior to anything currently possible here on Earth, Luther had seen this before.

"Thank you," he said. "It will always be nearby, but I hope we will never need it. I know that if the time comes when we do, however, we can count on you."

The droid seemed pleased by the words, saying, "ABCs and one, two, threes make—"

A red light began flashing within the droid's chest, cutting off the conversation.

"I must go," it told Luther, its tone never changing, but the urgency was evident, nonetheless.

Luther didn't understand how computers worked, much less the workings of an autonomous droid, but he knew the droid had just received a warning message of some kind.

XR737 turned and marched up the ramp into his ship. It was airborne seconds later, accelerating so quickly that the human could barely follow. In the blink of eye, it was gone.

Luther sighed, put the package in a satchel around his neck, and looked around the dark hillside. Construction equipment had cleared most of the trees. A paved road had already been built, and survey stakes marked the edges of lots where 100 houses would soon be built. To most, it would be yet another in a line of dozens of such developments popping up all over this city. No one would know the entire neighborhood was being constructed to provide secret cover for one house in particular.

Making his way into one of the few small patches of trees left standing, Luther ducked into the hidden entrance of the tunnel, where construction had recently been completed. He started the long journey back to headquarters.

* * *

XR737 pushed the scout ship to maximum speed. The ship's sensors had detected the telltale signature of an enemy intruder out over the ocean and was now moving to intercept. The frequency of appearances of Erdean scout ships had picked up drastically over the last few months. The Mondean leadership had grown concerned. That was why they had sent XR737 to deliver the latest version of the communications device to the group known as the Origin Society. But additional programming mandated that XR737 seek out and destroy, by any means necessary, *any* alien craft detected near or over the oceans. Their secret would never hold forever, but the longer they could prevent the Erdeans' investigation, the better the chances they could keep the humans safe from invasion.

As XR737 approached the target, it jammed all scanners and transmissions emanating from the enemy ship. The Erdean vessel was hovering just over the water. Its scanning interrupted, it turned in the air to face the incoming threat. Laser blasts rocketed from the enemy craft. Taking evasive action, XR737 made one simple mistake. It dove into the water. The laser blasts tracking the Mondean ship struck the water and dissipated. But the salt water itself transformed from liquid into a blue-tinged block of the most valuable resource in the galaxy. Although its scanners were jammed, the transformation was still captured by the Erdean ships' recording devices.

XR737 had no idea of the mistake. Following protocol would mean eliminating the risk of revealing the secret of the oceans, anyway. It activated the ship's own tracker, a device that would attract this ship like a magnet to that of the enemy craft. As long as they were within one Earth mile of each other, the Erdean vessel would never get away. All transmissions the enemy ship might want to make about what it had found were blocked, as well.

Or so it seemed.

* * *

Aboard the Erdean ship, the droid pilot activated visual recording. All efforts to send a message had failed after the arrival of the Mondean craft. The droid was unconcerned. Its transmission system had a redundancy built in. Although its long-range transmission were being blocked, it contained a short-range signal that could not be stopped. As soon as another Erdean ship entered the planetary system, it would receive the message. The secret of the mysterious blulex signature had been solved.

The pilot's mission to Earth was twofold, however. In addition to conducting yet another search of the planet for the elusive presence of blulex, the scout ship also contained a sample of the EncephaLink. It was time to start experimenting with Earthling mind control. If they were as susceptible to the technology as most other beings in the galaxy, this planet, despite its remoteness, might soon be a target for invasion. The intelligent life here seemed particularly suited for labor.

It was the second item on the agenda that concerned the Erdean pilot. It had not yet infected the first Earthling with the EncephaLink. It would need to escape its Mondean pursuer to complete the mission.

Rising high over the water, the ship accelerated toward the nearest land mass.

* * *

XR737 was within a mile of the Erdean ship and therefore locked on.

Both vessels were soon engaged in an aerial battle. The ships seemed evenly matched, and the battle was fierce. If not for the tracker in the cargo bay, the Erdean ship might have succeeded in getting away.

The battle ended minutes later over a small inland city called Ridgeport. The activity had not gone unnoticed by the Earthlings below.

* * *

Following the crash, but before shutting down, XR737 tapped into its own memory banks and made a modification. It was vital its own knowledge of Luther Grisham and the Origin Society be shielded from discovery. One final change to its own timeline ensured no connection could be accidentally made between itself, Grisham, and the Sparker. That accomplished, XR737 allowed protocol to take over. The blue lights in its eyes went dark, and the droid shut down.

CHAPTER 18
Plea for Help

Even after fighting and winning an aerial battle, simply landing the alien craft presented the biggest challenge for Jace. Once clear of the Erdeans, Jess had insisted that he take back over control. She had wanted to spend the travel time looking over the missing pages they had found inside the mannequin, but the trip had gone too fast. The ship responded to every thought, but Jace's problem was indecision on what exactly it was he wanted.

They wobbled in the air, straining the anti-gravity drive while they both looked for a good spot near the safehouse to set down. They finally found a small clearing in the trees close to where they had emerged from the secret garage.

"Who knows what's going on in the safehouse," Jace said. He nodded his head at the plexiglass case still containing the Sparker. "Want to do this here?"

Jess hesitated. It was what they'd been after, the very purpose of their mission back home, but a part of her was scared. One look out the still transparent walls of the ship was all the encouragement she needed, however. From their spot, she had a view over the drop-off to the river and the sprawling capital city below. The water level of the giant river was considerably lower than just a few hours ago. Ships lined up far beyond the horizon, waiting their turn to either siphon the liquid commodity or convert and harvest the massive supply of blulex.

Earth didn't have long.

Plus, Jace was right. They just didn't know what they were going to find in the Origin Society safehouse. If the President's people had made it through the tunnel and set up sentry in the house, they could be walking into a trap.

Jess was positive the giant book was worth the risk, though. It not only told the story of the OS and their history here on Earth, but it also apparently told the history of their family. That the two were intertwined only made it that much more intriguing. It was more pieces of the puzzle, but that wasn't top priority. They had to reach the Mondeans. They had to get help on its way as soon as possible. They couldn't risk being detained again.

She reached into the case and took hold of the crown. As she grasped it, though, it broke into two parts, each attached to one of the earpieces.

"It's a headset," Jace said in awe. "Two of them."

He was right. Jess had seen her brother wear one enough while playing his video games that she, too, recognized it for what it was. She handed one of the halves to Jace.

They looked at one another, hoping to see a certainty in the other's eyes that what they were doing was the right thing. Jace was absolutely certain, and Jess couldn't see another way.

"Ready?" she asked.

He nodded.

Simultaneously, they put their halves of the broken crown over their ears and inserted the earpieces. Not sure what to do next, Jess hovered a finger over the piece of blulex in her ear, hesitated for a deep breath, and tapped.

The world around them disappeared.

And time stopped.

* * *

When Jess had first touched the Sparker back in Ridgeport, it had activated the device itself. That was how the Erdeans had locked on to their location and started an all-out assault on the house and through the hidden tunnel.

There was a different reaction when she pressed the blulex stone in her ear, one neither of the twins were fully aware of at the time. Across the world, famous landmarks began to crumble, destroying the work that had kept alien structures hidden in plain sight for centuries.

In Egypt, huge blocks of stone broke into dust and fell to the desert as the Pyramids of Giza rose from the ground, not as an ancient wonder but as a technological marvel. A massive structure made of a metal-like material not of this world seemed to grow from the cloud of dust. The cone of the pyramid broke open, and the four sides expanded outward.

Halfway across the globe, El Mirador in Guatemala underwent the same transformation. It happened in China, Mexico, Italy, the United States, Cambodia, Peru, and Australia. Every continent. Every ocean.

Just off the coast of Cuba, in waters one mile deep—at the site believed to be the source of the Atlantis legend—pyramids on the sea floor broke open to reveal an alien construction. Sides of all of the pyramids broke open and spread out, like petals on a flower. Much like the Erdean transporters, these structures were part of a communications array, designed to send a powerful signal deep into space.

Unlike human-designed radio signals that would need hundreds, thousands, or millions of years to travel to the closest inhabited star system, this link was opened almost instantaneously. By using the interconnectedness of all dark matter in the universe, the Mondeans had created a means for overcoming the vastness of space.

In a small, plain room inside a much larger structure built above the waves of a watery planet, the link request sent from Jess's headset was accepted.

* * *

As if they were really there, Jace and Jess were looking inside a small, gray, mostly empty room. A tall man—for it really did appear to be a man—was the only occupant, living or otherwise. The person's back was turned, and he appeared to be pacing the room, walking away from the twins' perspective. With a languid motion, the person reached up with a long, skinny arm. A finger, much longer than a human's, extended and tapped its earpiece. A connection established, and the being turned around quickly and looked directly at the twins.

Jess gasped. She was looking at a person—a real person—but obviously not someone of this planet. The Mondean—for she was certain, without knowing how, that this person *was* Mondean—was very tall. Without physically standing beside him or having some reference point, she couldn't say for sure, but she guessed he was nearly eight feet tall. He moved with a graceful fluidity, his long, lean arms swinging rhythmically with each step closer. His skin was bluish gray, almost blending into the walls behind him. His nose and mouth were small, but the eyes were a bit bigger, lidless, and very dark. Still, there was an undeniable intelligence behind those eyes. The body appeared to be completely hairless, the skull smooth and slightly elongated. There was a familiarity about the being, like he was a mashup of all the ways aliens were portrayed in documentaries on the History Channel. He wore a silvery glittering shirt than extended far below his waist.

When he spoke, his voice was soft and high, his tone calm and measured. "Lysander and Axelia," he said, looking them in the eye as if they were actually in the room. "Jace and Jess Grisham. From the moment of the prophecy, we have been expecting your call."

With a wave of his right hand, the Mondean pulled from thin air a hologram. It looked like a star chart. Pinching his long fingers the same way Jace might zoom in for a closer look at a picture on his iPhone, the hologram focused in on a particular quadrant. As his fingers worked, he continued speaking.

"My name is Xanos," he said.

The hologram zoomed in more, until it was a view of what

appeared to be their own solar system, Jupiter and Saturn prominent with their unique features and unmistakable size.

"Zahnose?" Jace asked. "What kind—"

Jess elbowed him sharply in the ribs to get her brother to shut up. Now was not the time for jokes.

The gray man smiled, unoffended, and said, "The universe is full of strange beings with even stranger languages."

The hologram had focused in on what was clearly Earth. Like a globe rotating, the continents and oceans spun by until they had a view of North America. A small, blinking red light flashed like a beacon on the east coast of the United States. It was them.

"Even the Mondeans, who are more closely related to the humans of Earth than you have yet realized, have their own language and naming customs. Xanos is not truly my name, but it's the closest representation when translated to your English," Xanos said. "I can assure you the names Jace and Jess are equally unusual to my own ears."

"You speak English?" Jess asked, enthralled by the idea despite the desperation of their situation.

The Mondean paused a second and tilted his head. "Yes and no. The Sparker translates any known language into that of the listener. I am hearing the words you speak. I myself am speaking your language in return, but I can't say that I speak your English. I would not know what I am saying if I were to walk outside this room and speak the same words to another. The Sparker taps into our minds and does that work for us. Really remarkable."

"That's great and all," Jace said. "And I'm sure my sister would like to talk to you for hours about it, but we have a bit of a situation down here on Earth and don't exactly have time for small talk."

Jace tilted his head toward Jess and rolled his eyes.

The Mondean smiled patiently. "We have known this day would come. That you have searched out, found, and activated the Sparker suggests that our fears have come true. I imagine that your world is under attack by the scavenger Erdeans as we speak. We will get to that, I promise, but there is more to discuss. Your role is destined to be much larger than merely stopping the devastation taking place on your planet."

Jace was getting impatient and irritated, saying, "Yeah, yeah. Destiny, prophecy...whatever. We're watching giant ships suck the water out of a river. We've seen them turn the ocean into blocks of blulex—"

For the first time, the Mondean's facial expression turned from a mask of patience to one of concern as he said, "It is unfortunate that they have discovered that secret, but it's not unexpected. But you need to understand—"

"We don't have time for this!" Jace yelled.

Jess reached out and touched her brother's arm in an attempt to calm him, but her own voice was a little frantic, too.

"Believe me, I have a million questions," she said. "I desperately want to know more, but we're running out of time here. Every second we talk pushes our world closer to utter devastation."

The Mondean held out both hands in a calming gesture and said, "I apologize. I should have said this first. The Sparker is remarkable in another way. This conversation is happening outside of time. As long as we are linked, the world around you is essentially frozen. When the connection is broken, you will return to the very second we were connected."

"How is that possible?" Jess asked, still frantic but unable to control her curiosity.

"The physics is very complex, and the details of how are outside my realm of knowledge and understanding. It has to do with manipulation of the properties of dark matter and the untapped abilities of our brains," Xanos explained. "Have you ever had a dream, what seemed like a long dream, where you are building up to a moment when something bad is going to happen? Just before the bad thing happens, your alarm goes off, saving you at the last second."

"Yeah," Jace and Jess said at the same time.

Jace gave an example, saying, "I dreamed I was being chased. I couldn't see what was after me, but I knew my life depended on getting away. It didn't make sense, but dreams never do. I was trying to get out of a big warehouse. The next minute, I was in a jungle, trying to fight my way through vines and bushes. Then I was on the ledge of a cliff. Whatever was after me was about to emerge from the jungle and get me, but then the alarm went off."

Xanos nodded. "Exactly. That is the perfect example. We have done research. The entirety of your dream, even if it seemed like minutes or hours, occurred in the split second *after* your alarm went off but before your body could react to the sound. The same thing is happening here. This conversation is happening within a split second of the connection being established. As long as we stay connected, we have as long as we like to talk. What happens after that will be a bit more complicated, but it is important for you to understand why."

Jace was still trying to wrap his head around the fact that his dream had occurred after the alarm had saved him of his fate.

"I'm confused," Jace said.

Jess's face was blank as she responded, "I am, too."

The Mondean waved his hand, and the hologram went away. He crossed his arms in front of him and began to speak, saying, "The history of Mondea and Earth is long. We have a fleet of warships prepared and ready to come to your aide. We've known this day was coming. The prophecy predicted it, but prophecies, while almost always accurate, can be somewhat unreliable and vague. It's usually after an event occurs that a prophecy can be applied. A whole team of beings from every planet represented on the Supreme Planetary Council study the prophecies and try to decipher what they mean. It's inexact, to say the least. But when we caught an Erdean spy listening in on the council's recent emergency sessions, we were certain the prophecy about the two of you applied and that the Earth was likely in danger again."

"What *is* the prophecy about us?" Jess asked. "We know it exists, but we don't know what it is."

"That's a conversation for another time," Xanos said, choosing his words carefully. "It's best if the subjects of a prophecy don't know too much about it. Destiny rarely changes, but circumstances around it can. Often for the worst."

Jace started to argue, but Jess nodded in understanding. She didn't like it, but what the Mondean said made sense.

Xanos paused to make sure his point had been made, then continued, saying, "The Erdeans and Mondeans discovered the large quantities of blulex on Earth at about the same time. This was long, long ago. The war between Erdea and almost every other advanced civilization in the galaxy had been raging for quite some time. We were closely monitoring their movements and activities and knew they were planning an invasion. Fortunately, at about the same time, we discovered a method of masking the blulex: hiding it in plain sight.

"We beat the Erdeans to your planet and transformed the blulex into the massive oceans you have today. Needless to say, the Erdeans were disappointed. Unwilling to leave empty-handed, they started a campaign to enslave the indigenous inhabitants. They had sent a scavenging force, however, and not an army. They were unprepared to fight. Still, the war we fought on your soil was devastating. We barely won.

"We knew they'd come back eventually, so the decision was made to stunt the intellectual and technological advancement of the native species for as long as we could. Contrary to the history books and archaeological timelines you find in your museums today, the native Earthlings had advanced quite a bit. They were building cities and making advancements at a rapid pace. They were well on track to join the Planetary Council within a couple of centuries. The war, though, nearly wiped them out. The cities were mostly destroyed. For safety, the remaining Earthlings had moved back into the forests, back into caves, wherever they could find to hide. We covered up any sign of their advancements and did what we could to discourage future growth.

"We left a small group behind to control and monitor. If we could prevent the Earthlings from technological advancements that might draw attention to your wonderful planet, maybe we could keep the Erdeans away. It worked for many, many centuries. We were to observe and interfere only when necessary, but those we left behind fell in love with the planet. They grew to care for the Earthlings..."

Xanos paused, considering how much more to say, then said, "Mistakes were made."

"What mistakes?" Jess asked.

"That is not my place to say," Xanos said. "I feel that in time, you will come to learn everything. For now, though, I am only authorized to tell you what I have. I say this because you need to understand why the Planetary Council may choose not to allow us to come to your aide."

"WHAT?" Jace screamed. "We've gone through everything we have to get this Sparker thing, and you can't help us?"

"That decision has not been made," Xanos said calmly. "We are prepared to come. We are prepared to fight for the future of your planet and your people. Your people are our people. That's what we have to make the council understand. But as I told you, mistakes were made. The Terragoddrians are displeased, and our seat on the council is in jeopardy. There is so much more at play than you can possibly know."

"Then tell us," Jess pleaded. "Help us understand. Let us talk to your council."

"That time may come, but allow me—allow us—to do what we can first," Xanos said. "Procedures must be followed."

Jess was thinking furiously, trying to formulate an argument, a plea, that would convince the council to help them. There was just so much they didn't know, and Xanos didn't appear willing to tell them more.

"Who are you?" she asked.

"I am Xanos. I—"

"No, I know that. I mean, are you the Mondean representative on the council? Are you the president, or king, or ruler of Mondea?"

Xanos actually chuckled. "No, I do not hold the Mondean seat on the council. I am merely part of the Mondean delegation. I monitor... I..." He seemed unwilling to explain. Or uncertain of just how far he could go. "My role has been to wait on your call."

Jace furled his eyebrows and said, "Wait. Your job has been to stay in that room in case somebody on Earth found the Sparker?"

For the first time, Xanos truly looked uncomfortable. He moved closer to the monitor, or whatever it was in that gray room that allowed him to see and communicate with the twins, and spoke in a very low voice, almost a whisper, saying, "The universe if a big place. The creators have been busy, and the Erdeans are ruthless. Your planet is not the only one." Xanos looked around as if making sure he was truly alone in the room and couldn't be overheard. He backed up, resumed his air of calmness, and spoke in his regular voice. "I will inform the council of the situation on Earth. We will help if we are allowed. In the meantime, stay safe. It is imperative that you survive. The future of humanity is in your hands. I wish you luck."

The connection ended.

Jess looked at Jace, Xanos's words echoing in her head.

"It's truly us versus them," she said, struggling to accept the fact that help might not be coming.

Jace nodded and said, "Survival is up to us."

"Us."

CHAPTER 19
Back Again

Everything went quickly from there.

With Jace leading the way, because he held their lone weapon, they made their way to the front of the safehouse. They could see the outline of lights on inside, and there was a feel of occupancy, but the curtains were drawn, and there was no way to tell if there was someone there. Slowly and methodically, Jace tried the front doorknob. It turned in his hand. The door was unlocked.

"I say we bust in," Jace whispered.

Jess took just a second to think about it, then said, "No."

Jace was annoyed by the answer, but his sister quickly explained, saying, "If there are people in there, we'll have no idea if they are OS friendlies or if they are government forces being controlled by the Erdeans—or worse, Max."

The thought gave Jace pause. The look in his eyes and the set of his jaw were enough to convince Jess that he wanted to go in shooting. But the chance that he might get into a shooting match with the good guys held him back.

"Then what do we do?"

Jess knew that all of the curtains would be carefully closed. It would be a waste of time to go around the house checking. They only had one real option. Edging her brother out of the way, she took hold of the knob and eased the door open just a crack. The front room was empty. Still taking extreme care, she pushed it open just enough to slide through. Jace followed. Together, they moved on into the house, past the OS leadership wall and the giant book, going into the living area in the back. There was no sign of anyone, but they were not alone. A black ops uniform was spread out on the couch. A utility belt was draped across the back of the recliner. In the kitchen, a dirty plate with bread crusts was left on the table, along with an empty bag of chips.

A persistent and familiar sound was coming from the back of the house. Making sure all of the other rooms were clear, they moved that way. As they walked down the hall, the source of the sound was clear. It was a running shower, which cut off the second Jace reached for the door. They backed off into a dark bedroom across the hall and waited. Holding their alien laser weapon out in front of him, Jace waited for the door to open.

Max emerged from the bathroom, head down as he dried his hair with one towel, another towel wrapped around his body.

"Don't move!" Jace yelled, jumping out from the darkness.

Max staggered backward, ramming his back against the bathroom doorframe. He dropped one towel and almost lost the other one, grabbing it at the last possible second before it fell to the ground. He automatically reached to his side for a weapon that wasn't there. Training kicked in quickly. His wild eyes and look of fear were quickly replaced with calm control. Seeing who it was, he sighed deeply, secured the towel back around his waist, and held up his arms in the universal gesture of surrender.

"Jace. Jess. I'm so glad to see you," he said.

His tone was so convincing that Jess almost believed him. Almost.

"Shoot him, Jace," she said, surprising even her brother. He hesitated, but Jess pressed on. "He's one of them. He's a traitor. You saw him with the President. We can't trust him again."

"Wait!" Max yelled, torn between moving forward and keeping a safe distance. "Wait. I did what I did to save the President. And I succeeded. She's free of the EncephaLink and in a secure bunker at the White House. They can't get to her again."

"I don't believe it," Jess said coldly. "Shoot him."

This time, it was Jace who played the role of cool and calm. He leaned forward to look down the hallway and into the other bedrooms. They were all dark and likely empty.

"Where is everyone else?" he asked.

"Who?" Max said.

"The rest of Team Creepy," he said. "They were coming up the tunnel as we escaped earlier. Where are they?"

Max heaved a relieved sigh and said, "I sent them back. None of that team were members of the OS. They didn't know about the safe-house, and I didn't tell them. When I heard about the raid they were conducting, I left the President's side and joined them. I couldn't let them get to you or to this house. I convinced them the tunnel was a top-secret entrance to an extra supply of vehicles and weapons. Luckily, you were gone, and they bought it. They could see that the tunnel ended just ahead, and they believed me.

"I went back to the White House under the guise of telling the President I knew where you were headed, but because of the potential for spies, I said I could only tell her in private. She fell for it. Once alone, I tricked her into taking off the EncephaLink."

Jess stepped forward at this and said, "Uh-uh. No way. I remember what it felt like to hold Baby Mollie. Nothing would have convinced me to let her go."

Max smiled. "You never let her go, but you did hand her over. Didn't you?"

Jess stopped. She flashed back to the hospital. To sticking Baby Molly under the arm of Alfred Hammonds, the man who was dying after a severe heart attack. She never truly let her doll go, but...

Seeing Jess's understanding, Max pressed on with his story. "I told her my link was damaged and asked if she could shed a piece of hers. She believed me and held it out. I ripped it from her hands, grabbed her before she could scream, and held her until she calmed down. She is a mentally strong, highly motivated woman. It didn't take long for her to come back to her senses. She found a linen White House napkin and tied it around her neck to fool the rest of the team waiting outside the room. It was enough to get by them and into hiding."

Jess was torn. She'd been burned by this man too many times. She didn't want to risk believing him again. But Jace *did* seem to believe him. At least enough to allow Max to get dressed and move the conversation into the family room. To his credit, Jace kept his weapon on Max the whole time and didn't let him near the uniform or utility belt.

"So what next?" Jess asked, taking her turn holding the blaster while Jace went to the kitchen for food.

"You got here just in time," Max said. "I was getting ready to leave."

"Leave?" Jace asked from the other room. "Where were you going?"

Max looked uncomfortable as he answered, "To get as far out of this city and into the countryside as I can before 10:00 tomorrow morning."

"You're running away?" Jess asked, glaring at the supposed military leader in front of her. "The world is fighting for its very survival, and YOU'RE RUNNING AWAY."

Max was shaking his head. "I've told as many people as I could. Told them to tell others. We have to evacuate."

"Evacuate?" Jess asked, confused. "Why? We should be fighting!"

"We are fighting," Max said. "Before we split up, I was able to convince President Taylor to launch an attack."

Jess was shaking her head. "Our troops and our ships are no match for the Erdeans," she said. "We don't have a chance."

"No. We're not sending in our troops. Or our jets," Max said. "We're going with the weapon of last resort. It's the only way."

Jace dropped a plate in the kitchen, the sound of it shattering on the tile floor causing Jess to jump out of her seat, weapon shaking in her hand.

Jace raced into the room and got in Max's face, yelling, "You convinced her to nuke them?"

Max nodded. "It's the only way. We're targeting every transporter, every nest, and as many of their big ships as we can. I even found out we have a super-secret weapons system in orbit around the planet. It's not on any of the usual networks, so they've not been able to shut it down yet. We're going to launch nukes toward their base on the moon. That's where we believe they are sending their prisoners and creating their slaves. We believe those people would prefer—"

Jace's face was reddening, and he started shaking. He cut Max off midsentence. "If we nuke the transporters, we'll never get Dad back home."

"If we explode that many nukes in our country, there won't be a home to bring him back to," Jess said, her eyes filling with tears. "But you know that. That's why you're...why you are willing...why you're okay with blowing up the moon."

"There's no other option," Max said, lowering his head. "This decision wasn't made lightly. When we talked about it before, we were talking about nuking the transporter site in North Carolina and the nest there. One bomb, one place. Bad—terrible, actually—but survivable. This, though, I'm not sure. No one is. To have any chance at defeating the Erdeans, we'll have to detonate dozens, maybe even hundreds. We've contacted other nuclear nations. They are in agreement."

"That will destroy the world," Jess cried. "There won't be anything left."

"There won't be anything left if we don't," Max said. "It's a rotten choice, but at least this way we have a chance. If a few humans survive the invasion, the blasts, and fallout that will contaminate the planet for at least 100 years, just maybe the human race can survive and rebuild. If not, maybe our extinction will save another planet from the same fate."

"No," Jess whimpered.

"It's already done," Max said. "The President ordered me to go to a secret facility in West Virginia. It's deep under the mountains, built for this very thing. Come with me. We'll be the ones to restart the human race."

Jess tried to object, but no words would come out.

"No way," Jace said. "The prophecy says we're the ones to save the planet. We have to fight."

Jess looked at him with resignation and said, "Maybe this is what the prophecy meant. Maybe we're saving the world by being the ones to survive."

Jace was shaking his head. "No. I don't believe it. I'm not giving up like that. I'm going to save Dad, even if I have to fly to the moon in our Erdean ship and rescue him myself. We have to give the Mondeans time."

Max raced across the room and grabbed Jace by the shoulders, exclaiming, "What did you say?"

"I said I was going to save my dad," he said through gritted teeth. "Then I'm going to take the ship and find Mom and Uncle Urn."

But Max was shaking his head. "No. What did you say about the Mondeans?"

Jess found her voice. "We found the Sparker," she said. "We contacted them."

"The Mondeans are coming?" Max asked, half yelling, a sudden panic on his face.

"Well, we don't know for sure," Jace admitted. "They have to take it to the Planetary Council to decide. Something about interfering in the past."

"But they have an army ready to come as soon as they get approval," Jess added.

Max's hands flew to his head, trying to find enough of his shortly cropped hair to pull.

"This...this...changes everything."

Jess was trying to pull all of her thoughts together.

"We have to get to President Taylor. We have to stop her from launching those nukes," she said.

Max just nodded. He was pacing now, alternating between rubbing his head and tugging on his chin.

"You two have to come with me," he said at last. "It might be the only way to convince her."

Jace was shaking his head, but he didn't say anything. Jess could see him plotting, could see it in his eyes, but she didn't know what.

"You actually have an Erdean ship?" Max asked.

"Yeah," Jace said. "And I know how to fly it. We had to fight our way through a million other Erdeans to get here."

"Good," Max said. "That will save us time. I need you to fly us to the White House."

Jace started to object, then quickly shut his mouth. He understood what Max was doing and why he needed them to come along, but he had a plan of his own. He found himself doing what he swore he'd never do again: believing and trusting Max.

They raced for the door, pausing long enough for Max to grab his utility belt and pull two weapons from a secret compartment behind a decorative picture.

As they passed the hallway where past leaders of the OS hung on the wall and the giant history book rested on a table underneath, Jess paused and looked longingly. There was no time. Sighing, she pulled the missing pages from her pocket and tucked them inside the book. If they stopped the President from launching a nuclear attack, maybe she'd be able to come back and read it all. If not, it wouldn't matter.

CHAPTER 20
Separate Ways

The three of them stepped out of the alien ship and onto the White House lawn. A large contingent of Secret Service operatives stormed from every conceivable hiding place, weapons drawn. Fortunately, Max had called ahead and told them to expect an Erdean ship. Still, they were taking no chances. After a quick frisk to ensure none of them were secretly harboring one of the white cloth EncephaLinks, they were escorted quickly toward a side entrance of perhaps the most famous residence in the world.

Jace, however, pulled free from a black-suited man who had a strong grip on his elbow.

"I'm not going in," Jace argued.

Max tried again to talk him out of the crazy mission he seemed intent on undertaking, but Jess had given up that fight. If she could, she would go with him. The moon. Her brother was actually about to take an alien spaceship and fly it to the moon, and she was choosing to stay here on Earth. She looked skyward. The moon was a crescent just rising ahead of the sun. She hadn't really appreciated how beautiful it truly was. Jess knew, though, the importance of her role with Max and the President. Someone had to convince her not to launch the nuclear attack. Not only that, but they had to stop other countries from launching, as well. And time was winding down. The Doomsday Clock was ticking steadily toward 10:00. The first rays of light were breaking over the horizon.

Jess pulled free of her escort and raced across the perfectly manicured lawn, slamming into her brother with a mighty hug. Squeezing him tightly, choking back tears, she whispered in his ear, "Go get Dad." She sobbed. "But don't bring him back until after ten. If we fail here, stay away."

The gravity of the situation sank in on Jace. They were really splitting up. Any number of things could go wrong. He could get shot out of the sky. His ship could fail, and he could suffocate in deep space. He could lose the fight to free his dad from lunar enslavement.

The list was just as long and dire here. Max and Jess could fail to convince the President to change her mind. Even if they succeeded, there was no guarantee other world leaders would hold off. It was possible they could successfully prevent nuclear Armageddon and still see the world destroyed. There was no guarantee the Mondeans would come to their rescue, or win the battle if they did show up.

There were so many things that could go dreadfully wrong and so little pathways to success. For the first time, Jace seemed to realize this was not a video game. There were no do-overs, no resets. You didn't get to build up extra lives or resume play from the same spot if you got killed. But with that realization came a renewed confidence. Just because the stakes were real didn't mean the action wasn't going to be the same. He *was* a skilled gamer. Maybe the best. The odds might be heavily stacked against him, but at least he had a fighting chance. Humanity could do worse.

"We've got this, Lexy," he said with steely determination. "The prophecy says so." He gave her one last squeeze and stepped back. "Now go."

Nodding, tears in her eyes, she turned and allowed herself to be led into the White House. She didn't look back.

Jace watched her go for just a second, grinned, and boarded his ship, prepared for the greatest game he would ever play.

CHAPTER 21
Bunkers

In addition to gaming, Jace had already had an intense interest in space travel. He was too young to really remember the launches of the Space Shuttle, but he never missed a launch on NASA.gov. Watching the private companies like SpaceX and Blue Origin battle to be the first to send astronauts into space had been fascinating. Watching Elon Musk launch his own personal Tesla toward Mars had been one of the coolest things he'd ever seen. There was one thing those companies and NASA had in common when sending ships through Earth's atmosphere and into space: A massive amount of thrust was needed. Launches required perfect conditions, months of planning, and a tremendously high degree of risk.

As Jace sat in the cockpit of the stolen Erdean ship, he really wasn't worried about any of those things. While he couldn't be positive this ship was designed to carry a living pilot through the harsh conditions of space, the craft itself was made to do just that. As long as XR737 had been competent in fixing the ship, he should be fine.

Focusing his mind on the task at hand, he looked skyward, toward the sliver of moon gradually rising as day broke to the east. He willed the ship to lift off from the White House grounds and rocket toward his destination. As he climbed, he passed numerous Erdean ships going about their task of stripping Earth of all that made it special. None challenged his course. After escaping from the cave and fighting his way through an Erdean force, he had thought they might be on the lookout for one of their own ships behaving oddly. He was prepared to fight his way into space, but he was just one of many similar ships moving through the sky.

That bothered Jace more than if he'd had to fight. What did it mean if they weren't concerned that an enemy was moving around like one of their own? Were they so powerful and so certain that nothing could stop them?

As frightening as that was, Jace actually smiled. Countless times, he'd faced off against an opponent who underestimated him. He'd taken them down time after time. It was a lesson the Erdeans had not yet learned.

Well, he thought. *They're about to.*

The stolen ship rose as smoothly through the upper layers of the atmosphere as it did near the surface. The sun came into view, and the sky lit up around him in golds, reds, and blues shortly before going completely black again. He took a second to appreciate that he'd just become the first kid to travel into space.

He pushed the ship to maximum speed. And the moon drew nearer.

* * *

Jess followed as Max allowed the Secret Service agents to lead them first into the White House and then into the Oval Office itself. Having always been a history buff, despite the desperation of their situation, Jess wanted to pause to take it all in. This room *was* history. So many decisions that had shaped the country, and the world, had taken place in this very spot. Amazing.

As she was practically dragged through, however, she also realized the decision to launch nuclear weapons could've been made from this room, too. That brought her back to reality.

She knew there were saferooms in the White House, along with bunkers deep below, where the President could be whisked off to in the event of an emergency. Of course no one in the general public would know how to access these areas, but she always imagined it being a fake poker from the fireplace or a wall lamp that you pulled forward to release a secret door. Instead, one of the agents pulled a remote from his pocket, much like a car's key fob, and pressed a button. To their right, a section of wall fronted by a perfectly normal chair swung forward, revealing a small foyer.

An elevator door stood open and ready to receive them. Once inside, the door quickly slid shut, and they dropped immediately and quickly. Jess could feel the sensation of falling in her stomach. She could only guess how far down they had gone, but the drop had been really fast. She guessed that if there was an emergency so dire that it required the President to get underground, comfort wouldn't be high on the list when designing the escape route.

The doors opened, and they stepped into a hallway that could've been the interior of any government building. It was short but well lit, with several doors on both the left and right. Behind them, the elevator closed and ascended. A blast door fell into place, sealing the hallway from anything that might try to seep in from above.

The Secret Service left her and Max alone in the hallway, disappearing into the last room on the right. Jess's fascination must've shown on her face as she looked around, because Max noticed.

"As you've probably figured out, we're in an emergency bunker," he explained. "This was built in the 1950s."

Jess nodded. "During the Cold War. In case Russia launched a surprise nuclear attack. The President could be down here in seconds and still run the country. One of these rooms is a command center, isn't it?"

Max smiled. "Yes, one of these rooms is a command and control center, but no, the Cold War was not the reason it was built."

Jess cocked her head in confusion. Although it had never been confirmed, there were plenty of rumors that this underground facility really existed. Everything she'd seen or read suggested this was a nuclear shelter.

Max held out a hand and rolled it over, giving Jess the sign to keep thinking, to use her gift of logic to figure it out.

She thought. The 1950s were the beginning of the Cold War. Russia had been positioning itself as the greatest enemy to America, and the nuclear arms race was the greatest threat to the planet. But that wasn't true, was it? Something else had happened in the 1950s. There was a greater threat to the entire planet than two countries trying to one-up each other by building bigger, stronger bombs. The promise of mutually assured destruction—the thought that neither the Americans nor the Russians would ever attack with nuclear weapons, as both countries would be completely destroyed in the aftermath—was a stupid reason to make more weapons, but it would effectively keep both governments from ever making that critical mistake. But there was another threat that had emerged in the 50s, one that couldn't be controlled with threats. That was the decade the government had become aware of the Erdeans. If an alien species was so advanced that they could travel across the galaxy, then the likelihood of them backing off because we had powerful bombs was almost nil.

"Aliens," she said, putting her thoughts into a one-word answer for Max.

"Exactly," he said, nodding.

Jess's mind didn't stop turning, however. The Erdeans *wouldn't* be scared of any Earthling weapon, would they? Yet here they were. In just a couple of hours, nuclear-armed governments around the globe were scheduled to forego the concept of mutually assured destruction and launch an attack. She understood the thought process. If humans didn't have a future on this planet, then the least we could do was help make sure no other worlds suffered the same fate at the hands of the Erdeans. But that was an act of desperation. A last-ditch effort.

As bad as it looked on the surface at this moment, hope was not lost. They were not alone in their struggle against the Erdeans. The Mondeans were still out there. The Mondeans knew what was happening. All they needed was approval from the Supreme Planetary

Council, and they would send in the cavalry. They just needed time.

Jess realized she and Max were the only ones left to buy that time. That's why they were here. The very existence of the planet, and every person on it, depended on them, even if the world in general didn't know it.

The door at the end of hallway opened, and one of the agents stepped out.

"The President will see you now," he said. "You have five minutes."

* * *

Jace remembered that it took the Apollo mission astronauts three days to reach the moon. It was just short of 250,000 miles. With the advanced speed and technology of the Erdean ship, he had covered the distance in just over two hours. He barely had time to take in the wonders of what he was seeing. In transparent mode, he had a full 360 degree visual of actual space. Earth receded behind him, growing more impressive and beautiful the farther away he moved. The worries, the fighting, and the struggle for survival were all but invisible from here.

In front of him, the moon. Although only about a quarter of Earth's size, he was taken aback by how big it actually was. As his ship settled into a slower orbit around the satellite, the lunar landscape dominated his visual field.

The trip was not without its reminders of what was going on back home, though. Streaks of red light continuously shot past him in both directions. Transmissions continued unabated. Those were people being blasted apart on Earth, turned into particles of light, gathered in a giant receiver on the moon, and reassembled. It was here, Jace knew, that they were being turned into slaves, forced into the service of a hostile species.

There were dozens of ships hovering around the moon. Once the true invasion had started on Earth, they had dropped the cloaking shield around the moon. They had nothing to hide now. Most of the ships were massive transporters, but there were a few smaller ships zipping back and forth from the surface. As Jace navigated toward the seldom seen back side of the moon, he gasped at what he saw. Much of the surface had been hollowed out like a planet-sized crater. Inconceivably enormous beams, made from some kind of metal, extended out before meeting at a point miles above the ground. The moon had been turned into a giant transporter/receiver. Jace understood from what he had seen and learned earlier that this was how the Erdeans were bringing in the large ships and all of their soldiers, but actually seeing it took his breath away.

In full game mode, however, Jace kept his concentration on the task at hand. For everything he did see, there was a lot he didn't. For one, there didn't seem to be any attack ships up here. His was the only one. The other vessels were busy either preparing to make the short jump to Earth or unloading spoils recovered from the planet below.

Jace settled in behind one the large transporters, undoubtedly full of people, water, or blulex. Many of these ships were headed toward a monstrous mother ship that glided into view over the horizon. This ship was made for space. It was far too massive to entire Earth's atmosphere. It was nearly as big as the moon itself and easily a thousand times larger than the biggest ships hovering over Earth's oceans. This, Jace knew, was the ship that would collect everything and everyone stolen from home, then beam out once they had stripped the planet.

Not every ship was headed that way, however. The one Jace followed was moving toward the dusty gray surface. As they drew closer, Jace could see a base of some kind on the lunar ground. People—human people—were bustling around like ants. Although it wasn't visible, Jace assumed there was an artificial atmosphere, a bubble of some kind, in place. The people were not wearing spacesuits.

There was more construction taking place on the surface, keeping the enslaved people in constant motion. Off to the side, scattered about sporadically, were other humans carrying weapons. Undoubtedly under Erdean mind control, they were serving as guards or wardens, keeping the prisoners in line. But there didn't seem to be any dissention. All were working without so much as a single stray.

What Jace didn't see were Erdeans. While he was sure there were thousands, if not millions, in the ships overhead, there didn't seem to be any on the surface.

Jace broke away from the transport ship he had been following and navigated toward a large warehouse-type building, which most of the humans seemed to be emerging from. This, he thought, was where they would be keeping his dad. It was more than a guess. It was like he knew. His instincts were guiding him at this point.

As he neared the ground, Jace felt the ship wobble slightly and noticed a colorful shimmer of light sweep by. He was now inside the artificial atmosphere. He would be able to get out of the ship and walk on the moon. It should have been a thrilling thought, but he was in mission mode, and his focus was absolute.

The ship settled softly onto the muted gray surface, barely kicking up a puff of dust. Realizing he didn't really have a plan, Jace considered briefly before taking off a shoe. Peeling off a white tube sock, he tied it around his wrist. It wouldn't fool a suspicious guard, but it might help him move more freely around the facility if, at a glance, he appeared to be wearing an EncephaLink. If things went according to plan, he would already be on his way back to Earth before suspicion could be aroused.

He had no sooner exited the ship and taken his first step on the moon when his plan went awry. He didn't even get a second to appreciate where he was or what he was doing. His approach had not gone as unnoticed as he'd thought. As soon as he cleared the shadow of his ship and emerged in the open space around it, he was immediately surrounded by a dozen heavily armed, very hypnotized human adults. All weapons were aimed right at his chest.

* * *

Jess stepped into a room straight off of a TV show or movie set. There was a large, wooden table centered in a room, with at least 20 plush chairs spaced evenly around it. The lighting was sparse, making it easier to see that every inch of wall space was covered with monitors, each showing a different scene from around the world. One was even a feed from a telescope, showing activity on the moon. She wondered if Jace was there, if he had made it safely.

President Carmen Taylor sat at the head of the table on the far end. One other chair was occupied. An advisor Jess didn't recognize was seated to the President's left. Several folders and scattered bits of paper littered the table in front of him. Nothing was in front of the President.

The agent guided Max and Jess to seats to the right of the President, then disappeared through a door in the back of the room.

"Lieutenant. Mrs. Grisham," the President said in greeting. Her tone was stern and all business. "As you can imagine, the timing is not the best, but I understand that you now wish me to call off the coordinated launch after pushing so hard for the attack to begin with."

The woman was so intimidating that Jess could only sit quietly. Her arms and legs were shaking. Max, however, was prepared.

"Yes, ma'am," he said. "New information has come to light."

"Information we don't already have?" she asked doubtfully. "Information that caused you to completely change your tune in a matter of hours."

"Yes, ma'am," Max repeated.

The President sat back in her chair, steepling her fingers under her chin.

"As you know, the Grisham children have been deeply involved," Max began. "You also know of my role in the Origin Society."

The President nodded, encouraging him to go on.

First, Max turned to Jess and said, "I told the President as much as I knew about how the Mondeans saved the planet millennia ago and how they started the Origin Society, promising to look over us."

The President picked up the conversation. "You also said there was a way of contacting this other species but that you did not know where the communicator was. You said our best bet was to use every nuclear weapon at our disposal to drive away the Erdeans. Are you saying you have located this communication device."

Jess swallowed hard and found her voice. "My brother and I did, Miss President."

"Madam President," Max corrected, speaking under his breath.

"Oh, sorry. *Madam* President."

President Taylor waved it off and urged her to continue.

"The Sparker," Jess said. "Yes, ma'am. It was in our dad's house all along. We've learned that our grandfather was the leader of the Origin Society before Max, but he has disappeared. His picture was replaced with someone who looks just like my brother, but the picture is new. I—"

Max had cleared his throat, indicating that was a story for another time.

"Oh, sorry," Jess said. "Anyway, we found the Sparker and contacted the Mondeans."

The President leaned forward, eyes wide, and asked incredulously, "And they are coming?"

Jess sank back in her chair, afraid to go on. Max reached over and slid a hand behind her shoulder, urging her to sit up and continue.

"I don't know how much of the story Max told you, or even how much he knows himself," Jess said. "But the Mondean we spoke to told us they had to get approval from the Supreme Planetary Council before getting involved. It sounded very political. They even mentioned God getting involved."

Max cringed.

"God and politics," the President said, sinking back again. "I find it hard to believe that advanced species from other planets would get bogged down in such...*earthly*...trappings."

Max started to speak, but the President held out a hand to stop him.

"Where is this Sparker device?" she asked Jess.

"My brother has it," she responded.

It seemed to dawn on President Taylor for the first time that Jace wasn't there. She actually looked around the room as if expecting him to be hiding nearby.

"And where is your brother?"

Jess looked at Max. Max nodded, so she rose out of her chair and walked over to the wall of monitors, zeroing in on the one showing the moon.

"There," she said, pointing. "We stole an Erdean ship. He is flying it to the moon to rescue our dad."

* * *

Jace didn't know what to do. He couldn't believe he had walked himself into this trap. He looked desperately for a way out but was completely surrounded. Luckily, he had tucked his blaster into the waistband of his shorts. He could draw and start firing, but even the human zombies surrounding him wouldn't be so slow to act that he could take out 12 of them before getting shot himself.

Being a video game legend wasn't always about action, though. More often than not, it was about strategy. Although it wasn't his strong point, sometimes victory required patience. These were not Erdeans surrounding him. They were humans. The EncephaLink was an incredible mind control invention, but it didn't think *for* the person. It delivered instructions that the person followed. It was a minor difference, but it was one that might give him a slight window. For now, he'd go along and wait for that window to open.

Holding his hands up in surrender, he allowed the group to lead him into the warehouse-sized building. Inside, he saw it was a storage facility for all of the pieces and parts being used for the construction taking place out on the surface. All around, humans were being used as forced labor. Most seemed to be free of the EncephaLinks. Two things were keeping them in line. Armed guards, who were noticeably wearing the white cloths in some form on their bodies, were patrolling back and forth, keeping a close eye on the workers. Maybe more important, though, was the reality that there was nowhere to go. They could fight back. They could overwhelm the guards. But then what? They were on the moon. Jace was certain that somewhere nearby, an actual Erdean sat in a control booth. With a touch of a button, they could probably lift the artificial atmosphere, instantly killing every human. That was powerful motivation for them to follow orders.

Jace remembered the strange creatures he had seen in the forest near the original transporter. He had seen how they were chained together. The Erdeans were cruel and were only interested in getting what they wanted. If the human slaves didn't behave, there were no lengths they wouldn't go to in order to regain or retain control.

No one took notice of the newcomer. No one raised an eye in his direction.

Jace wasn't being led to the workers, however. He was taken to the center of the building. There, a platform enclosed with a short handrail rested just about the warehouse floor. Jace and four of his captors stepped onto the elevated surface. He could see now that it was an industrial elevator. With a jerk, he started to descend below the surface. Panic began creeping in. The deeper he was taken inside the Erdeans' lunar base, the harder it would be to fight his way out. But escape wasn't his goal at this moment. Somewhere here, he was certain, his father was being held. He had to be reasonable, though. He wouldn't be doing his father any good if he was forced into service.

One level below the surface, the lift dropped through another room as large as the warehouse above. Here, the nightmare was worse. Humans—thousands of them—were corralled in cages. Some looked to be sleeping. Others stood and clung to the cage wire in desperation. Moving steadily downward through this level, Jace only had a moment to take it all in, but the sight was heartbreaking. It looked like there were dozens of people in each cage, yet there was only truly enough room for a handful to lie down at a time.

Down through another level, and the nightmare grew worse. Another massive room. More cages. These, however, were filled with kids. The sound was worse than the sight. Screams and cries tore at Jace's ears. The smell that assaulted his nostrils was atrocious.

Still, though, down they went. The lift finally stopped on the third subterranean level. This area was smaller. There were more cages but fewer people in them. His guards led him to one of the segregated areas and stepped back. An Erdean—the first one Jace had seen—stepped forward, using four of its legs to walk. This alien was different than the ones he had seen on Earth. It was smaller, its color more tan or light brown.

This was not a soldier. Jace had the distinct impression this was a young female. He tried to remember back to science class in school, wishing he'd paid more attention to the life cycle of insects. He thought they started as larvae, or pupae, before emerging as adults, but he couldn't remember for sure. It also dawned on him that the life cycle of insects on Earth had no bearing on how these creatures developed.

From a pouch at its side, the Erdean pulled out a white cloth and attempted to hand it over to Jace. He stepped back, panicked. Being subjected to the cloth would end his mission. There would be no escape. He reached to the small of his back to pull his weapon and make his stand here and now, but he noticed that the Erdean reacted strangely, as well. She—for Jace was certain, without knowing how, that it was a female—pulled back and tilted her head. He almost laughed. The alien was looking at him like a confused puppy.

The realization hit Jace out of nowhere. The EncephaLink always presented itself as something desirable from the person's past. Instead of racing forward to accept the gift, Jace had stepped back. That had confused the Erdean.

Jace was confused, too. Why hadn't he seen Ranger Ron? Why wasn't he being pulled toward the link like a magnet?

The Erdean moved forward and forcibly placed the cloth in his hand, then stepped back to observe Jace's reaction.

He felt nothing. There was no connection; there was no link. He was still completely in control of himself. Acting on instinct, though, he grabbed the cloth and acted like it was the coolest thing in the world.

"Ranger Ron," he said. "I haven't seen one of these since I was a kid."

The Erdean continued to study him suspiciously. She wasn't buying his act. From another pouch, she took out a device about the size of a phone and studied the readout scrolling down the screen. It was in a language Jace didn't recognize. The Erdean's mouth flew open, but no words came out. She looked around, as if checking to see if anyone else was watching. Other than the few humans in the cages behind them, there was no one. She reached out and took Jace by the arm.

He started to pull back. His gut wanted him to reach for his hidden weapon and start firing. But there was something in her actions, something in the way she looked at him, that convinced Jace to remain patient.

A sound emerged from the Erdean girl's throat, a vibration that she was turning into words. She pulled him across the room, through a door, and into a hallway. Once alone, she let go and turned to face him. The vibrations had increased in pitch. She reached up with one arm and manipulated her throat. Words—English words—emerged.

"Coooommme withhhhh meeeee," she said. "Youuuu arrreee Grrisshammm."

Time for patience had run out. It was now or never for Jace. In one quick motion, like a gunslinger from the old west, Jace pulled his weapon from his waistband and prepared to fire.

The Erdean reacted quickly, too, but not in an aggressive manner. She placed her hand on Jace's arm, holding it down. The hand was cold and spiny. Tiny spikes up her forearm dug in but did not break the skin.

"Not alllll of usss agreeee with enslaving other woooorlds," she said. "Sssssome of ussss wisshhh toooo hellllp."

Jace kept his weapon pointed at her but relaxed the tension in his trigger finger. She was faster than him, stronger than him, and could have easily taken his gun, but she hadn't.

"Yooouuu ssshould noooot have commme heeere," she continued. "The oooothers will soooon knowww. Theee link is weeeeak, but the connnnection issss stillll there. Theyyyyy willll knowww."

"Why is the link weak?" Jace asked.

She reached one hand up and tapped the side of Jace's head. It wasn't his head, though. It was something else. The Sparker. He was still wearing the headset! There must be something about it that was protecting him from the Erdean EncephaLink.

He'd no sooner made the connection, though, when three human guards entered the hallway, weapons drawn and ready. Moving quicker than he would've thought possible, the Erdean took Jace's blaster from his grasp and fired three quick shots before Jace could even register the fact that he'd lost his weapon.

"Theeeey knowwww," she said, handing his gun back.

Taking his arm, she led him through a maze of corridors, deeper into the bunker. Twice, they ducked into empty rooms to avoid more guards.

Jace's mind was racing, trying to catch up with what was happening. He found himself trusting the young Erdean, but it wasn't like he really had a choice.

"If we're going to fight our way out of here together, I might as well know your name," Jace huffed, trying to catch his breath as they ran.

"Innnn your lannnnguage, Juxoria issss classest," she answered.

"Juzoo-what?" Jace asked, his eyebrows raised questioningly.

"Juxoria," she said again, slower, while urging him forward.

Back in the main hallway, they moved quickly, going deeper into the facility. She stopped in front of a door, and at first Jace thought it was to avoid more guards. This room wasn't empty, though. There was a man lying huddled in the corner.

Jace's heart pounded in his chest. His lungs refused to pull in air.

The man looked up, his face wearing the resigned expression of someone expecting torture.

"DAD!" Jace yelled.

Rick Grisham's eyes turned upward, not truly believing what they were seeing. He looked horrible. The effects of the disease, combined with everything he'd been through, had taken a crippling toll.

Jace dropped his weapon and ran to his father, falling to his knees as he embraced the man he hadn't been sure he would ever see again.

"What are you doing here?" Rick asked, his voice weaker than Jace had ever heard it.

"I've come to rescue you," he said, his chest swelling with pride.

Rick's chin sank, as if holding up his head was taking more energy than he possessed. His voice dropped to a whisper, his chest heaving with the effort it took to speak, and he asked, "Where is Lexy? Where is your sister? Is she okay?"

"She's fine," Jace said. "It's quite a story. I'll tell you on the way home, but for now we have to get out of here."

"No," Rick said, feebly shaking his head. "I'll never make it."

For the first time, Rick seemed to notice the Erdean standing in the doorway. Panicked, he tried to scramble to his feet but collapsed again. He whimpered, not in fear but in frustration.

"It's okay, Dad," Jace said. "She's been helping me."

"It's...It's a trap," Rick said, gasping. "They've held me to get to you and your sister."

"Trrruuue," the Erdean said from her position at the door. "Ooothers willlll beee cominggg, butttt I willll helllp. Weeeee muuust goooo noowww, thoughhhh."

Rick looked at the alien and nodded, then said, "I'm worse, Jace. My legs won't hold up. Thank you for coming. Thank you for giving me the gift of seeing you one more time, but you have to leave me. Go."

Jace covered his head with his hands. This wasn't right. This wasn't possible. He couldn't have come this far, done everything he'd done, only to find his dad and have it end this way.

"I'll carry you," he said, stooping to put his arm under his father's shoulder.

Rick weakly pushed him away.

"Weeeee mussst goooo," the Erdean said, checking the hallway. Her antennae fluttered as she used all of her senses to monitor the area. She was noticeably nearing a state of panic.

"No," Jace said, tears pooling in the corner of his eyes, unable to make himself get off the floor.

Rick reached out and grabbed Jace's arm, saying, "We'll always have a bond. We'll always—"

"THAT'S IT!" Jace yelled, his mind racing too fast for words to explain.

Not bothering to explain, he untied the EncephaLink from his wrist and carefully put it on the floor at his father's feet. He took the Sparker from his head and placed it on his father, helping him secure the earpiece. Rick looked confused but didn't fight it. Even the Erdean had moved into the room to see what he was doing. Jace had to fight to keep from looking at the cloth on the ground. From the corner of his eye, he clearly saw Ranger Ron lying there. His favorite toy. He wanted to pick it up. He wanted to play with it. It was right there. All he had to do was reach for it. But Jace fought back against those urges, wishing he had brought the other half of the Sparker with him. It remained in the ship where Jess had left it. He resisted looking directly at the Ranger Ron with everything in him.

"Take it, Dad," he said, nodding his chin toward the cloth on the ground.

Rick narrowed his eyes but didn't question the command. He took the cloth. The effect was instantaneous. Color returned to his pale cheeks. His yellow eyes transformed into a healthy white, and his labored breathing slowed to a deep and steady rhythm. Jace saw the pure white cloth turning black as it pulled the disease from Rick's body. Full recovery would take time they didn't have, but Jace just needed his father strong enough to walk. He pulled his dad to his feet with the help of Juxoria. Rick recoiled a little from the alien's touch but didn't resist. He wobbled for a second, then pulled his arms free and took two steady steps forward.

He nodded. "Let's go!"

* * *

"Do you want to repeat that?" the President demanded, placing both palms face down on the mahogany table.

Jess looked confused. "Which part?"

Max jumped in. "I told you about the prophecy, that there was more at play here than—"

President Taylor rose to her feet, her face turning red, and yelled, "I don't want to hear any more nonsense about a prophecy!" She slammed her hands on the table with each word. "This isn't a dysto- pian science fiction movie. This is the real world, with real people and real consequences." Max opened his mouth to argue, but she cut him off. "We are facing the possible extinction of our entire planet, and you don't think it important enough to tell me that these kids have an alien ship, that they can operate it, and that one of them just decided to fly it to the moon."

Her voice was raising, and her teeth were bared in fury. Jess slipped back to the table and shrank in her chair. The President of the United States was yelling at her.

Max maintained a level of respect in his tone, but he was accus- tomed to being yelled at. One didn't rise through the ranks of the military without learning how to take a butt chewing.

"Ma'am, listen to what you just said," he countered, his voice even and calm. "Two 11-year-old kids were able to steal a ship and escape an Erdean attack, and now one of them is FLYING THE SHIP TO THE MOON." He still didn't allow his voice to raise, but he put extra emphasis on each word. He repeated it to make sure his point sank in. "To the moon."

The President's face was still red, her teeth still clenched, but she dropped back into her own chair.

"How many of our best pilots have won a battle with the aliens? How many of their ships have our military commandeered?" Max continued. "But sitting here in front of you is one of two 11-year-olds who has done both of these things. I understand not believing in prophecies. I do. But at what point do you have to start thinking there's more to this than coincidence?" He looked over at Jess and smiled. He put his hand on top of hers and patted it. "These kids were tagged as the ones destined to save and protect Earth before they were even born. They've thwarted the Erdeans at every turn, escaped death many times already. If Miss Grisham says we should wait and not attack, I think the past few days have shown we should listen to her."

The President sighed. "Be that as it may, we don't have any evidence these Mondeans will be coming. Even Miss Grisham says she doesn't know." Jess sat up to argue, but President Taylor waved her off and continued. "You convinced me yourself, lieutenant, that this attack was our best chance. I was able to convince every significant world leader that we had to risk sacrificing our entire planet and the future of the human race for the good of whatever and whoever else is out there in the universe. I'm sorry. My mind is made up. The launch will happen as scheduled. We just can't take—"

The President stopped speaking because Max and Jess had stopped listening. They had risen from their chairs and moved toward the monitors hanging on the walls. Each showed a different location, but the scene unfolding was the same. Erdean tanker ships were rising, moving away from the oceans, lumbering around to uniformly face a common, unseen point in the distance. On other screens, the medium-sized transport ships ceased their search-and-seize mission along the surface. Their human captives were unceremoniously dumped to the ground, and hordes of Erdeans swarmed the landing zones to load onto the ships themselves. Smaller fighter craft began swarming the larger ships like worker bees circling a queen.

Something had happened. Something had changed.

Jess turned her attention to the shot of the moon. Where was Jace? What was going on?

* * *

Jace, his dad, and their Erdean helper had almost reached the elevator platform when the lights went out. They were immediately replaced with a dim orange lighting that cast an unsettling feel of danger.

"It's like their red alert," Rick said. "They know we're on the loose."

The Erdean girl was pressing the button that would call the elevator, but nothing was happening. She was screeching something that sounded like a curse in her own language.

From every corner of the room, human guards redirected from whatever job they were doing and moved into position, surrounding them. They were armed with rifle-sized blasters and were spreading out in such a symmetrical and coordinated manner that there was no doubt the instructions were being fed directly into their minds through the EncephaLinks. At least 20 Earthlings were closing the circle around them and closing in.

Jace held his own weapon ready. He was trying to recount a time in all of his video gaming where he'd experienced odds as bleak as these and still managed to come out on top. He was drawing a blank. Rick stepped in front of his son, spreading his arms out in a protective manner, but that only exposed Jace from behind. The Erdean moved in to fill that gap. Back to back to back in a triangle, they circled, looking for a gap through which they could escape.

The Erdean girl called out loudly in her own language, as if trying to command the guards. Nothing changed.

Jace didn't panic. Instead, he went into gaming mode. It might be slim, but they had a chance. After all, they were in the presence of an actual Erdean. He'd seen the alien soldiers in action. They were far superior physically than their human counterparts. Plus, he had a weapon. Together, maybe they could take out the guards. He didn't relish the thought. Although they were under Erdean control, these were still humans. He knew from personal experience that they were nothing more than puppets, not responsible for their own actions. Still, he had to find a way out of here. He had to get his dad back home to Earth. He had to buy time for the Mondeans to show up.

"Here's what we're going to do," he said, not worrying about being overheard.

Rick shushed him. "Wait. Be quiet," he said. "I can hear them."

"Hear who?" Jace asked.

Rick pointed to the EncephaLink tied around his neck and said, "I hear the instructions. I hear them talking to me. The guards on every level are on alert. They've turned off the lift. They're in every stairwell. They are to keep us in place until the Erdeans arrive. A ship of them just landed on the surface. They're on their way in now."

Juxoria was staring at him, listening to every word. Her exoskeleton prevented her face from showing any emotion, but she was clearly taking it all in. She looked from Rick to Jace to the circle of armed humans, like she was calculating her odds. In one blindingly swift motion, she launched herself into the air, wings unfurling at her back. Reaching the ceiling, she used two of her arms to sweep away tiles. Squeezing through the gap, she disappeared in the space between this and the floor above them.

The guards tracked her with their weapons but didn't fire. When she was gone from sight, they turned their attention fully back on Jace and Rick.

Jace was about to complain about being betrayed when the Erdean burst through the ceiling one row of tiles over. She was grasping a crossbeam with her offset rear legs, stretching out her middle and front legs as far she could. One set of claws grasped Jace's shoulders, and the other got ahold of Rick. Both were jerked off the floor and into the gap in the ceiling. Swinging her rear legs for momentum, she launched all three of them deeper into the gap between floors just as the first shots were fired by the guards below. Ripping a hole in the duct work, the alien continued to pull them quickly forward. Below, shot after shot of laser blasts ripped into the ceiling tile, but in the wrong spot.

The air ducts made a 90-degree turn up. There were no hand holds and no gaps to grasp, but the Erdean furiously beat her wings, propelling them upward toward the surface. Moments later, she kicked out a grate and finished pulling them onto the roof of the warehouse. The blackness of space was the sky above them. The moon spread out all around.

Crawling to the edge, all three looked over in time to see the last of the Erdean squad enter the facility below their hiding spot. Only two remained in the open, likely the pilots of the ship that had delivered the squadron. They stood at the base of a ramp underneath a cargo ship. Just yards past them, untouched and beckoning, was Jace's ship.

The girl tried to pull them in another direction, pointing toward a small gap in the lunar landscape. She revved up the vibrations that allowed her to speak and, as quietly as she could, uttered one word: "Hiiiddde."

Jace shook his head. "No," he said forcefully, pulling free from her grasp. "Leave!"

He pointed at his ship.

The Erdean shook her head and rubbed her throat to form more words, saying, "Eyeeee cannnottt defffffeattt a sssssoldierrr. Weeee musssst hiiiddde."

Jace was shaking his head, but Rick pulled him down flat on the roof. The Erdeans below must've heard the girl speak. They had wandered out from under their ship and were looking up in their general direction. Jace wasn't going to waste time arguing. Instinct was taking over. They might be alien soldiers, but it was now three on two. In a fair fight, that wouldn't be nearly enough, but his goal wasn't to defeat the soldiers; it was merely to get past them. If he could get to his ship, they could escape. But it wouldn't take long for the swarm that had just charged in the building to realize where they had gone. Timing was everything. Rising to his knees, Jace fired two shots from his own blaster. The first was a lucky shot, catching one of the pilots at the junction of head and thorax. It crumpled to the ground in a heap. The second shot missed the other Erdean but caused him to stumble backward.

Juxoria shrieked in her language again, directing her ire at Jace. Perhaps she, too, though, realized this was their only chance. She grasped both humans in her talons and launched off the roof toward Jace's ship.

The pilot had recovered and let out an ear-splitting warning. He didn't seem to be armed, but he was drawing the attention of those inside the giant warehouse. Erdean soldiers came streaming out as Jace dragged his dad up the ramp and into the cockpit of his ship.

"Shields forward," Jace yelled, falling into his seat.

He was just in time to see a barrage of laser blasts ricochet harmlessly off the hull. He willed the ramp to close and the ship to lift off the lunar surface. Outside, the Erdeans swarmed his ship from ground and air.

Beside him, Juxoria threw Rick from the co-pilot's chair and took his place.

"You know how to fly this thing?" Jace asked.

A voice responded, not from the alien herself but from the ship, saying, "No, but I have had training in our weapons systems. We must go now." The voice was computerized but clearly hers. She was able to think her words, and the ship translated. The communication was much quicker than the vibrations she used to speak out loud.

Jace willed the ship through the artificial atmosphere, toward the black sky of space. Looking down, he could see a swarm of Erdeans and humans alike pouring from the warehouse out onto the surface.

Some of the Erdeans were still firing toward them, but every time an Erdean fired a shot, free humans swallowed them up in a mass of humanity. Those who hadn't been mind slaves were fighting back.

"We can't leave them," Jace said. "There are thousands. They'll all die."

He actually started turning the ship back.

"I am not the only one," the computerized voice said. "There are others like me who will protect them. For now, you are the one my hive is after. We must—"

She stopped talking, and it only took Jace a split second to see why. The impossibly large mother ship had drifted around the horizon of the moon and into sight. What looked like giant puffs of smoke blew out from the middle of the ship.

"Zoom," Jace commanded, immediately wishing he hadn't.

Their view of the mother ship was magnified to the point that it looked like he could reach out and touch it. It wasn't smoke pouring from the ship. It was more ships. Fighters. Hundreds of them. Thousands. They closed the gap so fast that the first blasts from their cannons rocked his ship before he could blink away the magnification.

Juxoria whimpered and froze.

Jace, however, was in his element. First order of business was to try to put some distance between him and as much of the swarm as he could. The ship rocketed forward, banking only slightly to put it on a path directly toward home.

"Here we come," Jace yelled with a whoop of adrenalized excitement when Earth came into view around the moon.

Speed alone was not going to get them out of this, though.

"Weapons control!" he commanded, and his vision was instantly filled with targeting crosshairs.

Looking around, he sought out enemy ships and blinked to fire. Several shots found and destroyed targets, but they were taking a lot of fire, too. The ship was constantly rocked by enemy blasts. There were just too many. A warning blared through the ship. The shields were about to fail.

"Manual navigation!" Jace commanded, taking hold of the yoke.

He whipped the ship around, facing down his attackers. The dark void around him was lit up with hundreds of laser blasts. He bobbed and weaved. He twisted and turned. He took the fight right to the swarm, firing shot after shot. For a moment, despite being outnumbered thousands to one, he had the advantage. The Erdeans were confused and scrambling. There were so many that they were crashing into themselves.

Juxoria was shrieking, and it was coming through the ship's computer as very human-sounding screams. She was panicked, leaving Jace to do the flying *and* the fighting on his own. Behind them, Rick held on to anything he could find.

To Jace, it was the most realistic video game he'd ever played. His control of the ship was masterful. Not only was he locking on and destroying enemy ship after ship, but the Erdeans were having trouble tracking him. They were firing at themselves.

"Jace, Son," his dad said, finally speaking up. "You can't keep this up. There's too many of them. We have to find a way to disappear."

Jace couldn't slow down long enough to consider it. His flying and firing skills were keeping them alive for now. He'd worry about it later.

Juxoria sat up in her seat, though, and the vibrations began to build. She spoke in her own language, and the ship responded, "Identification code changed."

"What'd you do?" Jace yelled.

Her voice came through the ship. "Your father said we needed to disappear," she said. "That is impossible. But I made it possible."

"What? How?" Jace yelled. His adrenaline was pumping so hard that he couldn't control his tone.

"Every ship emits a unique signal. An identifying signature," she explained. "I asked the ship if it could change the code. The only way they can track us now is visually."

Jace smiled, impressed, and said, "Not for long."

Twisting the yoke, turning the ship this way and that, Jace whipped the vessel into a whirling dervish. He dove and spun. He wound his way around, through, and between his attackers. Having to concentrate on not running into one of their own, the Erdeans were forced to take evasive action. Just as suddenly, he stopped, settling the ship into position just off the rear of a five-ship formation. He matched his movements to theirs, blending in.

He looked over his seat at his dad, then smiled at the alien girl and said, "You did it! We've blended in."

"Yes," she said through the ship. "For now. But as soon you break free to head back to Earth, they'll be able to single us out again."

"And if they give up and head back to their mother ship, we can't follow," Rick said.

"But we're safe for now," Jace said with a sigh. "Give me a minute. I'll figure something out."

Before he could ask for advice, though, Rick screamed from the back and pressed his hands to his ears. He tore at the EncephaLink, ripping it off his wrist.

"Dad!" Jace yelled. "What is it? What's wrong?"

Rick kept screaming.

Outside, the Erdean swarm of ships suddenly changed directions as one, like a flock of birds. Jace didn't react in time and actually bumped into the closest enemy craft. The mistake went unnoticed. The other ships had all turned in a singular direction, facing toward deep space, pointing away from Earth *and* the moon.

Free from the link, Rick finally found his voice, but the look on his face scared Jace more than had the screams.

"Dad? What?"

"It was a warning," he said, heaving for breath. Gasping. "Like a million voices yelling at once."

"What voices? What were they saying?" Jace frantically asked.

He spared enough thought to turn his own ship like the others, but he was bobbing and weaving as his concentration slipped.

Juxoria's voice came through the speaker. One word. Then everything changed.

"Incoming!"

Before Jace could even question what she meant, the space all around was suddenly full of different ships. What could only be described as a fleet suddenly popped into existence out of nothing. Jace recognized the design differences immediately. He'd seen them before. In the cave. Even the larger ships hovering over them had the same unique features. They all looked like XR737's drone ship.

The Mondeans had arrived.

"We've gotta get out of here," Jace screamed as the first shots were fired in a new intragalactic war.

CHAPTER 22
A Planet in the Balance

"ABORT!" The President was screaming into a red phone. All around the room, suited men and women were scrambling from their seats, each with phones in hand and a mission to accomplish.

Max looked at the watch on his wrist. 9:57.

Across the world, final countdowns to launch had begun.

The underground bunker, so calm moments ago, was a hive of activity. Panic was so ripe in the air that Jess could almost smell it.

"Wh-what's going on?" she asked.

At first, no one responded. All eyes were either on phones or the monitors hanging around the room. All views of Earth showed Erdean craft moving into defensive positions. The hefty tankers were not war ships. They had shields and a number of cannons, but they would still be totally reliant on the smaller fighter craft for protection.

Jess's eyes shifted to the screen showing the moon. Only the natural satellite was barely visible. The screen was now full of ships. There was no mistaking their purpose. These crafts were made for war. Thousands of streaks of light, each representing a laser blast, filled the view. There were explosions all over as blasts hit their targets. Two distinctly different types of ships moved around each other like a coordinated dance. Her mind scrambling to process the sudden change in the bunker, Jess still hadn't put two and two together.

Max turned, his face lit up with a smile. He grasped Jess by the shoulders and pulled her into a hug, yelling, "You did it!" his voice rising above the cacophony of noise all around them.

"Mondeans?" she asked hesitantly.

"They came," Max said jubilantly. "You might have saved the human race, maybe the whole planet."

Max could barely contain his joy, but Jess peered over his shoulder. President Taylor did not have a joyous expression on her face. There was no mistaking her look of horror as one of the assistants whispered in her ear. Jess pulled away from Max and moved toward the President.

Retaking her seat at the head of the table, President Taylor pressed a green button on a control panel beside her.

"Control, give me anything we have on Pakistan on screen one. France on screen two." Her voice was calm and measured but was in no way indicative of what was clearly roiling inside her.

To their right, two screens went dark. After a moment of static, new images popped into view. The first showed one of the most recognizable structures in the world. Jess immediately recognized the Eiffel Tower. Just like everywhere else, the skies were full of Erdean ships, all facing skyward in anticipation.

Jess didn't recognize any buildings from the other screen, but she assumed the sprawling city, as seen from a hilltop view, was somewhere in Pakistan. As they watched, fiery streaks rose from the ground, tracking toward the Erdean ships hovering high above.

One. Two. Then five. Then more.

Missile launches. Pakistan had not been convinced to call off the attack in time.

The Erdean fleet responded, firing laser blasts at the incoming missiles. Most were blown out of the sky, but one made it through. A blinding flash of light was followed by darkness. The feed had been lost.

Jess slapped a shocked hand to her mouth. She turned to the shot of Paris. Similar streaks were converging on the Erdeans from all around.

"ABORT! ABORT! ABORT!" the President screamed into a phone.

The streaks came closer to the hovering ships. The Erdeans began firing, but before the missiles were in range, they began exploding in midair—conventional explosions, not the blinding flash of a nuclear blast.

"Report," President Taylor called.

Holding a laptop on his forearm, the man nearest her responded, his voice emotionless as he said, "One nuclear detonation in Karachi. Multiple launches in France, but a self-destruct signal was sent in time. All launches destroyed and accounted for. No other reports of launches."

"Thank goodness," the President said. "Please inform the Pakistani Prime Minister that the United States stands ready to assist in recovery as soon as...well...as soon as this whole mess ends."

There was little time for relief or celebration. On the screens around the room, the real battles had begun. Ships from two distant planets had engaged in battle in the skies above.

* * *

Jace took his hands off the yoke for a second and stared at the scene unfolding in the space between Earth and the moon. What appeared to be thousands of Mondean fighter ships poured from the larger transporters and engaged with an equal or greater number of Erdean vessels. Even then, more Mondean ships emerged and made a course for Earth. Several of the larger battleships also dropped into the planet's atmosphere. The darkness of space was lit up with green and red laser blasts, interspersed with brilliant flashes of yellow and orange as ships exploded.

The cluster Jace was hiding among began to assume an attack formation and, one by one, shot forward to engage the Mondeans.

"Jace," his dad said calmly from the back. "We—"

"Need to get out of here," Jace finished. "The Mondeans won't know we're the good guys in this ship."

Scanning all around, Jace spotted a convoy of Erdean vessels making a run to the blue planet below. Mustering enough concentration to regain navigational control of the ship, Jace willed them in that direction.

Juxoria stayed silent. The claw-like fingers on the ends of her middle arms nervously tapped the console in front of her.

"Ju," Jace said, taking his eyes off their flight path long enough to look at his co-pilot. "What's going on? What are they saying?"

She held her forearms up to her head, covering her eyes as she tried to cipher through all of the voices in her head. She didn't appear to be wearing any kind of earpiece, but she was tuned in to all of the Erdean chatter. Maybe it was coming from the ship, maybe she had some kind of implant, or maybe the Erdea were telepathic. Regardless, Jace was grateful for her intel.

"We weren't prepared for the full Mondean fleet," the ship's voice said, translating her projected explanation. "There is a lot of yelling, a lot of panic. It's hard to make out. The fighters we are following are headed to Earth to protect our cargo ships. We—they—want to make sure they take the blulex we've collected so far back to our planet until our war fleet has a chance to arrive."

They had settled in behind a group of 20 Erdeans fighters, but they seemed to be veering off to engage a group of Mondeans. One of the Mondeans' massive battleships had come under heavy attack. Spouts of fire leapt from the surface of the ship as its shields failed. The Mondean escorts were outnumbered here, as well.

They were entering the earth's atmosphere, the sky going from dark black to the faintest hints of blue. They were close enough to the planet that Jace should have been able to tell where they were going, but all he could see below were blues and browns. The shape of the land mass looked familiar, but geography wasn't his subject. He would recognize the shape of America. He knew Italy was shaped like a boot. Other than that, though, he had no idea. He needed Jess for stuff like this. Her mind was like a computer.

Computer. He had one of those. He gritted his teeth for not thinking of it right away.

"Where are we going?" he asked the ship, unsure if such a vague question could be answered.

But the ship seemed to read his mind.

"Based on the current trajectory and velocity, you will arrive in the city of Beijing in the Earth country of China in seven minutes," it said.

Beside him, Juxoria screeched something in her language, arms vibrating furiously over her throat.

The Mondean battleship was breaking apart, city-sized pieces separating from the whole. The sections, no longer protected by the ship's heat shields, burst into flames as they encountered atmospheric friction. As if sensing the weakness, the Erdean fighters went in for the kill. Dozens circled the larger vessel, firing blast after blast. The Mondean fighters continued their defense but began to back off as it became evident the battleship was going to explode.

Jace had managed to keep his distance from the fight, but the retreating Mondeans were now headed his way. They would notice him at any moment. This was where his video game skills were second to none. Being in an Erdean ship, he could have entered the fray, used the element of surprise to take out some of the Erdean attackers. The Mondean ship was already lost, though. Scanning the horizon, he could see many, many more approaching the surface.

Instead, he turned his ship away from the battle and accelerated to the west. There was going to be a time to engage, a time to take full advantage of being inside an enemy ship, but not yet.

"Where are we going?" Rick asked, his voice weak and strained as the healing power of the discarded EncephaLink waned.

Jace had already dictated directions to the ship with his mind. He turned to find Juxoria and his dad looking at him expectantly.

"We're going to get my sister."

* * *

Deep under the White House, Jess, Max, President Taylor, and nearly everyone else had stopped what they were doing and were glued to the TV monitors.

Jess was amazed at the number of camera shots and angles they had access to, especially considering that satellites had been taken out.

Reading her mind, Max answered, "Way before you were born, Ronald Reagan had the idea for attack satellites. He wanted to put weapons in space that could shoot down Russian missiles. If we could do that, Russia would then surely create a weapon of their own to counter it. We realized that being solely reliant on satellite communications was foolish. We have backup systems in place to keep us in touch with the world and what's going on. The Erdeans haven't discovered that signal."

Jess nodded. That was a better explanation for how they were able to see news reports on the tablet back at the safehouse long after the TV signal had gone down.

Every monitor was filled with images straight out of a science fiction movie. Impossibly large ships were hovering over Earth, fighting with weapons beyond Earth's capabilities. Mainly, she saw, it was lasers, but the Mondean battleships also appeared to be equipped with some other kind of bomb. From multi-shot cannons, trails of red-orange blobs emerged like slow-moving tracer fire. In a sea of lightning-quick laser fire, the plasma balls were comically slow but unaffected by any defensive efforts. The plasma balls were too slow to strike the smaller Erdean fighters, but when they made contact with the larger ships, the contact created a temporary hole in the shields. The bombs were immediately followed by incredibly concentrated volleys of laser fire, targeting the gap in the cargo ship's defenses. The results were spectacular. Ship after enemy ship was blasted from the sky, pieces raining down on ocean and land.

As a measure of defense, the Erdeans were moving their ships over cities. The Mondeans were reluctant to engage above heavily populated areas. It was here that the Erdeans were successfully fighting back.

Explanations of the strategy were being yelled across the conference table as the monitors shifted from scene to scene. Every chair in the command center was taken. The President remained at the head of the table, listening to three conversations at once. Jess was amazed at her ability to take it all in and remain calm. The other chairs were filled with men and women, some in casual clothes, others in suits, and the rest in military uniforms. The latter occupied the chairs closest to the President.

No one was giving Jess or Max so much as a sideways glance, but they were still doing all they could to stay out of the way. They were huddled under a bank of monitors in the corner of the room behind President Taylor.

There were gasps and moans, cheers and triumphant yells. There were explosions and scenes of death.

Despite the Mondean efforts to protect as many humans as possible, the Erdeans were using a different tactic. They aimed disabled ships, crashing them into streets and buildings. Undamaged Erdean vessels were evacuating from spots all over the globe. Their massive cargo ships—some completely loaded with water, blulex, and human—were disappearing as the ground-based transmitters triangulated positions and locked on. Jess watched as ships disappeared from one screen before reappearing almost instantly near the moon. She was following the progress screen to screen.

The scene around the moon was much the same. An intense war was being waged. There was so much going on that it was easy to get distracted, but the fate of her brother and father was never far from her mind. She continually studied the monitors focused on the moon in the hopes of seeing any sign of them, but they were a grain of sand on the beach.

The Erdeans were putting up a stout defense at the lunar base. The giant mother ship was more than a match for anything the Mondeans threw its way. Jess watched in horror as Erdean ships first appeared, then disappeared again, as the transporter array built into the far side of the moon launched them deep into the galaxy. All the while, Mondean attack vessels were deflected and destroyed.

At best, the battle out there appeared to be a standoff.

Back on Earth, Mondeans were gaining the upper hand all over the world. Erdean ships that weren't transported away were being destroyed by a relentless assault. On the largest monitor in the room, though, the scene wasn't as favorable. More and more Erdean ships were moving over Washington D.C., firing their weapons indiscriminately on ground-based targets. The largest of the ships were forming a circle around the city while hundreds of the smaller fighters weaved in and out, attacking any Mondeans that ventured too close.

Deep in the bunker beneath the White House, the walls shook. Faint explosions could be heard from the surface. This facility had been built to withstand nuclear war, but no one knew how it would hold up to alien battle capabilities.

Jess wondered how much longer the video feeds would last.

One by one, the skies above major cities and coastlines across the world cleared as the last of the Erdean ships were transported away or destroyed. Over D.C., however, the circling armada came to a hovering halt. Beams of light rose from the tops of the ships before joining at a singular point high above. From the point, a glowing shield cascaded down, covering all of the ships in a protective umbrella. Although far larger and more powerful than anything she'd seen before, Jess recognized the shield. It was the same as the cage Jace had used to capture them in the forest. The same one he had used to free them from the prison cell where they had been held. Only this was much, much larger.

Mondean efforts to penetrate the shield proved fruitless. Their plasma bombs failed to penetrate, and any ship that tried to fly through was incinerated. Erdean ships, however, moved in and out of the protective barrier at will, surgically striking at the Mondeans and ducking back into cover.

Meanwhile, a few of the medium-sized Erdean transports were

landing. Armed aliens were pouring out into the city. Jess didn't even have to think about what they were doing, what they were after. Or rather, who they were after. Capturing the US President, the most powerful person on the planet, could prove to be a valuable bargaining chip should they need it.

Getting one of the twins of the prophecy would be an added bonus, she thought wryly.

She eyed a small table standing beside the door through which they had entered. Resting there was her backpack. The Secret Service had taken it from her when they first entered but had left it here. Was the Mondean blaster still inside? If the aliens found the entrance to the bunker, they'd need all the firepower they could find. Careful not to draw attention to herself, she slid along the wall toward the table. She was almost there when she heard screams and shouts from the hallway beyond. There was an unmistakable whine of laser blasts and the return fire of conventional Earth weapons. Screams, yells, and explosions sounded throughout the bunker. Then the lights went out.

They'd been found!

* * *

Jace made his first miscalculation. It wasn't a mistake per se, but he had not anticipated that a single Erdean ship breaking free of the pack would draw Mondean attention. He was counting on a clear path back to America and Jess. Three Mondean fighters, however, had tracked his deviation and were closing ground.

"They'll be in firing range in seconds," Juxoria said, her vocal vibrations echoing through the ship's translator.

She activated the ship's targeting system and prepared to fire.

"No!" Jace yelled.

"It will do us no good to get shot down," she said, fear and panic clear even through the computerized voice.

Her throat heaved, and a high-pitched whistle started deep within her. If she couldn't control herself, reign in her fear, the full pitch of her call in the close confines of this ship would shatter his and Rick's eardrums. The throbbing vibrations reached her chest, and she gulped for breath as the ship's warning system indicated enemy weapons had locked on.

As confident as he was, as certain as he felt that not fighting his way through the Mondeans was the right choice, he whimpered as the ship's control console lit up red.

Rick leaned forward in his seat and put on hand on Jace's shoulder. Reluctantly, he placed his second hand on Juxoria, then said, "No Mondean life is worth less than our own. They came here to save us, and there is no justification for attempting to take their lives to save our own. I trust you, Son. You can get us out of this."

Jace tried to take a deep breath, but his rapid heartbeat kept his breathing coming in short, ragged gasps. He looked at the alien beside him. The *enemy* alien. She was scared, too, but had already sacrificed so much to save him. To save his dad. It was all for nothing if they were shot down over this foreign country. But his dad was right. Fighting these Mondeans just to save themselves ran counter to what they were fighting for. He had come to believe in the prophecy. If destiny had a larger role in store for him and Jess, his part in it would not end here, and it would not involve attacking his allies.

"Deactivate weapons system," he said out loud. "Transfer power to shields."

The first laser bolts from the pursuing Mondeans rocketed past, narrowly missing. Instead of scaring Jace and making his panic worse, it was almost as if the first volleys of the attack calmed him. He imagined the ship's yoke was his video game controller at home. This was just another game.

"Hold on to something," he warned.

As if sensing the danger, the ship responded to Jace's thought control almost before the plan formed in his head. He guided them into a steep dive, hurtling headlong toward the ground. Involuntarily,

Juxoria's call had become so shrill that it reached a painful threshold. He had to take control of their weapons system out of her hands, but his command to deactivate the weapons system had been a ruse. No sooner had he spoken the words out loud that he overrode the command with a thought. He had control of the weapons and the navigation, *and* he had a plan to get them out of this.

Just as he had counted on, his suicide dive to the surface had slowed the Mondean pursuit. Unsure if he was going to just plow into the ground, they had backed off to save themselves the same fate. Jace was putting a lot of faith in a machine pieced together by XR737 just hours ago. But the Erdean ship was fast and nimble. A pilot with enough nerve could pull off something that might seem impossible by human standards. No plane built on Earth could pull up from such a dive in time, but this ship wasn't built on Earth.

At the last possible moment, Jace urged the ship out of its dive. He had flown them into a valley between snow-covered mountain peaks higher than anything Jace had seen before. Glancing down through the transparent floor of the ship, he felt as if he could actually drag his toes in the grass. He'd managed an almost 90-degree turn at speeds exceeding 1,000 miles per hour. Far above, the Mondean ships fired again, but his daredevil flying had created enough distance that the shots missed.

Seeing the blasts impact into the side of the mountain gave Jace a new idea. Maybe he didn't have to outfly the Mondeans, after all. His original idea had been to get into the mountain valleys and outmaneuver the other pilots, use speed and daring to get away. There was another option. He laughed out loud as the pieces of a new plan came together.

A narrow road, wide enough for one car at most, followed the valley floor. Where there was a road, eventually there would be a gas station. He looked back and saw that the three Mondean ships had also leveled out, but at a safer speed. They were far enough back for now, but because three ships created a larger slipstream than one, they would be able to go faster and would gain on him before long.

He saw exactly what he was looking for around the next turn. Tucked up against a steep mountain slope was an old, wooden building. Out front was the unmistakable form of a gas pump.

Seeming to read his mind, Rick spoke from the back. "Fire at the mountain first," he said.

Juxoria looked around, confused, but the vibrations from deep within her had begun to subside. A silent calm had taken hold in the cockpit. That same calm resided inside Jace. Waiting until he had rounded the side of the mountain and moved out of sight of the pursuing Mondeans, he fired the ship's cannons. Two shots struck high up on the mountain slope. A third, triggered seconds later, impacted the base of the gas pump. Timing was crucial, but Jace knew he'd gotten it right. Massive chunks of snow and ice broke loose from the steep mountain slope and cascaded down to the valley floor below. Mere moments later, a tremendous explosion blew the gas station to splintered pieces of wood.

He brought his ship to the ground in a barely controlled skid, sliding them under the avalanche just as the Mondean ships rounded the turn.

"All systems off!" Jace yelled as tons of snow poured over them, and the ship went dark.

Understanding dawned on Juxoria. Unable to speak through the ship's computer, she began to rev up the vibrations at her throat. Moving her forearm up and down, she created English words, saying, "Ttthheeey willlll thinnnnk weeeee ccccrashhhhhed."

Jace smiled and nodded. The Mondeans would have seen Jace's reckless piloting, seen the explosion and all the debris. They would have seen the ship disappear from their targeting system. By shutting off all systems, there would be no signature to trace. The other pilots would believe their own eyes and return to their fleet. All Jace had to do now was wait. The ship would have no trouble plowing its way out of the snow and ice it was buried under. They'd be back on their way to America soon enough.

* * *

There was a scramble in the underground conference room. Flashlights were lighting up the room in narrow, crisscrossing beams. Several Secret Service agents emerged and grabbed the President under both arms, forcefully dragging her deeper into the secret facility. One of the agents noticed Jess and Max. Not willing to leave a child behind to fend for herself, they were urged to follow.

Jess pulled free from Max's grasp long enough to grab the backpack. She tore it open as they hurried through a dark hallway, flashlights up ahead the only light. Using sense of touch, Jess rummaged through the bag. Her fingers locked on something unexpected first. It was the glove XR737 had been using as a weapon and shield generator back in the cave. Jace must have hidden it here before heading out. She pulled it onto her right hand and kept digging through the bag with her left, finally grabbing hold of what she wanted: the laser blaster. Since she had the glove, she shoved the blaster into Max's hands.

The rest of the group had already passed through a feet-thick metal door. This was the room of last resort, a heavily shielded, impenetrable safe room within the bunker. Theoretically, once this door was closed, no one was getting in. But the Erdeans had already made it into the bunker itself. There was no guarantee anywhere was completely safe.

Max halted in the doorway.

"We're sitting ducks in here," he said to the agent, who was punching numbers on a keypad.

"There's not a human alive who can get in this room once the door is shut," the agent said reassuringly.

"If you hadn't noticed, those aren't humans," Max said, pointing back down the hallway. More sounds of weapons firing echoed loudly. They were getting closer. "No one was supposed to be able to get into this bunker, yet..."

Max let that stand. The agent stopped pressing buttons.

"They'll get in eventually," Jess said softly but confidently. "I'm betting there is another way out of here. We should keep moving."

The agent was no longer sure what to do. By the sounds of it, the fighting had reached the conference room. There was less and less conventional fire, but the sounds of laser blasts continued unabated. The Erdean troops were closing in.

Suddenly, the President was standing at their side. She eyed the weapon in Max's hands and made up her mind.

"Agent, wait until you see them enter the hallway and close this door," she commanded, her tone leaving little room for negotiation. "They'll assume we're all in here. It will buy us time. I know the way out, and I'll be in good hands with these two."

The agent shook his head. The Secret Service *never* left the President's side in times of crisis or danger, and they especially didn't leave the job to an 11-year-old girl.

"Madam President—"

"That's an order, agent," she said before turning to Jess and Max. "Now, let's go. This way."

She led them through a door to the left. They had just cleared the doorway when the Erdeans fought their way into the hall. There was a renewed cacophony of weapons firing, followed shortly by the heavy thud of the safe room door closing.

Jess found a flashlight in the bottom of her bag and turned it on. They were in a space intended to be a bedroom. A king-sized bed was flush against the wall to the left. The President led them to and through a secret panel in the back of the room. They found themselves in a space no larger than a closet. Squeezed together, Jess struggled to point the flashlight around. Trying to adjust to make more room, Max accidentally swung an elbow into her arm, causing Jess to drop the light. She reached in a desperate attempt to catch it, but there was a muffled bang as it struck the floor and extinguished. Something else, however, happened in the exchange. In her effort to grab the flashlight, Jess had squeezed her pinky and thumb of her gloved hand together. The glove lit up like a beacon, spreading light not only through the narrow confines of the closet but also upward.

Straight up. There was no ceiling, only a long, metal tube extending upward, with ladder rungs interspersed every two feet.

The President had already started climbing.

"Up we go," she huffed.

Max made Jess go next. He brought up the rear, climbing one-handed because he refused to let go of the weapon. Up and up they went. Jess's arms quickly became fatigued, but adrenaline kept her going. Down wasn't an option. Neither was staying where they were. She kept putting one hand in front of the other, pulling herself steadily upward for what seemed like hours. Until finally, she bumped into President Taylor.

"We're at the top," the President whispered. "Can you shine that glove up this way?"

Jess wrapped her left hand around the nearest rung to secure herself and leaned out until her right hand had a clear path to the top. There was some kind of complex latch that the President was working to release. The catch finally released a trap door the exact size of the tube. It slid to the side.

President Taylor leaned over to speak even more quietly to her two escorts. "I don't know what we're going to be walking into," she mouthed, her voice barely audible. "Lieutenant, give me your weapon."

Max was reluctant but complied, passing it up.

Up one more rung, President Taylor slid another barrier aside. A thin stream of light reached their eyes, and a cold rush of air cascaded over them. Jess pressed her pinky and thumb together again to turn off the glove. There was no more room to go up and no space to stand. The President held the weapon out in front and pushed her way forward. A door swung open, artificial light washed over them, and the President poured out onto a tiled floor. Jess could see her crouch in a defensive shooting position, but the room was clear. Jess climbed up to join her, followed quickly by Max, who immediately reclaimed the weapon.

They were in a large kitchen, industrial stainless-steel tables and appliances surrounded by sterilized white tile all around.

"The White House kitchen," President Taylor whispered.

Max nodded, and Jess looked behind her. They had emerged from an industrial-sized refrigerator, its false bottom slid to the side. Real shelves had flipped up, dumping their contents into a hidden compartment behind. Jess was certain that not even the cooks and serving staff would have suspected this fridge was anything other than what it appeared.

The President was already moving, not toward the dining room but back into the kitchen depths, through a pantry, and toward the garage door-sized service entrance. Sliding it up, the three stepped outside. Directly into a scene from another world.

The sky all around was full of giant Erdean ships, circling slowly around a central point. From underneath, the shield spread out like an umbrella from the converging beams above. Smaller ships darted in and out of the crackling blue shield. In the distance, Mondean ships helplessly stood sentry. Fighters of their own chased after the smaller Erdean ships, but the latter ducked through the shield every time danger got too close.

The Erdeans had circled the wagons. They were making their stand right here in Washington D.C. At least until they had acquired their target.

Little did they know that very target was now out in the open, staring helplessly skyward.

Erdean soldiers crawled all over the grounds. It would only be a matter of time before they were found. Max scanned for a place to hide, anywhere they could go that would buy them a little time. Kneeling behind a short row of hedges was the best they could do.

Jess hovered her first two fingers close to the pad of her thumb.

She knew what they did. The middle finger would produce a shield. The pointer finger created a laser blast, just like the weapon Max held. She had no idea what the ring finger would do, and now was not the time to experiment.

From their temporary place of concealment, the three took everything in. It was like a choreographed dance. The larger ships rotated slowly but steadily around an axis. The smaller ones continued to dart in and out, striking at the Mondeans when they saw an advantage.

It was rhythmic.

Until it wasn't.

A smaller Erdean ship entered the shield at full speed. And absolute havoc broke loose.

* * *

Jace wasted no time getting them to Washington. He pushed the Erdean ship to the very limits of its in-atmosphere speed capabilities. As they neared the capital, however, it was clear the battle was not going as well here as it was in other places. Along their way, they had seen Mondeans defeating the Erdeans. The enemy ships had either been destroyed in mass or were being chased off into space. They had witnessed the destruction of several transporters, their burning hulks all that remained of the structures. But D.C. was different. The Erdeans were not retreating. In fact, they seemed to have set up some kind of perimeter. Even from a distance, Juxoria had recognized the shield and explained its purpose to Jace and Rick.

Outside the barrier, the sky was full of Mondean ships, both the larger battle vessels and smaller fighters. They were helpless against the shield and the snake-like strikes of the Erdean/ attackers as they darted randomly from behind the shield, fired their weapons, and ducked back to safety.

"Stay back and try to keep out of sight," Rick advised from the back. His voice was wheezy, and the words came in ragged gasps. The price to pay for the healing properties of the EncephaLink was accelerated deterioration when separated. The ALS was progressing without resistance. "We need a plan."

Jace, though, already had a strategy. Well, not so much a strategy as a fly-by-the-seat-of-his-pants method of approaching every challenge. Off in the distance, more Mondean ships could be seen encroaching on the American capital. Fresh off victories won in other parts of the world, they were all converging on this point. The longer Jace waited outside the shielded boundary, the harder it would be to remain unnoticed.

It was now or never.

Maintaining their breakneck speed, Jace tore through gaps between the Mondean ships, racing toward the shield.

Mondean fighters reacted. A trio of the smaller craft moved into position to cut him off. Streaks of blue laser blasts narrowly missed them from behind as they rocketed into the middle of the convoy. Jace didn't let up. The shield was within their reach, but it was going to be close. Juxoria again tried to take control of the targeting computers, but Jace refused.

"We either make it, or we don't," he said, gritting his teeth with determination.

It wasn't easy putting your very survival on the line when the means to ensure it was literally at your fingertips. Three quick blasts would pave the road to safety behind the shield. The shots didn't have to hit the Mondeans; they merely needed to put them on the defensive long enough to slip by. But it wasn't worth the risk.

In response to the Mondeans, Jace adjusted their course slightly to the west. At any minute, the three sleek ships ahead would start firing at them. His timing would have to be absolutely perfect. They would have to adjust their own route to get a clear shot at him. Once they did, once their attention shifted to their targeting devices for even a fraction of a second, he would cut back hard. They were going so fast that the feint should be enough to get them to safety.

They were so close now. The shield loomed over them. Everything in the cockpit took on a blueish tinge. More Mondeans were firing from behind, but they were traveling nearly as fast as the blasts, and their own shields easily deflected the shots. The three Mondean ships ahead, now making the turn to track them, were the only true threat.

Juxoria had started vibrating again, the growing whine from within her drowning out the crackling of the giant shield toward which they hurtled. Jace tuned it all out. He was watching the Mondean ships intently. He put himself in their seats, his mind engrossed in video game mode. If he were them, when would he fire? Would he see the feint coming?

The answers were now and yes. Changing his mind at the last second, Jace willed the ship to dive at a steep angle. A volley of Mondean laser blasts streaked harmlessly over their heads. As he predicted, one of the ships anticipated Jace's move back to the east and concentrated his fire on the space where the Erdean ship would have been. Jace would've flown right into the laser blast, but instincts had guided him in an unexpected direction. In two seconds, they passed through the blue barrier with only the slightest of shakes.

Their speed was nearly too fast to control. Their new trajectory was hurtling them toward the ground. Jace envisioned another game he liked to play called Drifter. In that one, you drove souped up cars through narrow, windy streets. The goal was to complete a course as fast as possible without wrecking and without getting caught by police. By strategically applying the parking break, you could maintain speed into sharp turns, creating controlled slides.

The Erdean ship didn't have an emergency break, but it was flown with mind control. Jace imagined letting off the accelerator, pulling on the emergency break, yanking up on a yoke, and allowing the rear end of the ship to slide ahead of their projected path. It was so close that the bottom of the ship skidded twice along the grassy middle strip of the National Mall before the front end corrected. Once they were again pointing skyward, Jace mentally hit the gas, and the ship rose. A quick correction allowed them to narrowly avoid the tall obelisk of the Washington Monument.

All three occupants sighed with relief. They had reached their destination more or less in one piece. Now they faced their biggest problem yet. They were truly now in the belly of the whale.

* * *

Jess saw the daredevil maneuvers and reckless speed of the Erdean ship and knew right away who was in the pilot's seat. For a brief second, she forgot where she was.

"It's Jace!" she yelled, popping out from behind the row of hedges and pointing.

Max groaned and tried to pull her back, but it was too late. The momentary lapse was all it took. Erdean ground soldiers reacted quickly to her shout and closed in. Jess immediately recognized her mistake and froze. Erdeans scampered across the lawn in front of them. They climbed out windows and scaled down the White House walls behind them. Hundreds of them converged.

Max leapt into action, firing blast after blast from his weapon as he rotated in all directions. Most of the shots ricocheted harmlessly off the bugs' armored exoskeletons, but some found soft spots, and those Erdeans dropped.

Despite the horror she felt at making the mistake, Jess processed their predicament quickly. The prognosis was bleak, but they hadn't come this far and gotten this close to give up now. She tugged at the glove on her right hand to make sure it was secure, took aim, and squeezed her thumb and pointer finger. A tingle raced up the length of her arm, and her shoulder jerked slightly as a blue laser blast leapt from her fingertips and soared harmlessly over the heads of the encroaching swarm. She squeezed and fired again. And again. The shots didn't hold the same punch as Max's blaster, but solid contact slowed the Erdeans she hit. She even managed to separate one's head from its body. She permanently took out another when her shot broke the grip one alien had on the second story wall of the White House. Stunned from the blast, the bug didn't have a chance to unfurl its wings, and it crashed with a sickening crunch onto the concrete sidewalk below.

These were small victories, though. Dozens of laser blasts flashed all around as the Erdeans fired back.

President Taylor was not about to stay hidden in the shadows while others fought. She broke from cover and dashed into the open, grabbing a weapon of her own from a downed Erdean. An Army veteran herself, she was no stranger to guns. The blaster in her hands was a little bulkier than she was accustomed to, but it functioned much the same. She was firing almost instantly, standing back to back with Max to hold off the advancing aliens from all sides.

Jess was crouched just under their outstretched arms, squeezing off shots as quickly as she could. She noticed the blasts getting weaker. The glove was likely not meant for battlefield combat. The charge that gave it power would quickly deplete. They were so hopelessly outnumbered, however, that it soon wouldn't matter whether they were fighting with three weapons or two.

The Erdeans continued to close in, but they had stopped firing. A few were communicating in their shrill way.

"What's happening?" Jess asked, looking left and right.

The entire White House lawn was crawling with the soldiers. She could barely see the walls of the house itself. Even the sky above was becoming crowded with the winged creatures.

"They want the President alive," Max said.

Both he and President Taylor had stopped the rapid firing, only squeezing the trigger now when one of the Erdeans broke the closing circle and moved too close.

"We're going to need help from above to get out of this one," the President said.

* * *

THE ORIGIN SOCIETY: US

Above, Jace was weaving the stolen ship around the enclosed space over the capital. They had blasted several unsuspecting Erdean ships out of the sky and had managed to do it so far without attracting the attention of the fleet. That luck wouldn't hold out.

Frustration was setting in. There were just too many enemy ships. Once the Erdeans figured out they had an enemy among their ranks, they'd really be in trouble.

Most of the city was under the shield. Jace was flying low, staying just above the city streets, using the buildings to shield his attacks. As their flight path moved them back toward the National Mall, Rick pointed out unusual activity on the ground. Swarms of Erdeans, so thick the ground wasn't visible, were converging on the White House. Jace understood what it meant before the others

"Jess," he whispered.

Keeping low, he zipped in closer. Sure enough, close to the base of the East Wing, he saw three humans huddled together in the center of a closing ring.

"Visual zoom," he said aloud, and the transparent wall of the ship magnified, giving him a clear view of his sister, Max, and the President of United States. Jace blinked away the magnification. He turned to Juxoria. "How many laser cannons does this ship have?"

The alien shook her head. "It doesn't work that way," she explained, the ship's synthesized voice translating her thoughts. "The entire surface of the ship is part of the weapons system. It draws and stores energy from the friction of flight, concentrates it on a single point, and the shot emanates from there."

Jace curved the ship around the Capitol building and made a beeline directly for his sister, formulating a plan as he went.

"Can it fire from more than one place at the same time?"

"Yyyyeessss." The word vibrated from Juxoria's throat.

Jace responded immediately. "Weapons control, split to all three of us," he said aloud, knowing the ship's computer would understand his intentions.

"It's time to show ourselves," he said. "It's time to make our stand."

* * *

The Erdeans were moving forward cautiously, but the circle had closed enough that the nearest bugs could reach out and touch them. Max kept firing shots, but the swarm merely stepped over the fallen bodies and continued to close in. The President had lowered her weapon. This battle was lost, but maybe they could live to fight another day.

Jess closed her eyes and held her arms out in surrender, but the spiny hands of the aliens never grabbed her. Instead, an explosion rocked the ground so close that they were blown off their feet. An acrid smell of ozone and roasted bug filled her nostrils. The sky was full of alien body parts. A second blast did the same damage on the President's side of the circle, followed by a third. And a fourth. And a fifth.

President Taylor's help from above came in the form of an Erdean ship, skimming low. Blast after blast jumped from the underside of the fighter. It was also plowing through airborne Erdeans. Jace zoomed right over the center of the broken circle and turned on a dime to make another run.

The Erdeans forgot about the three humans on the ground and turned their attention to the sky. To them, it appeared one of their own was attacking. They tentatively started firing their weapons into the air.

In all of the commotion, Max spotted a clear path back into the White House. He pulled Jess and President Taylor down the path and back through the service entrance. Their escape didn't go totally unnoticed, but Jace was providing enough cover fire and enough of a distraction to keep the invading army occupied.

Back inside and safe for a moment, all they could do was hide and hope.

* * *

Just outside the giant shield, a Mondean captain watched helplessly as an Erdean ship seemed to turn on its own. The flying was impressive, but the revolt would be short-lived. A squadron of Erdean fighters had broken off perimeter patrol and were converging on the rogue ship. He paced his bridge, desperately wracking his brain for a way through the shield.

They had won the war. It had not been easy, but without the presence of the Erdeans' full armada, the Mondean fleet had managed to drive the invaders off the planet and into space. Reports from there were spotty as the battled raged on, but it seemed that despite heavy losses, they had the upper hand. The surviving Erdean ships were being transported out as quickly as they could reach the lunar transporter. The Earth city below was the only major hold out.

The captain shivered as he realized what it meant. The Erdeans were after the President; that was obvious. They would hope to use the Earth leader as a bargaining chip. From the captain's experience, though, the Erdeans didn't play politics. It wasn't their style. Although their invasion force was in retreat, they wouldn't just give up. Unless he was gravely mistaken, the circle of ships, the shield, and all of those troops on the ground weren't about taking a single hostage. That was a distraction. They were up to something else. But what was it? He paced and thought, watching with interest as the fighter squadron closed in on the rogue ship, and then another man burst through the bridge door at a run. The captain turned and faced him.

"Sir," Xanos said, setting a tablet down on the nearest flat surface. "I've found them."

A hologram emerged from the tablet and spread out like a bubble, hovering in the air over the device like a projection. It showed the same scene that was unfolding in person out the window. With one difference. A red dot was blinking in the exact spot where the rogue Erdean ship was taking out ground forces in waves.

"It's them," Xanos said. "The two. If they're inside that ship, it explains why I haven't been able to locate them. The Erdean tech was shielding the signal. I've just now broken through."

The captain ignored the hologram and raced to the bridge's viewscreen. He placed both hands on the transparent wall and stared helplessly as too many Erdean fighters to count converged on the one.

"Can you contact them?" the captain asked.

"I think so, but the signal will be weak," Xanos said. "That shield isn't letting much in or out."

"Try!" the captain said, panicked.

The hologram disappeared, and Xanos's fingers worked furiously on the tablet.

Inside the shield, the first of the Erdean fighters reached and started firing on the rogue ship.

* * *

Jace was expecting the attack and saw it coming. Hoping they had provided enough of a distraction to buy Jess some time to get into hiding, he rolled the ship away from the White House as the first wave came into range and accelerated down the mall. He transferred all weapons control to Juxoria and focused his concentration on aerial maneuvers. He'd seen documentaries on fighter jet dogfights where American F16s would twist and turn, dip and dive, and bob and weave while locked in combat with Soviet-made MiG jets. Outnumbered, the American pilots would use their tremendous skills and superior training to win.

Jace wasn't trained in aerial combat, but he was skilled, nevertheless. His mom often complained that he was wasting his life away playing those silly video games. All of those hours with a controller in his hand were the only things saving his life now.

He stayed two steps ahead of his pursuers. They were hopelessly outnumbered, however, and unless the Mondeans outside the shield pulled off a miracle, all he was really doing was delaying the inevitable. Best case scenario: He was buying Jess time to get away.

At first, he thought he was imagining the buzz in his ears. Then he thought maybe the vibration was something giving way in the ship itself. Finally, though, he remembered he was actually wearing a headset. Not sure what it could mean, he reached up and tapped the earpiece. Right in front of his eyes, a square of light appeared, like the screen of a monitor. Through static, Jace thought he could see movement, but the signal was too weak. He heard his dad gasp in the seat behind him.

"Son," Rick said, "are you seeing this?"

"All I see is static," Jace said, annoyed. "And I'm a little too busy right now to have something blocking my vision."

He tapped his ear again, and the screen went away. He resumed his evasive flying. Juxoria was firing on everything she could, but it was hard to lock onto a target when the pilot was turning and flipping them as quickly as the ship would allow.

Jace jumped in surprise and nearly lost his focus as his dad placed his half of the headset on Jace's head and fitted the earpiece in his left ear.

"Boost Mondean signal," Rick told the ship, having no idea if that was even possible.

Whether that did the trick, or whether it was connecting the two halves of the Sparker, he wasn't sure, but when Jace tapped the earpiece again, the screen reappeared, and he was greeted with a fuzzy image of Xanos, the Mondean he and Jess had first spoken to.

Xanos smiled and spoke to someone off screen, saying, "Communication established."

Another man shouldered his way into view, pushing Xanos to the side. Based on the impressive insignia on his uniform, this person held a high rank among the Mondeans. He wasted no time on introductions.

"Son," he said, his English accented slightly but otherwise perfect. "That's some amazing flying, but if you don't take the shield down, the rest of your life will be measured in seconds."

"The shield is coming from several of the giant Erdean ships!" Jace yelled. "It's hard enough battling these smaller ships. There's no way I can take out the bigger ones!"

"There's a way," the Mondean captain said.

He stepped back, and the screen image was replaced with an animated simulation.

"I can do that!" Jace said, slapping his leg in frustration.

It was so simple. Why hadn't he thought of it already? He used a hand to swipe away the image in front of his face. He could still hear the Mondeans in his ear, but he needed a full visual field to pull this off. He willed the ship into a steep vertical climb, the move causing two of the fighters behind him to collide and explode in midair.

Juxoria, who had been too busy targeting other ships to see the plan, squealed in surprise as Jace accelerated toward the underside of one of the giant Erdean vessels.

Without knowing how he knew, Jace realized the ship would not be able to use its own weapons systems while generating the shield. All of its power was focused on delivering the energy beam to the singular point centered high above all of the ships. The purpose of the shield was to keep enemies out. There would be no protection within, no shield for the shield itself. If he could break the connection at its origin, he could take it down. The smaller ships in pursuit stopped firing for fear of hitting the giant transporter. Jace took advantage, staying as close as he dared to the ship's underbelly.

"Weapon's control to pilot," he said calmly.

He would get one shot at this and only trusted himself to do it right. He felt the ship's power in his mind.

"Shields down. Transfer all power to weapons," he said.

Juxoria whimpered at the command. They'd be clear of the larger ship in seconds, and once in the open without shields, they would be easy pickings for the smaller ships on their tail.

Jace guided the stolen fighter out of the shadows and into two suns.

The first was the actual sun, shining brightly through the shield, bathing the ground below in warmth and natural light, as it had for millions of years. The second was the singularity, the converging point of the shield generating beams. Jace willed the ship directly at that point and closed his eyes. Timing was everything. Because of the little jail cell cube still in his pocket, he understood how these shields worked, and knew their weaknesses. Mere feet from the convergence point, he unleashed a blast straight into the center of the brilliant light source. He flew the ship into the temporary gap and issued a mental command to stop.

"SHIELDS UP!" he yelled.

Although not even a fraction as strong as the shield surrounding the city, the small fighter's shield was strong enough to deflect the beams coming from the larger ships. A dozen individual beams bounced back to their source. The cannons on those ships all exploded. The remnants of the shield evaporated, and the Mondeans, waiting for this very moment, poured in and engaged.

It was a battle like Jace had never witnessed before, not even in a video game or a movie. Despite being desperately outnumbered, the Erdeans still managed to put up a good fight. The Mondeans, however, just had too much fire power.

Jace moved his ship high above the fray, watching the battle unfold from up high. He itched to get involved, but he had one more mission to accomplish. He waited impatiently for a clear path to the ground. It didn't take long. The Mondeans were luring the Erdeans away from the city, to a place where crashing ships would do minimum damage on the ground below.

Once a clear window opened, Jace dove for the surface. His twin sister was down there, and he'd never wanted her by his side more than right now. Together, they'd find a way to heal their dad.

Jace turned in his seat. Rick was slumped over, but his eyes were open. There was no mistaking the pride evident there. The corners of his mouth twitched in an effort to smile.

Through tears, Jace smiled back.

CHAPTER 23
The Future of Us

Just two weeks ago, the scene would have been impossible to believe, one you'd find in a movie. A small group stood close together on the White House lawn. It was a diverse group, featuring the President of the United States, a special ops squad leader, two 11-year-old kids and their father, three aliens from the planet Mondea, and a young female from the planet Erdea.

Hovering high above, casting a shadow over a large portion of the Capitol, was a city-sized ship. A friendly one.

"On behalf of our entire planet, I thank you," President Taylor said, reaching out to shake the hand of Xanos, the Mondean standing slightly in front of two others.

Xanos turned and listened as one of the other tall gray-skinned beings spoke. The language was very similar in tone and cadence to Earth languages, but the words were foreign. Xanos nodded and translated through a device hanging from his neck. He worked words of English into his statement, clearly exhibiting a quick understanding of the language.

"We are committed to a peaceful universe," he said. "But we have a particular affinity for your planet. We have visited many times and have a history more intertwined that even you may realize."

"I would love to hear that history," the President said.

Xanos smiled. "We would be happy to return and share what we know, but that will have to be another day. We must return to the Planetary Council and answer for our...we'll call them transgressions."

President Taylor cocked her head in confusion.

Xanos smiled again. "We took advantage of the permission granted to us to come to Earth," he explained.

The President frowned. "You have this amazing technology, the unfathomable ability to travel the stars, the kindness of soul to come when the people of an inferior planet were most desperately in need, but you required permission?"

Xanos looked uncomfortable. He spoke again to the Mondean behind him.

"Again, our pasts are intertwined," he said. "In an early visit, our people broke one of the most sacred commandments of the Terragoddrians. We interfered in your development. I can't say more without telling the whole story."

"Does this have to do with Mondea protecting Earth from the Erdeans millennia ago?" Max asked, speaking for the first time. "Is it about how the Origin Society came to be?"

"It has everything to do with that," Xanos said without further explanation.

"So it's over now?" Jess asked. "We won?"

Juxoria cautiously stepped forward. Jace noticed the Mondeans move their hands closer to their holstered weapons. He had explained how the Erdean girl had helped him and his father escape, how there were others within the Erdean ranks who valued the lives of other species. Such a mentality was a rarity among the species, however, and the Mondeans didn't fully trust her.

"No," she said sternly, her antennae quivering in the light breeze. She held a small box by a handle. The device, similar to the one Xanos wore, was translating her words into mechanical English, the same way the ship had done. "Our people are relentless. They were defeated here, but this was not their first attempt to rob your planet, and it won't be the last. What you saw here was not even our army; it was just a scavenger crew, a small portion of our population."

The Mondeans shifted uncomfortably at this. They had sent their entire fleet to Earth and had sustained heavy losses in the victory. If this wasn't the Erdean army...

"Each attack is like a hammer probing for weaknesses," she continued. "They will keep pounding until they get what they want. While this was going on, the true Erdean army had taken over another planet close to our home world. Earth is full of life-sustaining resources and more blulex than has been discovered in the rest of the universe combined. This other planet is a staging area. If they are able to fulfill their plan of a militarized base of operations, an entire planet dedicated to creating an assembly line of warriors and warships to invade and take over planets, we—they—will never be stopped."

"So we can't win," Jess said matter-of-factly. "Earth is destined to fall."

Juxoria looked at her with disappointment, antennae sagging in response, and said, "I expected more from a chosen one. The only destiny is the one foretold about you."

Jace had a more confident take than his sister, and he said proudly, "No matter how big a force it was they sent here, we beat them. They're somewhere in outer space right now licking their wounds. If we give them time to recover, they *will* come back. I say we go finish them off before they get a chance."

Jess expected her brother's statement to be met with condescending smiles and polite pats on the back. Instead, he got nods of approval.

"I'm afraid it's the only way," Juxoria said. "We can only hope it's enough."

"So let's take the fight to them, whaddya say, Lexy?" Jace said, gently elbowing his sister.

"You mean we...us...you think we have to..."

She stopped talking and just stared at the giant ship hanging over the city.

"Yep," Jace nodded. "We have a pretty good army right here with the group of us. Let's take a little trip across the galaxy and end this war once and for all. Together, there's no way we can lose."

"I'm afraid I'll be sitting this one out," Rick said, using a cane to step forward.

He had improved some but was still extremely weak.

"No way, Dad," Jace said, shaking his head. "The Mondeans have to have medicine to make you better. You *have* to come."

Xanos started to speak, but Rick cut him off, saying, "All of this happened because of me. For my own selfish reasons, I started this war. I am responsible. The Erdeans might have come anyway, but if it hadn't been for me and my obsessions, maybe that wouldn't have happened for years. Maybe by then Earth would have been better prepared to stand up for ourselves."

"But, Dad..." Jace said, but no other words would come.

Jess walked over and put her arm around her father's waist, tears streaming down her face.

"You did it to have more time with us," Jess said through sobs. "We played our part in bringing the Erdeans here, too. But if we're the two of the prophecy, then this was our destiny. It's not your fault. You *have* to come with us."

Rick smiled warmly, tears of his own threatening to spill over, and said, "I want to find Aaron. I want to find your mother. I need to make things right with her before...while...while I still have time."

Wiping at his eyes, Rick walked away. He took a seat on a quaint little bench in a flower garden across the littered lawn.

President Taylor spoke again. "I'll be staying here, too. I have a country to rebuild. I can only imagine the death, damage, and destruction out there. Our people will be scared and need to know their leader is here to help piece it all back together. Our friends in Pakistan are going to need our support, as well."

Attention turned to Max, who reluctantly shook his head and said, "I'm out, too. There were Erdeans here before the full invasion. They had infiltrated our governments. Now there will be even more here. It'll be my job to exterminate them." He turned to Juxoria. "I do have a question for you, though. There appears to be a hole dug under the Lincoln Memorial. It's protected somehow. No one and nothing has been able to penetrate it. We found three sets of bodies of creatures not of this planet, chained together at the surface of the hole. Erdean slaves, no doubt."

The Mondean behind Xanos spoke rapidly. Xanos translated. "Our captain suspected the shield was about more than just getting to the kids or capturing your President. He felt like there was another reason."

"Do you know what this is about?" Max asked.

Erdeans weren't capable of expressing emotions with their facial features, but Juxoria turned her head away in a manner that didn't convince anyone she was telling the truth when she said, "No. I was not told of anything else."

Max opened his mouth to push for more but saw Jess shaking her head. If there was more to learn from Juxoria, they had a trip across the galaxy to learn about it.

"Juxoria will come," Jess said. "There's so much we can learn from her. But as far as Earthlings go, looks like it's just you and me, Lys."

Jace smiled and said, "Just the way I like it. The fate of the universe is up to us."

To be continued...

Coming Soon

Book Three in
The Origin Society

ABOUT THE AUTHOR

Billy Dixon is the author of several books, including the chapter book series' *Patty Paper* and *Backyard Bones*, as well as book one of *The Origin Society: They*. After a decade of working as a sports writer for the *Kingsport Times-News* in Tennessee, he shifted his career to the world of children's literature. He has performed author presentations at more than 300 schools and spoken to hundreds of thousands of students. Dixon now lives in Huntersville, NC with his wife Robin. He has two children, Reed and Allie, and an ever-increasing number of fur babies.